Tales From
the Dead of Night

CECILY GAYFORD studied English at Balliol College, Oxford, and now works in publishing. Her interest in Gothic and supernatural literature extends from Horace Walpole to Hilary Mantel. She once saw a ghost in a hotel in Ecuador. She lives in London.

TALES FROM THE DEAD OF NIGHT

THIRTEEN CLASSIC GHOST STORIES

Selected by Cecily Gayford

P

PROFILE BOOKS

This paperback edition published in 2018

First published in Great Britain in 2013 by
PROFILE BOOKS LTD
3 Holford Yard
Bevin Way
London WC1X 9HD
www.profilebooks.com

1 3 5 7 9 10 8 6 4 2

Typeset in Jenson by MacGuru Ltd
info@macguru.org.uk
Printed and bound in Great Britain by
CPI Group (UK) Ltd, Croydon CR0 4YY

A CIP catalogue record for this book is available from the British Library.

ISBN 978 1 78816 087 2
eISBN 978 1 84765 982 8

Two travellers sat alone in a train carriage.

'Do you believe in ghosts?' asked one, by way of conversation.

'Yes', said the other, and vanished.

Anon.

Contents

E. NESBIT

(1858–1924)

Best known now as the author of *The Railway Children*, Edith Nesbit was in her lifetime a formidable, and formidably eccentric, woman. She was a founder of the socialist Fabian Society, where she formed close relationships with George Bernard Shaw and H. G. Wells, as well as a writer of short stories, novels and poems and a mother to five children (two of whom were the illegitimate offspring of her husband, Hubert Bland). She was also intensely interested in the supernatural: there are suggestions that she was a member of the Hermetic Order of the Golden Dawn, where her fellow initiates included W. B. Yeats, Maud Gonne and the occultist Aleister Crowley, and she complained that Well Hall, where she wrote her most famous stories for children, was haunted by a ghost who sighed over her shoulder as she worked.

THE SHADOW

THIS IS NOT an artistically rounded-off ghost story, and nothing is explained in it, and there seems to be no reason why any of it should have happened. But that is no reason why it should not be told. You must have noticed that all the real ghost stories you have ever come close to, are like this in these respects – no explanation, no logical coherence. Here is the story.

There were three of us and another, but she had fainted suddenly at the second extra of the Christmas dance, and had been put to bed in the dressing room next to the room which we three shared. It had been one of those jolly, old-fashioned dances where nearly everybody stays the night, and the big country house is stretched to its utmost containing – guests harbouring on sofas, couches, settles and even mattresses on floors. Some of the young men actually, I believe, slept on the great dining table. We had talked of our partners, as girls will, and then the stillness of the manor house, broken only by the whisper of the wind in the cedar branches, and the scraping of their harsh fingers against our windowpanes, had pricked us to such luxurious confidence in our surroundings of bright chintz and candle-flame and firelight, that we had dared to talk of ghosts – in which, we all said, we did not believe one bit. We had told the story of the phantom coach, and the horribly strange bed, and the lady in the sacque, and the house in Berkeley Square.

We none of us believed in ghosts, but my heart, at least, seemed to leap to my throat and choke me there when a tap came to our door – a tap faint, not to be mistaken.

'Who's there?' said the youngest of us, craning a lean neck towards the door. It opened slowly, and I give you my word the instant of suspense that followed is still reckoned among my life's least confident moments. Almost at once the door opened fully, and Miss Eastwich, my aunt's housekeeper, companion and general stand-by, looked in on us.

We all said, 'Come in,' but she stood there. She was, at all normal hours, the most silent woman I have ever known. She stood and looked at us, and shivered a little. So did we – for in those days corridors were not warmed by hot-water pipes and the air from the door was keen.

'I saw your light,' she said at last, 'and I thought it was late for you to be up – after all this gaiety. I thought perhaps –' her glance turned towards the door of the dressing room.

'No,' I said, 'she's fast asleep.' I should have added a goodnight, but the youngest of us forestalled my speech. She did not know Miss Eastwich as we others did; did not know how her persistent silence had built a wall round her – a wall that no one dared to break down with the commonplaces of talk, or the littlenesses of mere human relationship. Miss Eastwich's silence had taught us to treat her as a machine; and as other than a machine we never dreamed of treating her. But the youngest of us had seen Miss Eastwich for the first time that day. She was young, crude, ill-balanced, subject to blind, calf-like impulses. She was also the heiress of a rich tallow-chandler, but that has nothing to do with this part of the story. She jumped up from the hearth rug, her unsuitably rich silk lace-trimmed dressing gown falling back from her thin collarbones, and ran to the door and put an arm round Miss Eastwich's prim, lisse-encircled neck. I gasped. I should as soon have dared to embrace Cleopatra's Needle. 'Come in,' said the youngest of us – 'come in and get warm. There's lots of cocoa left.' She drew Miss Eastwich in and shut the door.

The vivid light of pleasure in the housekeeper's pale eyes went through my heart like a knife. It would have been so easy to put an arm round her neck, if one had only thought she wanted an arm there. But it was not I who had thought that – and indeed, my arm might not have brought the light evoked by the thin arm of the youngest of us.

'Now,' the youngest went on eagerly, 'you shall have the very biggest, nicest chair, and the cocoa pot's here on the hob as hot as hot – and we've all been telling ghost stories, only we don't believe in them a bit; and when you get warm you ought to tell one too.'

Miss Eastwich – that model of decorum and decently done duties – tell a ghost story!

'You're sure I'm not in your way,' Miss Eastwich said, stretching her hands to the blaze. I wondered whether housekeepers have fires in their rooms even at Christmas time. 'Not a bit,' I said it, and I hope I said it as warmly as I felt it. 'I – Miss Eastwich – I'd have asked you to come in other times – only I didn't think you'd care for girls' chatter.'

The third girl, who was really of no account, and that's why I have not said anything about her before, poured cocoa for our guest. I put my fleecy Madeira shawl round her shoulders. I could not think of anything else to do for her and I found myself wishing desperately to do something. The smiles she gave us were quite pretty. People can smile prettily at forty or fifty, or even later, though girls don't realise this. It occurred to me, and this was another knife thrust, that I had never seen Miss Eastwich smile – a real smile – before. The pale smiles of dutiful acquiescence were not of the same blood as this dimpling, happy, trans-figuring look.

'This is very pleasant,' she said, and it seemed to me that I had never before heard her real voice. It did not please me to think that at the cost of cocoa, a fire, and my arm round her neck, I might have heard this new voice any time these six years.

'We've been telling ghost stories,' I said. 'The worst of it is, we don't believe in ghosts. No one we know has ever seen one.'

'It's always what somebody told somebody, who told somebody you know,' said the youngest of us, 'and you can't believe that, can you?'

'What the soldier said is not evidence,' said Miss Eastwich. Will it be believed that the little Dickens quotation pierced one more keenly than the new smile or the new voice?

'And all the ghost stories are so beautifully rounded off – a murder committed on the spot – or a hidden treasure, or a warning … I think that makes them harder to believe. The most horrid ghost story I ever heard was one that was quite silly.'

'Tell it.'

'I can't – it doesn't sound anything to tell. Miss Eastwich ought to tell one.'

'Oh, do,' said the youngest of us, and her salt cellars loomed dark, as she stretched her neck eagerly and laid an entreating arm on our guest's knee.

'The only thing that I ever knew of was – was hearsay,' she said slowly, 'till just the end.'

I knew she would tell her story, and I knew she had never before told it, and I knew she was only telling it now because she was proud, and this seemed the only way to pay for the fire and the cocoa and the laying of that arm round her neck.

'Don't tell it,' I said suddenly. 'I know you'd rather not.'

'I dare say it would bore you,' she said meekly, and the youngest of us, who, after all, did not understand everything, glared resentfully at me.

'We should just *love* it,' she said. '*Do* tell us. Never mind if it isn't a real, proper, fixed-up story. I'm certain anything *you* think ghostly would be quite too beautifully horrid for anything.'

Miss Eastwich finished her cocoa and reached up to set the cup on the mantelpiece.

'I can't do any harm,' she said half to herself, 'they don't believe in ghosts, and it wasn't exactly a ghost either. And they're all over twenty – they're not babies.'

There was a breathing time of hush and expectancy. The fire crackled and the gas suddenly glared higher because the billiard lights had been put out. We heard the steps and voices of the men going along the corridors.

'It is really hardly worth telling,' Miss Eastwich said doubtfully, shading her faded face from the fire with her thin hand.

We all said, 'Go on – oh, go on – do!'

'Well,' she said, 'twenty years ago – and more than that – I had two friends, and I loved them more than anything in the world. And they married each other –'

She paused, and I knew just in what way she had loved each of them. The youngest of us said, 'How awfully nice for you. Do go on.'

She patted the youngest's shoulder, and I was glad that I had understood, and that the youngest of all hadn't. She went on.

'Well, after they were married, I did not see much of them for a year or two; and then he wrote and asked me to come and stay, because his wife was ill, and I should cheer her up, and cheer him up as well; for it was a gloomy house, and he himself was growing gloomy too.'

I knew, as she spoke, that she had every line of that letter by heart.

'Well, I went. The address was in Lee, near London; in those days there were streets and streets of new villa houses growing up round old brick mansions standing in their own grounds, with red walls round, you know, and a sort of flavour of coaching days, and post-chaises, and Blackheath highwaymen about them. He had said the house was gloomy, and it was called The Firs, and I imagined my cab going through a dark, winding shrubbery, and drawing up in front of one of these sedate, old, square houses. Instead, we drew up in front of a large, smart villa, with iron railings, gay encaustic tiles leading from the iron gate to the stained-glass-panelled door, and for shrubbery only a few stunted cypresses and aucubas in the tiny front garden. But inside it was all warm and welcoming. He met me at the door.'

She was gazing into the fire and I knew she had forgotten us. But the youngest girl of all still thought it was to us she was telling her story.

'He met me at the door,' she said again, 'and thanked me for coming, and asked me to forgive the past.'

'What past?' said that high priestess of the *inàpropos*, the youngest of all.

'Oh – I suppose he meant because they hadn't invited me before, or something,' said Miss Eastwich worriedly, 'but it's a very dull story, I find, after all, and –'

'Do go on,' I said – then I kicked the youngest of us, and got up to rearrange Miss Eastwich's shawl, and said in blatant dumb show, over the shawled shoulder, 'Shut up, you little idiot!'

After another silence, the housekeeper's new voice went on.

'They were very glad to see me and I was very glad to be there. You girls, now, have such troops of friends, but these two were all I had – all I had ever had. Mabel wasn't exactly ill, only weak and excitable. I thought he seemed more ill than she did. She went to bed early and before she went, she asked me to keep him company through his last pipe, so we went into the dining room and sat in the two armchairs on each side of the fireplace. They were covered with green leather, I remember. There were bronze groups of horses and a black marble clock on the mantelpiece – all wedding presents. He poured out some whisky for himself, but he hardly touched it. He sat looking into the fire.

At last I said, "What's wrong? Mabel looks as well as you could expect."

'He said, "Yes – but I don't know from one day to another that she won't begin to notice something wrong. That's why I wanted you to come. You were always so sensible and strong-minded, and Mabel's like a little bird on a flower."

'I said yes, of course, and waited for him to go on. I thought he must be in debt, or in trouble of some sort. So I just waited. Presently he said, "Margaret, this is a very peculiar house –" He always called me Margaret. You see, we'd been such old friends. I told him I thought the house was very pretty, and fresh, and home-like – only a little too new – but that fault would mend with time. He said, "It *is* new: that's just it. We're the first people who've ever lived in it. If it were an old house, Margaret, I should think it was haunted."

'I asked if he had seen anything. "No," he said, "not yet."

'"Heard then?" said I.

'"No – not heard either," he said, "but there's a sort

❖ 8 ❖

of feeling: I can't describe it – I've seen nothing and I've heard nothing, but I've been so near to seeing and hearing, just near, that's all. And something follows me about – only when I turn round, there's never anything, only my shadow. And I always feel that I *shall* see the thing next minute – but I never do – not quite – it's always just not visible."

'I thought he'd been working rather hard – and tried to cheer him up by making light of all this. It was just nerves, I said. Then he said he had thought I could help him, and did I think anyone he had wronged could have laid a curse on him, and did I believe in curses. I said I didn't – and the only person anyone could have said he had wronged forgave him freely, I knew, if there was anything to forgive. So I told him this too.'

It was I, not the youngest of us, who knew the name of that person, wronged and forgiving.

'So then I said he ought to take Mabel away from the house and have a complete change. But he said no; Mabel had got everything in order, and he could never manage to get her away just now without explaining everything – "and, above all," he said, "she mustn't guess there's anything wrong. I dare say I shan't feel quite such a lunatic now you're here."

'So we said goodnight.'

'Is that all the story!' said the third girl, striving to convey that even as it stood it was a good story.

'That's only the beginning,' said Miss Eastwich. 'Whenever I was alone with him he used to tell me the same thing over and over again, and at first when I began to notice things, I tried to think that it was his talk that had upset my nerves. The odd thing was that it wasn't only at night – but in broad daylight – and particularly on the stairs and passages. On the staircase the feeling used to be so awful that I have had to bite my lips till they bled to keep myself from running upstairs at full speed. Only I knew if I did I should go mad at the top. There was always something behind me – exactly as he had said – something that one could just not see. And a sound that one could just not hear. There was a long corridor at the top of the house. I have sometimes almost seen something – you know how one sees things without looking – but if I turned round, it seemed as if the thing drooped and melted into my shadow. There was a little window at the end of the corridor.

'Downstairs there was another corridor, something like it, with a cupboard at one end and the kitchen at the other. One night I went down into the kitchen to heat some milk for Mabel. The servants had gone to bed. As I stood by the fire, waiting for the milk to boil, I glanced through the open door and along the passage. I never could keep my eyes on what I was doing in that house. The cupboard door was partly open; they used to keep empty boxes and things in it. And, as I looked, I knew that now it was not going to be "almost" any more. Yet I said, "Mabel?" not because I thought it could be Mabel who was crouching down there, half in and half out of the cupboard. The thing was grey at first, and then it was black. And when I whispered, "Mabel", it seemed to sink down till it lay like a pool of ink on the floor, and then its edges drew in, and it seemed to flow, like ink when you tilt up the paper you have spilt it on, and it flowed into the cupboard till it was all gathered into the shadow there. I saw it go quite plainly. The gas was full on in the kitchen. I screamed aloud, but even then, I'm thankful to say, I had enough sense to upset the boiling milk, so that when he came downstairs three steps at a time, I had the excuse for my scream of a scalded hand. The explanation satisfied Mabel, but next night he said, "Why didn't you tell me? It was that cupboard. All the horror of the house comes out of that. Tell me – have you seen anything yet? Or is it only the nearly seeing and nearly hearing still?"

'I said, "You must tell me first what you've seen." He told me, and his eyes wandered, as he spoke, to the shadows by the curtains, and I turned up all three gas lights, and lit the candles on the mantelpiece. Then we looked at each other and said we were both mad, and thanked God that Mabel at least was sane. For what he had seen was what I had seen.

'After that I hated to be alone with a shadow, because at any moment I might see something that would crouch, and sink, and lie like a black pool, and then slowly draw itself into the shadow that was nearest. Often that shadow was my own. The thing came first at night, but afterwards there was no hour safe from it. I saw it at dawn and at noon, in the dusk and in the firelight, and always it crouched and sank, and was a pool that flowed into some shadow and became part of it. And always I saw it with a straining of the eyes – a pricking and aching. It seemed as though I could only just see it, as if my sight, to see it, had to be strained to the uttermost. And still the sound was in the house – the sound that I could just not hear. At last, one morning early, I did hear it. It was close behind me, and it was only a sigh. It was worse than the thing that crept into the shadows.

'I don't know how I bore it. I couldn't have borne it, if I hadn't been so fond of them both. But I knew in my heart that, if he had no one to whom he could speak openly, he would go mad, or tell Mabel. His was not a very strong character; very sweet, and kind, and gentle, but not strong. He was always easily led. So I stayed on and bore up, and we were very cheerful, and made little jokes, and tried to be amusing when Mabel was with us. But when we were alone, we did not try to be amusing. And sometimes a day or two would go by without our seeing or hearing anything, and we should perhaps have fancied that we had fancied what we had seen and heard – only there was always the feeling of there being something about the house, that one could just not hear and not see. Sometimes we used to try not to talk about it, but generally we talked of nothing else at all. And the weeks went by, and Mabel's baby was born. The nurse and the doctor said that both mother and child were doing well. He and I sat late in the dining room that night. We had neither of us seen or heard anything for three days; our anxiety about Mabel was lessened. We talked of the future – it seemed then so much brighter than the past. We arranged that, the moment she was fit to be moved, he should take her away to the sea, and I should superintend the moving of their furniture into the new house he had already chosen. He was gayer than I had seen him since his marriage – almost like his old self. When I said goodnight to him, he said a lot of things about my having been a comfort to them both. I hadn't done anything much, of course, but still I am glad he said them.

'Then I went upstairs, almost for the first time without that feeling of something following me. I listened at Mabel's door. Everything was quiet. I went on towards my own room, and in an instant I felt that there *was* something behind me. I turned. It was crouching there; it sank, and the black fluidness of it seemed to be sucked under the door of Mabel's room.

'I went back. I opened the door a listening inch. All was still. And then I heard a sigh close behind me. I opened the door and went in. The nurse and the baby were asleep. Mabel was asleep too – she looked so pretty – like a tired child – the baby was cuddled up into one of her arms with its tiny head against her side. I prayed then that Mabel might never know the terrors that he and I had known. That those little ears might never hear any but pretty sounds, those clear eyes never see any but pretty sights. I did not dare to pray for a long time after that. Because my prayer was answered. She never saw, never heard anything more in this world. And now I could do nothing more for him or for her.

'When they had put her in her coffin, I lighted wax candles round her, and laid the horrible white flowers that people will send near her, and then I saw he had followed me. I took his hand to lead him away.

'At the door we both turned. It seemed to us that we heard a sigh. He would have sprung to her side in I don't know what mad, glad hope. But at that instant we both saw it. Between us and the coffin, first grey, then black, it crouched an instant, then sank and liquefied – and was gathered together and drawn till it ran into the nearest shadow. And the nearest shadow was the shadow of Mabel's coffin. I left the next day. His mother came. She had never liked me.'

Miss Eastwich paused. I think she had quite forgotten us.

'Didn't you see him again?' asked the youngest of us all.

'Only once,' Miss Eastwich answered, 'and something black crouched then between him and me. But it was only his second wife, crying beside his coffin. It's not a cheerful story, is it? And it doesn't lead anywhere. I've never told anyone else. I think it was seeing his daughter that brought it all back.'

She looked towards the dressing-room door.

'Mabel's baby?'

'Yes – and exactly like Mabel, only with his eyes.'

The youngest of all had Miss Eastwich's hands and was petting them.

Suddenly the woman wrenched her hands away and stood at her gaunt height, her hands clenched, eyes straining. She was looking at something that we could not see, and I know what the man in the Bible meant when he said, 'The hair of my flesh stood up.'

What she saw seemed not quite to reach the height of the dressing-room door handle. Her eyes followed it down, down – widening and widening. Mine followed them – all the nerves of them seemed strained to the uttermost – and

I almost saw – or did I quite see? I can't be certain. But we all heard the long-drawn, quivering sigh. And to each of us it seemed to be breathed just behind us.

It was I who caught up the candle – it dripped all over my trembling hand – and was dragged by Miss Eastwich to the girl who had fainted during the second extra. But it was the youngest of all whose lean arms were round the housekeeper when we turned away, and that have been round her many a time since, in the new home where she keeps house for the youngest of us.

The doctor who came in the morning said that Mabel's daughter had died of heart disease – which she had inherited from her mother. It was that that had made her faint during the second extra. But I have sometimes wondered whether she may not have inherited something from her father. I had never been able to forget the look on her dead face.

W. F. HARVEY
(1885–1937)

Born into a wealthy Quaker family, William Fryer Harvey enjoyed an idyllic childhood on the edge of Ilkley Moor. After studying at Balliol College, Oxford, and taking a medical degree at Leeds University, he travelled around the world; on his return his first book of short stories, *Midnight House*, was published. At the outbreak of war he joined the Friends' Ambulance Service and served in Ypres on the Western Front and then with the Royal Navy as a surgeon-lieutenant. He was awarded the Albert Medal for Lifesaving after an accident at Scapa Flow in which he amputated the arm of a stoker trapped below decks in the foundering ship. Smoke inhalation sustained during the rescue damaged his lungs permanently; his ghost stories, of which the most famous remains 'The Beast with Five Fingers', were written at a sanatorium in Switzerland where he lived for much of his later life. Suffering from homesickness, he returned to England in 1937, and died at Letchworth.

The Clock

I LIKED YOUR DESCRIPTION of the people at the *pension*. I can just picture that rather sinister Miss Cornelius, with her toupee and clinking bangles. I don't wonder you felt frightened that night when you found her sleepwalking in the corridor. But after all, why shouldn't she sleepwalk? As to the movements of the furniture in the lounge on the Sunday, you are, I suppose, in an earthquake zone, though an earthquake seems too big an explanation for the ringing of that little handbell on the mantelpiece. It's rather as if our parlourmaid – another new one! – were to call a stray elephant to account for the teapot we found broken yesterday. You have at least escaped the eternal problem of maids in Italy.

Yes, my dear, I most certainly believe you. I have never had experiences quite like yours, but your mention of Miss Cornelius has reminded me of something rather similar that happened nearly twenty years ago, soon after I left school. I was staying with my aunt in Hampstead. You remember her, I expect; or, if not her, the poodle, Monsieur, that she used to make perform such pathetic tricks. There was another guest, whom I had never met before, a Mrs Caleb. She lived in Lewes and had been staying with my aunt for about a fortnight, recuperating after a series of domestic upheavals, which had culminated in her two servants leaving her at an hour's notice, without any reason, according to Mrs Caleb; but I wondered. I had never seen the maids; I had seen Mrs Caleb and, frankly, I disliked her. She left the same sort of impression on me as I gather your Miss Cornelius leaves on you – something queer and secretive; underground, if you can use the expression, rather than underhand. And I could feel in my body that she did not like me.

It was summer. Joan Denton – you remember her; her husband was killed in Gallipoli – had suggested that I should go down to spend the day with her. Her people had rented a little cottage some three miles out of Lewes. We arranged a day. It was gloriously fine for a wonder, and I had planned to leave that stuffy old Hampstead house before the old ladies were astir. But Mrs Caleb waylaid me in the hall, just as I was going out.

'I wonder,' she said, 'I wonder if you could do me a small favour. If you do have any time to spare in Lewes – only if you do – would you be so kind as to call at my house? I left a little travelling clock there in the hurry of parting. If it's not in the drawing room, it will be in my bedroom or in one of the maids' bedrooms. I know I lent it to the cook, who was a poor riser, but I can't remember if she returned it. Would it be too much to ask? The house has been locked up for twelve days, but everything is in order. I have the keys here; the large one is for the garden gate, the small one for the front door.'

I could only accept, and she proceeded to tell me how I could find Ash Grove House.

'You will feel quite like a burglar,' she said. 'But mind, it's only if you have time to spare.'

As a matter of fact I found myself glad of any excuse to kill time. Poor old Joan had been taken suddenly ill in the night – they feared appendicitis – and though her people were very kind and asked me to stay to lunch, I could see that I should only be in the way, and made Mrs Caleb's commission an excuse for an early departure.

I found Ash Grove without difficulty. It was a medium-sized red-brick house, standing by itself in a high-walled garden that bounded a narrow lane. A flagged path led from the gate to the front door, in front of which grew, not an ash, but a monkey puzzle, that must have made the rooms unnecessarily gloomy. The side door, as I expected, was locked. The dining room and drawing room lay on either side of the hall and, as the windows of both were shuttered, I left the hall door open, and in the dim light looked round hurriedly for the clock, which, from what Mrs Caleb had said, I hardly expected to find in either of the downstairs rooms. It was neither on table nor mantel-piece. The rest of the furniture was carefully covered over with white dustsheets. Then I went upstairs. But, before doing so, I closed the front door. I did in fact feel rather like a burglar, and I thought that if anyone did happen to see the front door open, I might have difficulty in explaining things. Happily the upstairs windows were not shuttered. I made a hurried search of the principal bedrooms. They had been left in apple-pie order; nothing was out of place; but there was no sign of Mrs Caleb's clock. The impression that the house gave me – you know the sense of personality that a house conveys – was neither pleasing nor displeasing, but it was stuffy, stuffy from the absence of fresh air, with an additional stuffiness added that seemed to come out from the hangings and quilts and antimacassars. The corridor, on to which the bedrooms I had examined opened, communicated with a smaller wing, an older part of the house, I imagined, which contained a box room and the maids' sleeping quarters. The last door that I unlocked – (I should say that the doors of all the rooms were locked, and relocked by me after I had glanced inside them) – contained the object of my search. Mrs Caleb's travelling clock was on the mantelpiece, ticking away merrily.

That was how I thought of it at first. And then for the first time I realised that there was something wrong. The clock had no business to be ticking. The house had been shut up for twelve days. No one had come in to air it or to light fires. I remembered how Mrs Caleb had told my aunt that if she left the keys with a neighbour, she was never sure who might get hold of them. And yet the clock was going. I wondered if some vibration had set the mechanism in motion, and pulled out my watch to see the time. It was five minutes to one. The clock on the mantelpiece said four minutes to the hour. Then, without quite knowing why, I shut the door on to the landing, locked myself in, and again looked round the room. Nothing was out of place. The only thing that might have called for remark was that there appeared to be a slight indentation on the pillow and the bed; but the mattress was a feather mattress, and you know how difficult it is to make them perfectly smooth. You won't need to be told that I gave a hurried glance under the bed – do you remember your supposed burglar in Number Six at St Ursula's? – and then, and much more reluctantly, opened the doors of two horribly capacious cupboards, both happily empty, except for a framed text with its face to the wall. By this time I really was frightened. The clock went ticking on. I had a horrible feeling that an alarm might go off at any moment, and the thought of being in that empty house was almost too much for me. However, I made an attempt to pull myself together. It might after all be a fourteen-day clock. If it were, then it would be almost run down. I could roughly find out how long the clock had been going by winding it up. I hesitated to put the matter to the test; but the uncertainty was too much for me. I took it out of its case and began to wind. I had scarcely turned the winding screw twice when it stopped. The clock clearly was not running down; the hands had been set in motion probably only an hour or two before. I felt cold and faint and, going to the window, threw up the sash, letting in the sweet, live air of the garden. I knew now that the house was queer, horribly queer. Could someone be living in the house? Was someone else in the house now? I thought that I had been in all the rooms, but had I? I had only just opened the bathroom door, and I had certainly not opened any cupboards, except those in the room in which I was. Then, as I stood by the open window, wondering what I should do next and feeling that I just couldn't go down that corridor into the darkened hall to fumble at the latch of the front door with I don't know what behind me, I heard a noise. It was very faint at first, and seemed to be coming from the stairs. It was a curious noise – not the noise of anyone climbing up the stairs, but – you will laugh if this letter reaches you by a morning post – of something hopping up the stairs, like a very big bird would hop. I heard it on the landing; it stopped. Then there was a curious scratching noise against one of the bedroom doors, the sort of noise you can make with the nail of your little finger scratching polished wood. Whatever it was was coming slowly down the corridor, scratching at the doors as it went. I could stand it no longer. Nightmare pictures of locked doors opening filled my brain. I took up the clock, wrapped it in my mackintosh, and dropped it out of the window on to a flowerbed. Then I managed to crawl out of the window and, getting a grip of the sill, 'successfully negotiated', as the journalists would say, 'a twelve-foot drop'. So much for our much abused gym at St Ursula's. Picking up the mackintosh, I ran round to the front door and locked it. Then I felt I could breathe, but not until I was on the far side of the gate in the garden wall did I feel safe.

Then I remembered that the bedroom window was open. What was I to do? Wild horses wouldn't have dragged me into that house again unaccompanied. I made up my mind to go to the police station and tell them everything. I should be laughed at, of course, and they might easily refuse to believe my story of Mrs Caleb's commission. I had actually begun to walk down the lane in the direction of the town, when I chanced to look back at the house. The window that I had left open was shut.

No, my dear, I didn't see any face or anything dreadful like that … and, of course, it may have shut by itself. It was an ordinary sash window, and you know they are often difficult to keep open.

And the rest? Why, there's really nothing more to tell. I didn't even see Mrs Caleb again. She had had some sort of fainting fit just before lunchtime, my aunt informed me on my return, and had had to go to bed. Next morning I travelled down to Cornwall to join mother and the children. I thought I had forgotten all about it, but when three years later Uncle Charles suggested giving me a travelling clock for a twenty-first birthday present, I was foolish enough to prefer the alternative that he offered, a collected edition of the works of Thomas Carlyle.

E. F. BENSON
(1867–1940)

The novelist Edward Frederic 'Fred' Benson is best known now for his 'Mapp and Lucia' series. The son of the fearsome Archbishop of Canterbury Edward White Benson, as a young man he was a friend of Oscar Wilde, a keen archaeologist – at one point accompanying Wilde's lover, Lord Alfred Douglas, on a trip to the pyramids – and a champion figure skater. During the First World War he was sent to Capri to report on the morale of the Italian civilians; the Foreign Office described his reports as 'preposterous'. Written near the end of his life, 'Pirates' is set in a version of Lis Escop, the Bensons' family home in Truro (where a young M. R. James often visited his school friend, Benson's older brother Arthur). Benson's fond memories of his childhood gave way to sadness in adulthood: two of his siblings died young, while another two struggled with a family tendency to severe depression. It is perhaps not surprising that 'Pirates' so powerfully evokes a desire for reconciliation and the simplicity and joy of youth restored in age.

PIRATES

F OR MANY YEARS this project of sometime buying
back the house had simmered in Peter Graham's
mind, but whenever he actually went into the idea with
practical intention, stubborn reasons had presented themselves to deter him. In the first place it was very far off from
his work, down in the heart of Cornwall, and it would be
impossible to think of going there just for weekends, and
if he established himself there for longer periods what on
earth would he do with himself in that soft remote Lotus-
land? He was a busy man who, when at work, liked the
diversions of his club and of the theatres in the evening,
but he allowed himself few holidays away from the City,
and those were spent on salmon river or golf links with
some small party of solid and like-minded friends. Looked
at in these lights, the project bristled with objections.

Yet through all these years, forty of them now, which
had ticked away so imperceptibly, the desire to be at home
again at Lescop had always persisted, and from time to
time it gave him shrewd little unexpected tugs, when his
conscious mind was in no way concerned with it. This

desire, he was well aware, was of a sentimental quality, and often he wondered at himself that he, who was so well-armoured in the general jostle of the world against that type of emotion, should have just this one joint in his harness. Not since he was sixteen had he set eyes on the place, but the memory of it was more vivid than that of any other scene of subsequent experience. He had married since then, he had lost his wife, and though for many months after that he had felt horribly lonely, the ache of that loneliness had ceased and now, if he had ever asked himself the direct question, he would have confessed that bachelor existence was more suited to him than married life had ever been. It had not been a conspicuous success and he never felt the least temptation to repeat the experiment.

But there was another loneliness which neither married life nor his keen interest in his business had ever extinguished and this was directly connected with his desire for that house on the green slope of the hills above Truro. For only seven years had he lived there, the youngest but one of a family of five children, and now out of all that gay company he alone was left. One by one they had dropped off the stem of life, but as each in turn went into this silence, Peter had not missed them very much: his own life was too occupied to give him time really to miss anybody and he was too vitally constituted to do otherwise than look forwards.

None of that brood of children except himself, and he childless, had married, and now, when he was left without intimate tie of blood to any living being, a loneliness had gathered thickly around him. It was not in any sense a tragic or desperate loneliness: he had no wish to follow them on the unverified and unlikely chance of finding them all again. Also, he had no use for any disembodied existence: life meant to him flesh and blood and material interests and activities, and he could form no conception of life apart from such. But sometimes he ached with this dull gnawing ache of loneliness, which is worse than all others, when he thought of the stillness that lay congealed like clear ice over these young and joyful years when Lescop had been so noisy and alert and full of laughter, with its garden resounding with games, and the house with charades and hide-and-seek and multitudinous plans. Of course there had been rows and quarrels and disgraces, hot enough at the time, but now there was no one to quarrel with. 'You can't really quarrel with people whom you don't love,' thought Peter, 'because they don't matter.' ... Yet it was ridiculous to feel lonely; it was even more than ridiculous, it was weak, and Peter had the kindly contempt of a successful and healthy and unemotional man for weaknesses of that kind. There were so many amusing and interesting things in the world, he had so many irons in the fire to be beaten, so to speak, into gold when he was working, and so many palatable diversions when he was not (for he still brought a boyish enthusiasm to work and play alike), that there was no excuse for indulging in sentimental sterilities. So, for months together, hardly a stray thought would drift towards the remote years lived in the house on the hillside above Truro.

He had lately become chairman of the board of that new and highly promising company, the British Tin

Syndicate. Their property included certain Cornish mines which had been previously abandoned as non-paying propositions, but a clever mineralogical chemist had recently invented a process by which the metal could be extracted far more cheaply than had hitherto been possible. The British Tin Syndicate had bought the patent and, having acquired these derelict Cornish mines, were getting very good results from ore that had not been worth treating. Peter had very strong opinions as to the duty of a chairman to make himself familiar with the practical side of his concerns and was now travelling down to Cornwall to make a personal inspection of the mines where this process was at work. He had with him certain technical reports which he had received to read during the uninterrupted hours of his journey and it was not till his train had left Exeter behind that he finished his perusal of them and, putting them back in his dispatch case, turned his eye at the swiftly passing panorama of travel. It was many years since he had been to the West Country and now, with the thrill of vivid recognition, he found the red cliffs round Dawlish, interspersed between stretches of sunny sea beach, startlingly familiar. Surely he must have seen them quite lately, he thought to himself, and then, ransacking his memory, he found it was forty years since he had looked at them, travelling back to Eton from his last holidays at Lescop. The intense sharp-cut impressions of youth!

His destination tonight was Penzance and now, with a strangely keen sense of expectation, he remembered that just before reaching Truro station the house on the hill was visible from the train, for often on these journeys to and from school he had been all eyes to catch the first sight of it and the last. Trees perhaps would have grown up and intervened, but as they ran past the station before Truro he shifted across to the other side of the carriage and once more looked out for that glimpse ... There it was, a mile away across the valley, with its grey stone front and the big beech tree screening one end of it, and his heart leaped as he saw it. Yet what use was the house to him now? It was not the stones and the bricks of it, nor the tall hay fields below it, nor the tangled garden behind that he wanted, but the days when he had lived in it. Yet he leaned from the window till a cutting extinguished the view of it, feeling that he was looking at a photograph that recalled some living presence. All those who had made Lescop dear and still vivid had gone, but this record remained, like the image on a plate ... And then he smiled at himself with a touch of contempt for his sentimentality.

The next three days were a whirlwind of enjoyable occupation: tin mines in the concrete were new to Peter, and he absorbed himself in these, as in some new game or ingenious puzzle. He went down the shafts of mines which had been opened again, he inspected the new chemical process, seeing it at work and checking the results, he looked into running expenses, comparing them with the value of the metal recovered. Then, too, there were substantial traces of silver in some of these ores, and he went eagerly into the question as to whether it would pay to extract it. Certainly even the mines which had previously been closed down ought to yield a decent dividend with this process, while those where the lode was richer would vastly increase their profits. But economy, economy ... Surely it would save in the end, though at considerable capital expenditure now, to lay a light railway from the works to the railhead instead of employing these motor lorries. There was a piece of steep gradient, it was true, but a small detour, with a trestle bridge over the stream, would avoid that.

He walked over the proposed route with the engineer and scrambled about the stream bank to find a good take-off for his trestle bridge. And all the time at the back of his head, in some almost subconscious region of thought, were passing endless pictures of the house and the hill, its rooms and passages, its fields and garden, and with them, like some accompanying tune, ran that ache of loneliness. He felt that he must prowl again about the place: the owner, no doubt, if he presented himself, would let him just stroll about alone for half an hour. Thus he would see it all altered and overscored by the life of strangers living there, and the photograph would fade into a blur and then blankness. Much better that it should.

It was in this intention that, having explored every avenue for dividends on behalf of his company, he left Penzance by an early train in order to spend a few hours in Truro and go up to London later in the day. Hardly had he emerged from the station when a crowd of memories, forty years old, but more vivid than any of those of the last day or two, flocked around him with welcome for his return. There was the level-crossing and the road leading down to the stream where his sister Sybil and he had caught a stickleback for their aquarium, and across the bridge over it was the lane sunk deep between high crumbling banks that led to a footpath across the fields to Lescop. He knew exactly where was that pool with long ribands of water-weed trailing and waving in it, which had yielded them that remarkable fish: he knew how campions red and white would be in flower on the lane-side, and in the fields the meadow-orchis. But it was more convenient to go first into the town, get his lunch at the hotel, and to make enquiries from a house agent as to the present owner of Lescop; perhaps he would walk back to the station for his afternoon train by that short cut.

Thick now as flowers on the steppe when spring comes, memories bright and fragrant shot up around him. There was the shop where he had taken his canary to be stuffed (beautiful it looked!): and there was the shop of the 'undertaker and cabinetmaker', still with the same name over the door, where on a memorable birthday, on which his amiable family had given him, by request, the tokens of their goodwill in cash, he had ordered a cabinet with five drawers and two trays, varnished and smelling of newly cut wood, for his collections of shells ... There was a small boy in jersey and flannel trousers looking in at the window now, and Peter suddenly said to himself, 'Good Lord, how like I used to be to that boy: same kit, too.' Strikingly like indeed he was, and Peter, curiously interested, started to cross the street to get a nearer look at him. But it was market day, a drove of sheep delayed him, and when he got across the small boy had vanished among the passengers. Further along was a dignified house front with a flight of broad steps leading up to it, once the dreaded abode of

Mr Tuck, dentist. There was a tall girl standing outside it now, and again Peter involuntarily said to himself, 'Why, that girl's wonderfully like Sybil!' But before he could get more than a glimpse of her, the door was opened and she passed in, and Peter was rather vexed to find that there was no longer a plate on the door indicating that Mr Tuck was still at his wheel ... At the end of the street was the bridge over the Fal just below which they used so often to take a boat for a picnic on the river. There was a jolly family party setting off just now from the quay, three boys, he noticed, and a couple of girls, and a woman of young middle-age. Quickly they dropped downstream and went forth, and with half a sigh he said to himself, 'Just our number with Mamma.'

He went to the Red Lion for his lunch: that was new ground and uninteresting, for he could not recall having set foot in that hostelry before. But as he munched his cold beef there was some great fantastic business going on deep down in his brain: it was trying to join up (and believed it could) that boy outside the cabinetmaker's, that girl on the threshold of the house once Mr Tuck's, and that family party starting for their picnic on the river. It was in vain that he told himself that neither the boy nor the girl nor the picnic party could possibly have anything to do with him: as soon as his attention relaxed that burrowing underground chase, as of a ferret in a rabbit hole, began again ... And then Peter gave a gasp of sheer amazement, for he remembered with clear-cut distinctness how on the morning of that memorable birthday, he and Sybil started earlier than the rest from Lescop, he on the adorable errand of ordering his cabinet, she for the dolorous visit to Mr Tuck. The others followed half an hour later for a picnic on the Fal to celebrate the great fact that his age now required two figures (though one was for nought) for expression. 'It'll be ninety years, darling,' his mother had said, 'before you want a third one, so be careful of yourself.'

Peter was almost as excited when this momentous memory burst on him as he had been on the day itself. Not that it meant anything, he said to himself, as there's nothing for it to mean. But I call it odd. It's as if something from those days hung about here still ...

He finished his lunch quickly after that, and went to the house agent's to make his enquiries. Nothing could be easier than that he should prowl about Lescop, for the house had been untenanted for the last two years. No card 'to view' was necessary, but here were the keys: there was no caretaker there.

'But the house will be going to rack and ruins,' said Peter indignantly. 'Such a jolly house, too. False economy not to put a caretaker in. But of course it's no business of mine. You shall have the keys back during the afternoon: I'll walk up there now.'

'Better take a taxi, sir,' said the man. 'A hot day, and a mile and a half up a steep hill.'

'Oh, nonsense,' said Peter. 'Barely a mile. Why, my brother and I used to often do it in ten minutes.'

It occurred to him that these athletic feats of forty years ago would probably not interest the modern world ...

Pyder Street was as populous with small children as ever, and perhaps a little longer and steeper than it used to be. Then turning off to the right among strange new-built suburban villas he passed into the well-known lane, and in five minutes more had come to the gate leading into the short drive up to the house. It drooped on its hinges, he must lift it off the latch, sidle through and prop it in place again. Overgrown with grass and weeds was the drive, and with another spurt of indignation he saw that the stile to the pathway across the field was broken down and had dragged the wires of the fence with it. And then he came to the house itself, and the creepers trailed over the windows, and, unlocking the door, he stood in the hall with its discoloured ceiling and patches of mildew growing on the damp walls. Shabby and ashamed it looked, the paint perished from the window sashes, the panes dirty and in the air the sour smell of chambers long unventilated. And yet the spirit of the house was there still, though melancholy and reproachful, and it followed him wearily from room to room – 'You are Peter, aren't you?' it seemed to say. 'You've just come to look at me, I see, and not to stop. But I remember the jolly days just as well as you.' … From room to room he went, dining room, drawing room, his mother's sitting room, his father's study: then upstairs to what had been the schoolroom in the days of governesses, and had then been turned over to the children for a playroom. Along the passage was the old nursery and the night nursery, and above that attic rooms, to one of which, as his own exclusive bedroom, he had been promoted when he went to school. The roof of it had leaked, there was a brown-edged stain on the sagging ceiling just above where his bed had been. 'A nice state to let my room get into,' muttered Peter. 'How am I to sleep underneath that drip from the roof? Too bad!'

The vividness of his own indignation rather startled him. He had really felt himself to be not a dual personality, but the same Peter Graham at different periods of his existence. One of them, the chairman of the British Tin Syndicate, had protested against young Peter Graham being put to sleep in so damp and dripping a room, and the other (oh, the ecstatic momentary glimpse of him!) was indeed young Peter back in his lovely attic again, just home from school and now looking round with eager eyes to convince himself of that blissful reality, before bouncing downstairs again to have tea in the children's room. What a lot of things to ask about! How were his rabbits, and how were Sybil's guinea pigs, and had Violet learned that song 'Oh 'tis nothing but a shower', and were the wood pigeons building again in the lime tree? All these topics were of first importance ...

Peter Graham the elder sat down on the window seat. It overlooked the lawn and just opposite was the lime tree, a drooping lime making a green cave inside the skirt of its lower branches, but with those above growing straight, and he heard the chuckling coo of the wood pigeons coming from it. They were building there again then: that question of young Peter's was answered.

'Very odd that I should just be thinking of that,' he said to himself: somehow there was no gap of years between him and young Peter, for his attic bridged over the decades which in the clumsy material reckoning of time intervened between them. Then Peter the elder seemed to take charge again.

The house was a sad affair, he thought: it gave him a stab of loneliness to see how decayed was the theatre of their joyful years, and no evidence of newer life, of the children of strangers and even of their children's children growing up here could have overscored the old sense of it so effectually. He went out of young Peter's room and paused on the landing: the stairs led down in two short flights to the storey below, and now for the moment he was young Peter again, reaching down with his hand along the banisters and preparing to take the first flight in one leap. But then old Peter saw it was an impossible feat for his less supple joints.

Well, there was the garden to explore, and then he would go back to the agent's and return the keys. He no longer wanted to take that short cut down the steep hill to the station, passing the pool where he and Sybil had caught the stickleback, for his whole notion, sometimes so urgent, of coming back here, had wilted and withered. But he would just walk about the garden for ten minutes, and as he went with sedate step downstairs, memories of the garden, and of what they all did there, began to invade him. There were trees to be climbed, and shrubberies – one thicket of syringa particularly where goldfinches built – to be searched for nests and moths, but above all there was that game they played there, far more exciting than lawn tennis or cricket in the bumpy field (though that was exciting enough) called Pirates ... There was a summer house, tiled and roofed and of solid walls, at the top of the garden and that was 'home' or 'Plymouth Sound', and from there ships (children that is) set forth at the order of the Admiral to pick a trophy without being caught by the Pirates. There were two Pirates, who hid anywhere in the garden and jumped out, and (counting the Admiral, who, after giving his orders, became the flagship) three ships, which had to cruise to orchard or flowerbed or field and bring safely home a trophy culled from the ordained spot. Once, Peter remembered, he was flying up the winding path to the summer house with a pirate close on his heels, when he fell flat down, and the humane pirate leaped over him for fear of treading on him and fell down too. So Peter got home, because Dick had fallen on his face and his nose was bleeding …

'Good Lord, it might have happened yesterday,' thought Peter. 'And Harry called him a bloody pirate, and Papa heard and thought he was using shocking language till it was explained to him.'

The garden was even worse than the house, neglected utterly and rankly overgrown, and to find the winding path at all, Peter had to push through briar and thicket. But he persevered and came out into the rose garden at the top, and there was Plymouth Sound with roof collapsed and walls bulging, and moss growing thick between the tiles of the floor.

'But it must be repaired at once,' said Peter aloud … 'What's that?' He whisked around towards the bushes through which he had pushed his way, for he had heard a voice, faint and far off coming from there, and the voice was familiar to him, though for thirty years it had been dumb. For it was Violet's voice which had spoken and she had said, 'Oh Peter: *here* you are!'

He knew it was her voice, and he knew the utter impossibility of it. But it frightened him, and yet how absurd it was to be frightened, for it was only his imagination, kindled by old sights and memories, that had played him a trick. Indeed, how jolly to even have imagined that he had heard Violet's voice once again.

'Vi!' he called aloud, but of course no one answered. The wood pigeons were cooing in the lime, there was a hum of bees and a whisper of wind in the trees and all round the soft enchanted Cornish air, laden with dream-stuff.

He sat down on the step of the summer house and demanded the presence of his own common sense. It had been an uncomfortable afternoon, he was vexed at this ruin of neglect into which the place had fallen and he did not want to imagine these voices calling to him out of the past, or to see these odd glimpses which belonged to his boyhood. He did not belong any more to that epoch over which grasses waved and headstones presided, and he must be quit of all that evoked it, for, more than anything else, he was director of prosperous companies with big interests dependent on him. So he sat there for a calming five minutes, defying Violet, so to speak, to call to him again. And then, so unstable was his mood today, that presently he was listening for her. But Violet was always quick to see when she was not wanted and she must have gone to join the others ...

He retraced his way, fixing his mind on material environments. The golden maple at the head of the walk, a sapling like himself when last he saw it, had become a stout-trunked tree, the shrub of bay a tall column of fragrant leaf, and just as he passed the syringa a goldfinch dropped out of it with dipping flight. Then he was back at the house again where the climbing fuchsia trailed its sprays across the window of his mother's room and hot thick scent (how well remembered!) spilled from the chalices of the great magnolia.

'A mad notion of mine to come and see this house again,' he said to himself. 'I won't think about it any more: it's finished. But it was wicked not to look after it.'

He went back into the town to return the keys to the house agent.

'Much obliged to you,' he said. 'A pleasant house, when I knew it years ago. Why was it allowed to go to ruin like that?'

'Can't say, sir,' said the man. 'It has been let once or twice in the last ten years, but the tenants have never stopped long. The owner would be very pleased to sell it.'

An idea, fanciful, absurd, suddenly struck Peter.

'But why doesn't he live there?' he asked. 'Or why don't the tenants stop long? Was there something they didn't like about it? Haunted: anything of that sort? I'm not going to take it or purchase it: so that won't put me off.'

The man hesitated a moment.

'Well, there were stories,' he said, 'if I may speak confidentially. But all nonsense, of course.'

'Quite so,' said Peter. 'You and I don't believe in such rubbish. I wonder now: was it said that children's voices were heard calling in the garden?'

The discretion of the house agent reasserted itself.

'I can't say, sir, I'm sure,' he said. 'All I know is that the house is to be had very cheap. Perhaps you would take our card.'

Peter arrived back in London late that night. There was a tray of sandwiches and drinks waiting for him, and having refreshed himself, he sat smoking awhile, thinking of his three days' work in Cornwall at the mines: there must be a directors' meeting as soon as possible to consider his suggestions ... Then he found himself staring at the round rosewood table where his tray stood. It had been in his mother's sitting room at Lescop, and the chair in which he sat, a fine Stuart piece, had been his father's chair at the dinner table, and that bookcase had stood in the hall, and his Chippendale card table ... he could not remember exactly where that had been. That set of Browning's poems had been Sybil's: it was from the shelves in the children's room. But it was time to go to bed, and he was glad he was not to sleep in young Peter's attic.

It is doubtful whether, if once an idea has really thrown out roots in a man's mind, he can ever extirpate it. He can cut off its sprouting suckers, he can nip off the buds it bears, or, if they come to maturity, destroy the seed, but the roots defy him. If he tugs at them something breaks, leaving a vital part still embedded, and it is not long before some fresh evidence of its vitality pushes up above the ground where he least expected it. It was so with Peter now: in the middle of some business meeting, the face of one of his co-directors reminded him of that of the coachman of Lescop; if he went for a weekend of golf to the Dormy House at Rye, the bow window of the billiard room was in shape and size that of the drawing room there, and the bank of gorse by the tenth green was no other than the clump below the tennis court: almost he expected to find a tennis ball there when he had need to search it. Whatever he did, wherever he went, something called him from Lescop, and in the evening when he returned home, there was the furniture, more of it than he had realised, asking to be restored there: rugs and pictures and books, the silver on his table all joined in the mute appeal. But Peter stopped his ears to it: it was a senseless sentimentality, and a purely materialistic one, to imagine that he could recapture the life over which so many years had flowed, and in which none of the actors but himself remained, by restoring to the house its old amenities and living there again. He would only emphasise his own loneliness by the visible contrast of the scene, once so alert and populous, with its present emptiness. And this 'butting in' (so he expressed it) of materialistic sentimentality only confirmed his resolve to have done with Lescop. It had been a bitter sight but tonic, and now he would forget it.

Yet even as he sealed his resolution, there would come to him, blown as a careless breeze from the west, the memory of that boy and girl he had seen in the town, of the gay family starting for their river picnic, of the faint welcoming call to him from the bushes in the garden, and, most of all, of the suspicion that the place was supposed to be haunted. It was just because it was haunted that he longed for it, and the more savagely and sensibly he assured himself of the folly of possessing it, the more he yearned after it, and constantly now it coloured his dreams. They were happy dreams; he was back there with the others, as in old days, children again in holiday time, and like himself they loved being at home there again, and they made much of Peter because it was he who had arranged it all. Often in these dreams he said to himself, 'I have dreamed this before, and then I woke and found myself elderly and lonely again, but this time it is real!'

The weeks passed on, busy and prosperous, growing into months, and one day in the autumn, on coming home from a day's golf, Peter fainted. He had not felt very well for some time, he had been languid and easily fatigued, but with his robust habit of mind he had labelled such symptoms as mere laziness, and had driven himself with the whip. But now it might be as well to get a medical over-hauling just for the satisfaction of being told there was nothing the matter with him. The pronouncement was not quite that ...

'But I simply can't,' he said. 'Bed for a month and a winter of loafing on the Riviera! Why, I've got my time filled up till close on Christmas, and then I've arranged to go with some friends for a short holiday. Besides, the Riviera's a pestilent hole. It can't be done. Supposing I go on just as usual: what will happen?'

Dr Dufflin made a mental summary of his wilful patient.

'You'll die, Mr Graham,' he said cheerfully. 'Your heart is not what it should be, and if you want it to do its work, which it will for many years yet, if you're sensible, you must give it rest. Of course, I don't insist on the Riviera: that was only a suggestion, for I thought you would probably have friends there, who would help to pass the time for you. But I do insist on some mild climate, where you can loaf out of doors. London with its frosts and fogs would never do.'

Peter was silent for a moment.

'How about Cornwall?' he asked.

'Yes, if you like. Not the north coast of course.'

'I'll think it over,' said Peter. 'There's a month yet.'

Peter knew that there was no need for thinking it over. Events were conspiring irresistibly to drive him to that which he longed to do, but against which he had been struggling, so fantastic was it, so irrational. But now it was made easy for him to yield and his obstinate colours came down with a run. A few telegraphic exchanges with the house agent made Lescop his, another gave him the address of a reliable builder and decorator, and with the plans of the house, though indeed there was little need of them, spread out on his counterpane, Peter issued urgent orders. All structural repairs, leaking roofs and dripping ceilings, rotted woodwork and crumbling plaster must be tackled at once, and when that was done, painting and papering followed. The drawing room used to have a Morris paper; there were spring flowers on it, black-thorn, violets and fritillaries, a hateful wriggling paper, so he thought it, but none other would serve. The hall was painted duck-egg green, and his mother's room was pink, 'a beastly pink, tell them,' said Peter to his secretary, 'with a bit of blue in it: they must send me samples by return of post, big pieces, not snippets' … Then there was furniture: all the furniture in the house here which had once been at Lescop must go back there. For the rest, he would send down some stuff from London, bedroom appurtenances, and linen and kitchen utensils: he would see to carpets when he got there. Spare bedrooms could wait; just four servants' rooms must be furnished and also the attic, which he had marked on the plan and which he intended to occupy himself. But no one must touch the garden till he came: he would superintend that himself, but by the middle of next month there must be a couple of gardeners ready for him.

'And that's all,' said Peter, 'just for the present.' 'All?' he thought, as, rather bored with the direction of matters that usually ran themselves, he folded up his plans. 'Why, it's just the beginning: just underwriting.'

The month's rest cure was pronounced a success, and with strict orders not to exert mind or body, but to lie fallow, out of doors whenever possible, with quiet strolls and copious restings, Peter was allowed to go to Lescop, and on a December evening he saw the door opened to him and the light of welcome stream out on to his entry. The moment he set foot inside he knew, as by some interior sense, that he had done right, for it was not only the warmth and the ordered comfort restored to the deserted house that greeted him, but the firm knowledge that they whose loss made his loneliness were greeting him … That came in a flash, fantastic and yet soberly convincing; it was fundamental, everything was based on it. The house had been restored to its old aspect, and though he had ventured to turn the small attic next door to young Peter's bedroom into a bathroom, 'after all,' he thought, 'it's my house, and I must make myself comfortable. They don't want bathrooms, but I do, and there it is.' There indeed it was, and there was electric light installed, and he dined, sitting in his father's chair, and then pottered from room to room, drinking in the old friendly atmosphere, which was round him wherever he went, for they were pleased. But neither voice nor vision manifested that, and perhaps it was only his own pleasure at being back that he attributed to them. But he would have loved a glimpse or a whisper, and from time to time, as he sat looking over some memoranda about the British Tin Syndicate, he peered into corners of the room, thinking that something moved there, and when a trail of creeper tapped against the window he got up and looked out. But nothing met his scrutiny but the dim starlight falling like dew on the neglected lawn. 'They're here, though,' he said to himself, as he let the curtain fall back.

The gardeners were ready for him the next morning, and under his directions began the taming of the jungly wildness. And here was a pleasant thing, for one of them was the son of the cowman, Calloway, who had been here forty years ago, and he had childish memories still of the garden where with his father he used to come from the milking shed to the house with the full pails. And he remembered that Sybil used to keep her guinea pigs on the drying ground at the back of the house. Now that he said that Peter remembered it too, and so the drying ground all overgrown with brambles and rank herbage must be cleared.

'Iss, sure, nasty little vermin I thought them,' said Calloway the younger, 'but 'twas here Miss Sybil had their hutches and a wired run for 'em. And a rare fuss there was when my father's terrier got in and killed half of 'em, and the young lady crying over the corpses.'

That massacre of the innocents was so dim to Peter; it must have happened in term time when he was at school, and by the next holidays, to be sure, the prolific habits of her pets had gladdened Sybil's mourning.

So the drying ground was cleared and the winding path up the shrubbery to the summer house which had been home to the distressed vessels pursued by pirates. This was being rebuilt now, the roof timbered up, the walls rectified and whitewashed, and the steps leading to it and its tiled floor cleaned of the encroaching moss. It was soon finished, and Peter often sat there to rest and read the papers after a morning of prowling and supervising in the garden, for an hour or two on his feet oddly tired him, and he would doze in the sunny shelter. But now he never dreamed about coming back to Lescop or of the welcoming presences. 'Perhaps that's because I've come,' he thought, 'and those dreams were only meant to drive me. But I think they might show that they're pleased: I'm doing all I can.'

Yet he knew they were pleased, for as the work in the garden progressed, the sense of them and their delight hung about the cleared paths as surely as the smell of the damp earth and the uprooted bracken which had made such trespass. Every evening Calloway collected the gleanings of the day, piling them on the bonfire in the orchard.

The bracken flared, and the damp hazel stems fizzed and broke into flame, and the scent of the woodsmoke drifted across to the house. And after some three weeks' work all was done, and that afternoon Peter took no siesta in the summer house, for he could not cease from walking through flower garden and kitchen garden and orchard now perfectly restored to their old order. A shower fell, and he sheltered under the lime where the pigeons built, and then the sun came out again, and in that gleam at the close of the winter day he took a final stroll to the bottom of the drive, where the gate now hung firm on even hinges. It used to take a long time in closing, if, as a boy, you let it swing, penduluming backwards and forwards with the latch of it clicking as it passed the hasp: and now he pulled it wide, and let go of it, and to and fro it went in lessening movement till at the last it clicked and stayed. Somehow that pleased him immensely: he liked accuracy in details.

But there was no doubt he was very tired: he had an unpleasant sensation, too, as of a wire stretched tight across his heart, and of some thrumming going on against it. The wire dully ached, and this thrumming produced little stabs of sharp pain. All day he had been conscious of something of the sort, but he was too much taken up with the joy of the finished garden to heed little physical beckonings. A good long night would make him fit again, or, if not, he could stop in bed tomorrow. He went upstairs early, not the least anxious about himself, and instantly went to sleep. The soft night air pushed in at his open window, and the last sound that he heard was the tapping of the blind tassel against the sash.

He woke very suddenly and completely, knowing that somebody had called him. The room was curiously bright, but not with the quality of moonlight; it was like a valley lying in shadow, while somewhere, a little way above it, shone some strong splendour of noon. And then he heard again his name called, and knew that the sound of the voice came in through the window. There was no doubt that Violet was calling him: she and the others were out in the garden.

'Yes, I'm coming,' he cried, and he jumped out of bed. He seemed – it was not odd – to be already dressed: he had on a jersey and flannel trousers, but his feet were bare and he slipped on a pair of shoes, and ran downstairs, taking the first short flight in one leap, like young Peter. The door of his mother's room was open, and he looked in, and there she was, of course, sitting at the table and writing letters.

'Oh, Peter, how lovely to have you home again,' she said. 'They're all out in the garden, and they've been calling you, darling. But come and see me soon, and have a talk.'

Out he ran along the walk below the windows, and up the winding path through the shrubbery to the summer house, for he knew they were going to play Pirates. He must hurry, or the Pirates would be aboard before he got there, and as he ran, he called out, 'Oh, do wait a second: I'm coming.'

He scudded past the golden maple and the bay tree, and there they all were in the summer house which was home. And he took a flying leap up the steps and was among them.

*

It was there that Calloway found him next morning. He must indeed have run up the winding path like a boy, for the new-laid gravel was spurned at long intervals by the toe-prints of his shoes.

MARJORIE BOWEN

(1885–1952)

Gabrielle Margaret Campbell, who wrote under the name of Marjorie Bowen (among others), was born between 'All Saints and All Souls', which, as she remarked in her autobiography, 'is supposed to give the gift of second sight'. Her childhood was poverty-stricken and nomadic, driven by the need to escape debts; at one point the family lived in a house in St John's Wood, north London, which was haunted by 'all the usual psychic phenomena', including a 'hooded figure'. From an early age Bowen was the sole breadwinner for her sister and mother and she continued to publish prolifically throughout her life. One of her lasting literary legacies was to inspire Graham Greene, who described reading her first book, *The Viper of Milan*, aged fourteen: 'From that moment I began to write. All the other possible futures slid away …'

THE CROWN DERBY PLATE

MARTHA PYM SAID that she had never seen a ghost and that she would very much like to do so, 'particularly at Christmas, for, you can laugh as you like, that is the correct time to see a ghost'.

'I don't suppose you ever will,' replied her cousin Mabel comfortably; while her cousin Clara shuddered and said that she hoped they would change the subject, for she disliked even to think of such things.

The three elderly, cheerful women sat round a big fire, cosy and content after a day of pleasant activities. Martha was the guest of the other two, who owned the handsome, convenient country house; she always came to spend her Christmas with the Wyntons, and found the leisurely country life delightful after the bustling round of London, for Martha managed an antiques shop of the better sort and worked extremely hard. She was, however, still full of zest for work or pleasure, though sixty years old, and looked backwards and forwards to a succession of delightful days.

The other two, Mabel and Clara, led quieter but none-theless agreeable lives; they had more money and fewer interests, but nevertheless enjoyed themselves very well.

'Talking of ghosts,' said Mabel, 'I wonder how that old woman at Hartleys is getting on – for Hartleys, you know, is supposed to be haunted.'

'Yes, I know,' smiled Miss Pym; 'but all the years we have known of the place we have never heard anything definite, have we?'

'No,' put in Clara; 'but there *is* that persistent rumour that the house is uncanny, and for myself, *nothing* would induce me to live there.'

'It is certainly very lonely and dreary down there on the marshes,' conceded Mabel. 'But as for the ghost – you never hear *what* it is supposed to be, even.'

'Who has taken it?' asked Miss Pym, remembering Hartleys as very desolate indeed and long shut up.

'A Miss Lefain, an eccentric old creature – I think you met her here once two years ago –'

'I believe that I did, but I don't recall her at all.'

'We have not seen her since. Hartleys is so ungetatable and she didn't seem to want visitors. She collects china, Martha, so really you ought to go and see her and talk shop.'

With the word 'china' some curious associations came into the mind of Martha Pym; she was silent while she strove to put them together, and after a second or two they all fitted together into a very clear picture.

She remembered that thirty years ago – yes, it must be thirty years ago, when, as a young woman, she had put all her capital into the antiques business and had been staying with her cousins (her aunt had then been alive) – she had driven across the marsh to Hartleys, where there was an auction sale; all the details of this she had completely forgotten, but she could recall quite clearly purchasing a set of gorgeous china which was still one of her proud delights, a perfect set of Crown Derby save that one plate was missing.

'How odd,' she remarked, 'that this Miss Lefain should collect china too, for it was at Hartleys that I purchased my dear old Derby service – I've never been able to match that plate.'

'A plate was missing? I seem to remember,' said Clara. 'Didn't they say that it must be in the house somewhere and that it should be looked for?'

'I believe they did; but of course I never heard any more, and that missing plate has annoyed me ever since. Who had Hartleys?'

'An old connoisseur, Sir James Sewell. I believe he was some relation to this Miss Lefain, but I don't know –'

'I wonder if she has found the plate,' mused Miss Pym. 'I expect she has turned out and ransacked the whole place.'

'Why not trot over and ask?' suggested Mabel. 'It's not much use to her if she has found it, one odd plate.'

'Don't be silly,' said Clara. 'Fancy going over the marshes in this weather to ask about a plate missed all those years ago. I'm sure Martha wouldn't think of it.'

But Martha did think of it; she was rather fascinated by the idea. How queer and pleasant it would be if, after all these years, nearly a lifetime, she should find the Crown Derby plate, the loss of which had always irked her! And this hope did not seem so altogether fantastical; it was quite likely that old Miss Lefain, poking about in the ancient house, had found the missing piece.

And, of course, if she had, being a fellow collector, she would be quite willing to part with it to complete the set.

Her cousin endeavoured to dissuade her; Miss Lefain, she declared, was a recluse, an odd creature who might greatly resent such a visit and such a request.

'Well, if she does I can but come away again,' smiled Miss Pym. 'I suppose she can't bite my head off, and I rather like meeting these curious types – we've got a love for old china in common, anyhow.'

'It seems so silly to think of it after all these years – a plate!'

'A Crown Derby plate,' corrected Miss Pym. 'It is certainly strange that I did not think of it before, but now that I have got it into my head I can't get it out. Besides,' she added hopefully, 'I might see the ghost.'

So full, however, were the days with pleasant local engagements that Miss Pym had no immediate chance of putting her scheme into practice; but she did not relinquish it and she asked several different people what they knew about Hartleys and Miss Lefain.

And no one knew anything except that the house was supposed to be haunted and the owner 'cracky'.

'Is there a story?' asked Miss Pym, who associated ghosts with neat tales into which they fitted as exactly as nuts into shells.

But she was always told, 'Oh no, there isn't a story; no one knows anything about the place, don't know how the idea got about; old Sewell was half crazy, I believe. He was buried in the garden and that gives a house a nasty name.'

'Very unpleasant,' said Martha Pym, undisturbed.

This ghost seemed too elusive for her to track down; she would have to be content if she could recover the Crown Derby plate; for that at least she was determined to make a try and also to satisfy that faint tingling of curiosity roused in her by this talk about Hartleys and the remembrance of that day, so long ago, when she had gone to the auction sale at the lonely old house.

So the first free afternoon, while Mabel and Clara were comfortably taking their afternoon repose, Martha Pym, who was of a more lively habit, got out her little governess cart and dashed away across the Essex flats.

She had taken minute directions with her, but she soon lost her way.

Under the wintry sky, which looked as grey and hard as metal, the marshes stretched bleakly to the horizon; the olive-brown broken reeds were harsh as scars on the saffron-tinted bogs, where the sluggish waters that rose so high in winter were filmed over with the first stillness of a frost. The air was cold, but not keen; everything was damp. Faintest of mists blurred the black outlines of trees that rose stark from the ridges above the stagnant dykes; the flooded fields were haunted by black birds and white birds, gulls and crows, whining above the high ditch grass and wintry wastes.

Miss Pym stopped the little horse and surveyed this spectral scene, which had a certain relish about it to one sure to return to a homely village, a cheerful house and good company.

A withered and bleached old man, in colour like the dun landscape, came along the road between the spare alders.

Miss Pym, buttoning up her coat, asked the way to Hartleys as he passed her; he told her, straight on, and she proceeded, straight indeed along the road that went with undeviating length across the marshes.

'Of course,' thought Miss Pym, 'if you live in a place like this you are bound to invent ghosts.'

The house sprang up suddenly on a knoll ringed with rotting trees, encompassed by an old brick wall that the perpetual damp had overrun with lichen, blue, green, white, colours of decay.

Hartleys, no doubt; there was no other residence or human being in sight in all the wide expanse; besides, she could remember it, surely, after all this time – the sharp rising out of the marsh, the colony of tall trees; but then fields and trees had been green and bright – there had been no water on the flats, it had been summertime.

'She certainly,' thought Miss Pym, 'must be crazy to live here. And I rather doubt if I shall get my plate.'

She fastened up the good little horse by the garden gate, which stood negligently ajar, and entered. The garden itself was so neglected that it was quite surprising to see a trim appearance in the house – curtains at the windows and a polish on the brass door-knocker, which must have been recently rubbed there, considering the taint in the sea damp which rusted and rotted everything.

It was a square-built, substantial house with 'nothing wrong with it but the situation', Miss Pym decided, though it was not very attractive, being built of that drab, plastered stone so popular a hundred years ago, with flat windows and door; while one side was gloomily shaded by a large evergreen tree of the cypress variety which gave a blackish tinge to that portion of the garden. There was no pretence at flowerbeds nor any manner of cultivation in this garden, where a few rank weeds and straggling bushes matted together above the dead grass. On the enclosing wall, which appeared to have been built high as protection against the ceaseless winds that swung along the flats, were the remains of fruit trees; their crucified branches, rotting under the great nails that held them up, looked like the skeletons of those who had died in torment.

Miss Pym took in these noxious details as she knocked firmly at the door; they did not depress her; she merely felt extremely sorry for anyone who could live in such a place.

She noticed at the far end of the garden, in the corner of the wall, a headstone showing above the sodden, colourless grass, and remembered what she had been told about the old antiquary being buried there, in the grounds of Hartleys.

As the knock had no effect, she stepped back and looked at the house: it was certainly inhabited – with those neat windows, white curtains and drab blinds all pulled to precisely the same level. And when she brought her glance back to the door she saw that it had been opened and that someone, considerably obscured by the darkness of the passage, was looking at her intently.

'Good afternoon,' said Miss Pym cheerfully. 'I just thought I would call and see Miss Lefain – it is Miss Lefain, isn't it?'

'It's my house,' was the querulous reply.

Martha Pym had hardly expected to find any servants here, though the old lady must, she thought, work pretty hard to keep the house so clean and tidy as it appeared to be.

'Of course,' she replied. 'May I come in? I'm Martha Pym, staying with the Wyntons. I met you there –'

'Do come in,' was the faint reply. 'I get so few people to visit me, I'm really very lonely.'

'I don't wonder,' thought Miss Pym; but she had resolved to take no notice of any eccentricity on the part of her hostess, and so she entered the house with her usual agreeable candour and courtesy.

The passage was badly lit, but she was able to get a fair idea of Miss Lefain. Her first impression was that this poor creature was most dreadfully old, older than any human being had the right to be; why, she felt young in comparison – so faded, feeble and pallid was Miss Lefain.

She was also monstrously fat; her gross, flaccid figure was shapeless and she wore a badly cut, full dress of no colour at all, but stained with earth and damp where, Miss Pym supposed, she had been doing futile gardening; this gown was doubtless designed to disguise her stoutness, but had been so carelessly pulled about that it only added to it, being rucked and rolled 'all over the place', as Miss Pym put it to herself.

Another ridiculous touch about the appearance of the poor old lady was her short hair; decrepit as she was and lonely as she lived, she had actually had her scanty relics of white hair cropped round her shaking head.

'Dear me, dear me,' she said in her thin, treble voice. 'How very kind of you to come. I suppose you prefer the parlour? I generally sit in the garden.'

'The garden? But not in this weather?'

'I get used to the weather. You've no idea how used one gets to the weather.'

'I suppose so,' conceded Miss Pym doubtfully. 'You don't live here quite alone, do you?'

'Quite alone, lately. I had a little company, but she was taken away – I'm sure I don't know where. I haven't been able to find a trace of her anywhere,' replied the old lady peevishly.

'Some wretched companion that couldn't stick it, I suppose,' thought Miss Pym. 'Well, I don't wonder – but someone ought to be here to look after her.'

They went into the parlour, which, the visitor was dismayed to see, was without a fire, but otherwise well kept.

And there, on dozens of shelves, was a choice array of china, at which Martha Pym's eyes glistened.

'Aha!' cried Miss Lefain. 'I see you've noticed my treasures. Don't you envy me? Don't you wish that you had some of those pieces?'

Martha Pym certainly did, and she looked eagerly and greedily round the walls, tables and cabinets, while the old woman followed her with little thin squeals of pleasure.

It was a beautiful little collection, most choicely and elegantly arranged, and Martha thought it marvellous that this feeble, ancient creature should be able to keep it in such precise order as well as doing her own housework.

'Do you really do everything yourself here and live quite alone?' she asked, and she shivered even in her thick coat and wished that Miss Lefain's energy had risen to a fire, but then probably she lived in the kitchen, as these lonely eccentrics often did.

'There was someone,' answered Miss Lefain cunningly, 'but I had to send her away. I told you she's gone; I can't find her and I am so glad. Of course,' she added wistfully, 'it leaves me very lonely, but then I couldn't stand her impertinence any longer. She used to say that it was *her* house and her collection of china! Would you believe it? She used to try and chase me away from looking at my own things!'

'How very disagreeable,' said Miss Pym, wondering which of the two women had been crazy. 'But hadn't you better get someone else?'

'Oh no,' was the jealous answer. 'I would rather be alone with my things. I daren't leave the house for fear someone takes them away – there was a dreadful time once when an auction sale was held here –'

'Were you here then?' asked Miss Pym; but indeed she looked old enough to have been anywhere.

'Yes, of course,' Miss Lefain replied rather peevishly, and Miss Pym decided that she must be a relation of old Sir James Sewell. Clara and Mabel had been very foggy about it all. 'I was very busy hiding all the china – but one set they got – a Crown Derby tea service …'

'With one plate missing!' cried Martha Pym. 'I bought it, and do you know, I was wondering if you'd found it –'

'I hid it,' piped Miss Lefain.

'Oh, you did, did you? Well, that's rather funny behaviour. Why did you hide the stuff away instead of buying it?'

'How could I buy what was mine?'

'Old Sir James left it to you, then?' asked Martha Pym, feeling very muddled.

'*She* bought a lot more,' squeaked Miss Lefain, but Martha Pym tried to keep her to the point.

'If you've got the plate,' she insisted, 'you might let me have it – I'll pay quite handsomely. It would be so pleasant to have it after all these years.'

'Money is no use to me,' said Miss Lefain mournfully. 'Not a bit of use. I can't leave the house or the garden.'

'Well, you have to live, I suppose,' said Martha Pym cheerfully. 'And, do you know, I'm afraid you are getting rather morbid and dull, living here all alone – you really ought to have a fire – why, it's just on Christmas and very damp.'

'I haven't felt the cold for a long time,' replied the other; she seated herself with a sigh on one of the horsehair chairs and Miss Pym noticed with a start that her feet were covered only by a pair of white stockings. 'One of those nasty health fiends,' thought Miss Pym; 'but she doesn't look too well for all that.'

'So you don't think that you could let me have the plate?' she asked briskly, walking up and down, for the dark, clean, neat parlour was very cold indeed, and she thought that she couldn't stand this much longer; as there seemed no sign of tea or anything pleasant and comfortable, she had really better go.

'I might let you have it,' sighed Miss Lefain, 'since you've been so kind as to pay me a visit. After all, one plate isn't much use, is it?'

'Of course not, I wonder you troubled to hide it.'

'I couldn't *bear*,' wailed the other, 'to see the things going out of the house!'

Martha Pym couldn't stop to go into all this; it was quite clear that the old lady was very eccentric indeed and that nothing very much could be done with her; no wonder that she had 'dropped out' of everything and that no one ever saw her or knew anything about her; though Miss Pym felt that some effort ought really to be made to save her from herself.

'Wouldn't you like a run in my little governess cart?' she suggested. 'We might go to tea with the Wyntons on the way back, they'd be delighted to see you; and I really think that you do want taking out of yourself.'

'I was taken out of myself some time ago,' replied Miss Lefain. 'I really was; and I couldn't leave my things – though,' she added with pathetic gratitude, 'it is very, very kind of you –'

'Your things would be quite safe, I'm sure,' said Martha Pym, humouring her. 'Whoever would come up here this hour of a winter's day?'

'They do, oh, they do! And *she* might come back, prying and nosing and saying it was all hers, all my beautiful china here!'

Miss Lefain squealed in her agitation, and rising up ran round the wall fingering with flaccid, yellow hands the brilliant glossy pieces on the shelves.

'Well, then, I'm afraid that I must go. They'll be

expecting me, and it's quite a long ride; perhaps some other time you'll come and see us?'

'Oh, must you go?' quavered Miss Lefain dolefully. 'I do like a little company now and then, and I trusted you from the first – the others, when they do come, are always after my things and I have to frighten them away.'

'Frighten them away!' replied Martha Pym. 'However do you do that?'

'It doesn't seem difficult. People are so easily frightened, aren't they?'

Miss Pym suddenly remembered that Hartleys had the reputation of being haunted – perhaps the queer old thing played on that; the lonely house with the grave in the garden was dreary enough to create a legend.

'I suppose you've never seen a ghost?' she asked pleasantly. 'I'd rather like to see one, you know –'

'There is no one here but myself,' said Miss Lefain.

'So you've never seen anything? I thought it must be all nonsense. Still, I do think it rather melancholy for you to live here all alone.'

Miss Lefain sighed. 'Yes, it's very lonely. Do stay and talk to me a little longer.' Her whistling voice dropped cunningly. 'And I'll give you the Crown Derby plate!'

'Are you sure you've really got it?' Miss Pym asked.

'I'll show you.'

Fat and waddling as she was, she seemed to move lightly as she slipped in front of Miss Pym and conducted her from the room, going slowly up the stairs – such a gross, odd figure in that clumsy dress with the fringe of white hair hanging on to her shoulders.

The upstairs of the house was as neat as the parlour – everything well in its place; but there was no sign of occupancy; the beds were covered with dustsheets. There were no lamps or fires set ready. 'I suppose,' said Miss Pym to herself, 'she doesn't care to show me where she really lives.'

But as they passed from one room to another, she could not help saying, 'Where do you live, Miss Lefain?'

'Mostly in the garden,' said the other.

Miss Pym thought of those horrible health huts that some people indulged in.

'Well, sooner you than I,' she replied cheerfully.

In the most distant room of all, a dark, tiny closet, Miss Lefain opened a deep cupboard and brought out a Crown Derby plate, which her guest received with a spasm of joy, for it was actually that missing from her cherished set.

'It's very good of you,' she said in delight. 'Won't you take something for it or let me do something for you?'

'You might come and see me again,' replied Miss Lefain wistfully.

'Oh yes, of course I should like to come and see you again.'

But now that she had got what she had really come for – the plate – Martha Pym wanted to be gone; it was really very dismal and depressing in the house, and she began to notice a fearful smell – the place had been shut up too long, there was something damp rotting somewhere – in this horrid little dark closet no doubt.

'I really must be going,' she said hurriedly.

Miss Lefain turned as if to cling to her, but Martha Pym moved quickly away.

'Dear me,' wailed the old lady. 'Why are you in such haste?'

'There's – a smell,' murmured Miss Pym rather faintly.

She found herself hastening down the stairs, with Miss Lefain complaining behind her.

'How peculiar people are! *She* used to talk of a smell –'

'Well, you must notice it yourself.'

Miss Pym was in the hall; the old woman had not followed her but stood in the semi-darkness at the head of the stairs, a pale, shapeless figure.

Martha Pym hated to be rude and ungrateful, but she could not stay another moment; she hurried away and was in her cart in a moment – really, that smell …

'Goodbye!' she called out with false cheerfulness. 'And thank you *so* much!'

There was no answer from the house.

Miss Pym drove on; she was rather upset and took another way than that by which she had come – a way that led past a little house raised above the marsh. She was glad to think that the poor old creature at Hartleys had such near neighbours, and she reined up the horse, dubious as to whether she should call someone and tell them that poor old Miss Lefain really wanted a little looking after, alone in a house like that and plainly not quite right in her head.

A young woman, attracted by the sound of the governess cart, came to the door of the house and, seeing Miss Pym, called out, asking if she wanted the keys of the house.

'What house?'

'Hartleys, mum. They don't put a board out, as no one

is likely to pass, but it's to be sold. Miss Lefain wants to sell or let it –'

'I've just been up to see her –'

'Oh no, mum; she's been away a year, abroad somewhere – couldn't stand the place. It's been empty since then; I just run in every day and keep things tidy.'

Loquacious and curious, the young woman had come to the fence; Miss Pym had stopped her horse.

'Miss Lefain is there now,' she said. 'She must have just come back –'

'She wasn't there this morning, mum. 'Tisn't likely she'd come, either – fair scared she was, mum, fair chased away, didn't dare move her china. Can't say I've noticed anything myself, but I never stay long; and there's a smell –'

'Yes,' murmured Martha Pym faintly, 'there's a smell. What – what – chased her away?'

The young woman, even in that lonely place, lowered her voice.

'Well, as you aren't thinking of taking the place, she got an idea in her head that old Sir James ... well, he couldn't bear to leave Hartleys, mum. He's buried in the garden, and she thought he was after her, chasing round them bits of china –'

'Oh!' cried Miss Pym.

'Some of it used to be his, she found a lot stuffed away; he said they were to be left in Hartleys, but Miss Lefain would have the things sold, I believe – that's years ago.'

'Yes, yes,' said Miss Pym with a sick look. 'You don't know what he was like, do you?'

'No, mum; but I've heard tell he was very stout and very old – I wonder who it was you saw up at Hartleys?'

Miss Pym took a Crown Derby plate from her bag.

'You might take that back when you go,' she whispered. 'I shan't want it, after all.'

Before the astonished young woman could answer, Miss Pym had darted off across the marsh; that short hair, that earth-stained robe, the white socks, 'I generally live in the garden ...'

Miss Pym drove away at breakneck speed, frantically resolving to mention to no one that she had paid a visit to Hartleys, nor lightly again to bring up the subject of ghosts.

She shook and shuddered in the damp, trying to get out of her clothes and her nostrils that indescribable smell.

Hugh Walpole

(1884–1941)

Born in New Zealand, Hugh Walpole was educated in England, where he found boarding school an experience of 'sheer, stark, unblinking terror', exacerbated by a series of nightmares which continued into later life and 'took exactly the sense of sudden death'. In adult life he became a prolific and successful novelist, cultivating close friendships with other writers such as Arnold Bennett, Joseph Conrad and Henry James, the last of whom he addressed as '*très cher maître*' in his letters. Although one of the most prominent literary figures of his age, he complained of feeling as if he had 'my true self jumping up inside me and saying, "Well, you know you're not a writer of the first rank, you know."' His reputation suffered a fatal blow when W. Somerset Maugham caricatured him as the sycophantic and mediocre novelist Alroy Kear in *Cakes and Ale*. Walpole's diary reveals his emotions on opening the book for the first time: 'Read on with increasing horror. Unmistakeable portrait of myself. Never slept!'

THE TARN

I

As Foster moved unconsciously across the room, bent towards the bookcase and stood leaning forward a little, choosing now one book, now another with his eye, his host, seeing the muscles of the back of his thin, scraggy neck stand out above his low flannel collar, thought of the ease with which he could squeeze that throat, and the pleasure, the triumphant, lustful pleasure, that such an action would give him.

The low, white-walled, white-ceilinged room was flooded with the mellow, kindly Lakeland sun. October is a wonderful month in the English Lakes, golden, rich and perfumed, slow suns moving through apricot-tinted skies to ruby evening glories; the shadows lie then thick about that beautiful country, in dark purple patches, in long web-like patterns of silver gauze, in thick splotches of amber and grey. The clouds pass in galleons across the mountains, now veiling, now revealing, now descending with ghost-like armies to the very breast of the plains, suddenly rising to the softest of blue skies and lying thin in lazy languorous colour.

Fenwick's cottage looked across to Low Fells; on his right, seen through side windows, sprawled the hills above Ullswater.

Fenwick looked at Foster's back and felt suddenly sick, so that he sat down, veiling his eyes for a moment with his hand. Foster had come up there, come all the way from London, to explain. It was so like Foster to want to explain, to want to put things right. For how many years had he known Foster? Why, for twenty at least, and during all those years Foster had been forever determined to put things right with everybody. He could never bear to be disliked; he hated that anyone should think ill of him; he wanted everyone to be his friend. That was one reason, perhaps, why Foster had got on so well, had prospered so in his career; one reason, too, why Fenwick had not.

For Fenwick was the opposite of Foster in this. He did not want friends, he certainly did not care that people should like him – that is, people for whom, for one reason or another, he had contempt – and he had contempt for quite a number of people.

Fenwick looked at that long, thin, bending back and felt his knees tremble. Soon Foster would turn round and that high, reedy voice would pipe out something about the books. 'What jolly books you have, Fenwick!' How many, many times in the long watches of the night, when Fenwick could not sleep, had he heard that pipe sounding close there – yes, in the very shadows of his bed! And how many times had Fenwick replied to it, 'I hate you! You are the cause of my failure in life! You have been in my way always. Always, always, always! Patronising and pretending, and in truth showing others what a poor thing you thought me, how great a failure, how conceited a fool! I know. You can hide nothing from me! I can hear you!'

For twenty years now Foster had been persistently in Fenwick's way. There had been that affair, so long ago now, when Robins had wanted a subeditor for his wonderful review, the *Parthenon*, and Fenwick had gone to see him and they had had a splendid talk. How magnificently Fenwick had talked that day; with what enthusiasm he had shown Robins (who was blinded by his own conceit, anyway) the kind of paper the *Parthenon* might be; how Robins had caught his own enthusiasm, how he had pushed his fat body about the room, crying, 'Yes, yes, Fenwick – that's fine! That's fine indeed!' – and then how, after all, Foster had got that job.

The paper had only lived for a year or so, it is true, but the connection with it had brought Foster into prominence just as it might have brought Fenwick!

Then, five years later, there was Fenwick's novel, *The Bitter Aloe* – the novel upon which he had spent three years of blood-and-tears endeavour – and then, in the very same week of publication, Foster brings out *The Circus*, the novel that made his name; although, heaven knows, the thing was poor enough sentimental trash. You may say that one novel cannot kill another – but can it not? Had not *The Circus* appeared would not that group of London know-alls – that conceited, limited, ignorant, self-satisfied crowd, who nevertheless can do, by their talk, so much to affect a book's good or evil fortunes – have talked about *The Bitter Aloe* and so forced it into prominence? As it was, the book was stillborn and *The Circus* went on its prancing, triumphant way.

After that there had been many occasions – some small, some big – and always in one way or another that thin, scraggy body of Foster's was interfering with Fenwick's happiness.

The thing had become, of course, an obsession with Fenwick. Hiding up there in the heart of the Lakes, with no friends, almost no company and very little money, he was given too much to brooding over his failure. He *was* a failure and it was not his own fault. How could it be his own fault with his talents and his brilliance? It was the fault of modern life and its lack of culture, the fault of the stupid material mess that made up the intelligence of human beings – and the fault of Foster.

Always Fenwick hoped that Foster would keep away from him. He did not know what he would not do did he see the man. And then one day, to his amazement, he received a telegram:

Passing through this way. May I stop with you Monday and Tuesday? – Giles Foster.

Fenwick could scarcely believe his eyes, and then – from curiosity, from cynical contempt, from some deeper, more mysterious motive that he dared not analyse – he had telegraphed, 'Come.'

And here the man was. And he had come – would

you believe it? – to 'put things right'. He had heard from Hamlin Eddis that Fenwick was hurt with him, had some kind of grievance.

'I didn't like to feel that, old man, and so I thought I'd just stop by and have it out with you, see what the matter was and put it right.'

Last night after supper Foster had tried to put it right. Eagerly, his eyes like a good dog's who is asking for a bone that he knows he thoroughly deserves, he had held out his hand and asked Fenwick to 'say what was up'.

Fenwick simply had said that nothing was up; Hamlin Eddis was a damned fool.

'Oh, I'm glad to hear that!' Foster had cried, springing up out of his chair and putting his hand on Fenwick's shoulder. 'I'm glad of that, old man. I couldn't bear for us not to be friends. We've been friends so long.'

Lord! How Fenwick hated him at that moment!

II

'What a jolly lot of books you have!' Foster turned round and looked at Fenwick with eager, gratified eyes. 'Every book here is interesting! I like your arrangement of them, too, and those open bookshelves – it always seems to me a shame to shut up books behind glass!'

Foster came forward and sat down quite close to his host. He even reached forward and laid his hand on his host's knee. 'Look here! I'm mentioning it for the last time – positively! But I do want to make quite certain. There *is* nothing wrong between us, is there, old man? I know you assured me last night, but I just want –'

Fenwick looked at him and, surveying him, felt suddenly an exquisite pleasure of hatred. He liked the touch of the man's hand on his knee; he himself bent forward a little and, thinking how agreeable it would be to push Foster's eyes in, deep, deep into his head, crunching them, smashing them to purple, leaving the empty, staring, bloody sockets, said, 'Why, no. Of course not. I told you last night. What could there be?'

The hand gripped the knee a little more tightly.

'I *am* so glad! That's splendid! Splendid! I hope you won't think me ridiculous, but I've always had an affection for you ever since I can remember. I've always wanted to know you better. I've admired your talent so greatly. That novel of yours – the – the – the one about the aloe –'

'*The Bitter Aloe?*'

'Ah, yes, that was it. That was a splendid book. Pessimistic, of course, but still fine. It ought to have done better. I remember thinking so at the time.'

'Yes, it ought to have done better.'

'Your time will come, though. What I say is that good work always tells in the end.'

'Yes, my time will come.'

The thin, piping voice went on: 'Now, I've had more success than I deserved. Oh yes, I have. You can't deny it. I'm not falsely modest. I mean it. I've got some talent, of course, but not so much as people say. And you! Why, you've got so *much* more than they acknowledge. You have, old man. You have indeed. Only – I do hope you'll forgive my saying this – perhaps you haven't advanced quite as you might have done. Living up here, shut away here, closed in by all these mountains, in this wet climate – always raining – why, you're out of things! You don't see people, don't talk and discover what's really going on. Why, look at me!'

Fenwick turned round and looked at him.

'Now, I have half the year in London, where one gets the best of everything, best talk, best music, best plays; and then I'm three months abroad, Italy or Greece or somewhere, and then three months in the country. Now, that's an ideal arrangement. You have everything that way.'

Italy or Greece or somewhere!

Something turned in Fenwick's breast, grinding, grinding, grinding. How he had longed, oh, how passionately, for just one week in Greece, two days in Sicily! Sometimes he had thought that he might run to it, but when it had come to the actual counting of the pennies … And how this fool, this fathead, this self-satisfied, conceited, patronising …

He got up, looking out at the golden sun.

'What do you say to a walk?' he suggested. 'The sun will last for a good hour yet.'

III

As soon as the words were out of his lips he felt as though someone else had said them for him. He even turned half round to see whether anyone else were there. Ever since Foster's arrival on the evening before he had been conscious of this sensation. A walk? Why should he take Foster for a walk, show him his beloved country, point out those curves and lines and hollows, the broad silver shield of Ullswater, the cloudy purple hills hunched like blankets about the knees of some recumbent giant? Why? It was as though he had turned round to someone behind him and had said, 'You have some further design in this.'

They started out. The road sank abruptly to the lake, then the path ran between trees at the water's edge. Across the lake tones of bright yellow light, crocus-hued, rode upon the blue. The hills were dark.

The very way that Foster walked bespoke the man. He was always a little ahead of you, pushing his long, thin body along with little eager jerks, as though, did he not hurry, he would miss something that would be immensely to his advantage. He talked, throwing words over his shoulder to Fenwick as you throw crumbs of bread to a robin.

'Of course I was pleased. Who would not be? After all, it's a new prize. They've only been awarding it for a year or two, but it's gratifying – really gratifying – to secure it. When I opened the envelope and found the cheque there – well, you could have knocked me down with a feather. You could, indeed. Of course, a hundred pounds isn't much. But it's the honour –'

Whither were they going? Their destiny was as certain as though they had no free will. Free will? There is no free will. All is Fate. Fenwick suddenly laughed aloud.

Foster stopped.

'Why, what is it?'

'What's what?'

'You laughed.'

'Something amused me.'

Foster slipped his arm through Fenwick's.

'It *is* jolly to be walking along together like this, arm in arm, friends. I'm a sentimental man. I won't deny it. What I say is that life is short and one must love one's fellow beings, or where is one? You live too much alone, old man.' He squeezed Fenwick's arm. 'That's the truth of it.'

It was torture, exquisite, heavenly torture. It was wonderful to feel that thin, bony arm pressing against his. Almost you could hear the beating of that other heart. Wonderful to feel that arm and the temptation to take it in your hands and to bend it and twist it and then to hear the bones crack ... crack ... crack ... Wonderful to feel that temptation rise through one's body like boiling water and yet not to yield to it. For a moment Fenwick's hand touched Foster's. Then he drew himself apart.

'We're at the village. This is the hotel where they all come in the summer. We turn off at the right here. I'll show you my tarn.'

IV

'Your tarn?' asked Foster. 'Forgive my ignorance, but what *is* a tarn exactly?'

'A tarn is a miniature lake, a pool of water lying in the lap of the hill. Very quiet, lovely, silent. Some of them are immensely deep.'

'I should like to see that.'

'It is some little distance – up a rough road. Do you mind?'

'Not a bit. I have long legs.'

'Some of them are immensely deep – unfathomable – nobody touched the bottom – but quiet, like glass, with shadows only –'

'Do you know, Fenwick, I have always been afraid of water – I've never learned to swim. I'm afraid to go out of my depth. Isn't that ridiculous? But it is all because at my private school, years ago, when I was a small boy, some big fellows took me and held me with my head under the water and nearly drowned me. They did indeed. They went further than they meant to. I can see their faces.'

Fenwick considered this. The picture leaped to his mind. He could see the boys – large, strong fellows, probably – and this skinny thing like a frog, their thick hands about his throat, his legs like grey sticks kicking out of the water, their laughter, their sudden sense that something was wrong, the skinny body all flaccid and still –

He drew a deep breath.

Foster was walking beside him now, not ahead of him, as though he were a little afraid and needed reassurance. Indeed, the scene had changed. Before and behind them stretched the uphill path, loose with shale and stones. On their right, on a ridge at the foot of the hill, were some quarries, almost deserted, but the more melancholy in the fading afternoon because a little work still continued there; faint sounds came from the gaunt listening chimneys, a stream of water ran and tumbled angrily into a pool below, once and again a black silhouette, like a question mark, appeared against the darkening hill.

It was a little steep here and Foster puffed and blew.

Fenwick hated him the more for that. So thin and spare, and still he could not keep in condition! They stumbled, keeping below the quarry, on the edge of the running water, now green, now a dirty white-grey, pushing their way along the side of the hill.

Their faces were set now towards Helvellyn. It rounded the cup of hills, closing in the base and then sprawling to the right.

'There's the tarn!' Fenwick exclaimed – and then added, 'The sun's not lasting as long as I had expected. It's growing dark already.'

Foster stumbled and caught Fenwick's arm.

'This twilight makes the hills look strange – like living men. I can scarcely see my way.'

'We're alone here,' Fenwick answered. 'Don't you feel the stillness? The men will have left the quarry now and gone home. There is no one in all this place but ourselves. If you watch you will see a strange green light steal down over the hills. It lasts for but a moment and then it is dark.

'Ah, here is my tarn. Do you know how I love this place, Foster? It seems to belong especially to me, just as much as all your work and your glory and fame and success seem to belong to you. I have this and you have that. Perhaps in the end we are even, after all. Yes …

'But I feel as though that piece of water belonged to me and I to it, and as though we should never be separated – yes … Isn't it black?

'It is one of the deep ones. No one has ever sounded it. Only Helvellyn knows, and one day I fancy that it will take me, too, into its confidence, will whisper its secrets –'

Foster sneezed.

'Very nice. Very beautiful, Fenwick. I like your tarn. Charming. And now let's turn back. That is a difficult walk beneath the quarry. It's chilly, too.'

'Do you see that little jetty there?' Fenwick led Foster by the arm. 'Someone built that out into the water. He had a boat there, I suppose. Come and look down. From the end of the little jetty it looks so deep and the mountains seem to close round.'

Fenwick took Foster's arm and led him to the end of the jetty. Indeed, the water looked deep here. Deep and very black. Foster peered down, then he looked up at the hills that did indeed seem to have gathered close around him. He sneezed again.

'I've caught a cold, I am afraid. Let's turn homewards, Fenwick, or we shall never find our way.'

'Home, then,' said Fenwick, and his hands closed about the thin, scraggy neck. For the instant the head half turned, and two startled, strangely childish eyes stared; then, with a push that was ludicrously simple, the body was impelled forward, there was a sharp cry, a splash, a stir of something white against the swiftly gathering dusk, again and then again, then far-spreading ripples, then silence.

V

The silence extended. Having enwrapped the tarn, it spread as though with finger on lip to the already quiescent hills. Fenwick shared in the silence. He luxuriated in it. He did not move at all. He stood there looking upon the inky water of the tarn, his arms folded, a man lost in intensest thought. But he was not thinking. He was only conscious of a warm, luxurious relief, a sensuous feeling that was not thought at all.

Foster was gone – that tiresome, prating, conceited, self-satisfied fool! Gone, never to return. The tarn assured him of that. It stared back into Fenwick's face approvingly as though it said, 'You have done well – a clean and necessary job. We have done it together, you and I. I am proud of you.'

He was proud of himself. At last he had done something definite with his life. Thought, eager, active thought, was beginning now to flood his brain. For all these years he had hung around in this place doing nothing but cherish grievances, weak, backboneless – now at last there was action. He drew himself up and looked at the hills. He was proud – and he was cold. He was shivering. He turned up the collar of his coat. Yes, there was that faint green light that always lingered in the shadows of the hills for a brief moment before darkness came. It was growing late. He had better return.

Shivering now so that his teeth chattered, he started off down the path, and then was aware that he did not wish to leave the tarn. The tarn was friendly – the only friend he had in all the world. As he stumbled along in the dark this sense of loneliness grew. He was going home to an empty house. There had been a guest in it last night. Who was it? Why, Foster, of course – Foster with his silly laugh and amiable, mediocre eyes. Well, Foster would not be there now. No, he never would be there again.

And suddenly Fenwick started to run. He did not know why, except that, now that he had left the tarn, he was lonely. He wished that he could have stayed there all night, but because it was cold he could not, and so now he was running so that he might be at home with the lights and the familiar furniture – and all the things that he knew to reassure him.

As he ran the shale and stones scattered beneath his feet. They made a tit-tattering noise under him, and someone else seemed to be running too. He stopped, and the other runner also stopped. He breathed in the silence. He was hot now. The perspiration was trickling down his cheeks. He could feel a dribble of it down his back inside his shirt. His knees were pounding. His heart was thumping. And all around him the hills were so amazingly silent, now like India-rubber clouds that you could push in or pull out as you do those India-rubber faces, grey against the night sky of a crystal purple, upon whose surface, like the twinkling eyes of boats at sea, stars were now appearing.

His knees steadied, his heart beat less fiercely, and he began to run again. Suddenly he had turned the corner and was out at the hotel. Its lamps were kindly and reassuring. He walked then quietly along the lake-side path, and had it not been for the certainty that someone was treading behind him he would have been comfortable and at his ease. He stopped once or twice and looked back, and once he stopped and called out, 'Who's there?' Only the rustling trees answered.

He had the strangest fancy, but his brain was throbbing so fiercely that he could not think, that it was the tarn that was following him, the tarn slipping, sliding along the road, being with him so that he should not be lonely. He could almost hear the tarn whisper in his ear, 'We did that together, and so I do not wish you to bear all the responsibility yourself. I will stay with you, so that you are not lonely.'

He climbed down the road towards home, and there were the lights of his house. He heard the gate click behind him as though it were shutting him in. He went into the sitting room, lighted and ready. There were the books that Foster had admired.

The old woman who looked after him appeared.

'Will you be having some tea, sir?'

'No, thank you, Annie.'

'Will the other gentleman be wanting any?'

'No; the other gentleman is away for the night.'

'Then there will be only one for supper?'

'Yes, only one for supper.'

He sat in the corner of the sofa and fell instantly into a deep slumber.

VI

He woke when the old woman tapped him on the shoulder and told him that supper was served. The room was dark save for the jumping light of two uncertain candles. Those two red candlesticks – how he hated them up there on the mantelpiece! He had always hated them, and now they seemed to him to have something of the quality of Foster's voice – that thin, reedy, piping tone.

He was expecting at every moment that Foster would enter, and yet he knew that he would not. He continued to turn his head towards the door, but it was so dark there that you could not see. The whole room was dark except just there by the fireplace, where the two candlesticks went whining with their miserable twinkling plaint.

He went into the dining room and sat down to his meal. But he could not eat anything. It was odd – that place by the table where Foster's chair should be. Odd, naked, and made a man feel lonely.

He got up once from the table and went to the window, opened it and looked out. He listened for something, A trickle as of running water, a stir, through the silence, as though some deep pool were filling to the brim. A rustle in the trees, perhaps. An owl hooted. Sharply, as though someone had spoken unexpectedly behind his shoulder, he closed the windows and looked back, peering under his dark eyebrows into the room.

Later on he went up to his bed.

VII

Had he been sleeping, or had he been lying lazily, as one does, half dozing, half luxuriously not thinking? He was wide awake now, utterly awake, and his heart was beating with apprehension. It was as though someone had called him by name. He slept always with his window a little open and the blind up. Tonight the moonlight shadowed in sickly fashion the objects in his room. It was not a flood of light nor yet a sharp splash, silvering a square, a circle, throwing the rest into ebony darkness. The light was dim, a little green, perhaps, like the shadow that comes over the hills just before dark.

He stared at the window, and it seemed to him that something moved there. Within, or rather against the green-grey light, something silver-tinted glistened. Fenwick stared. It had the look, exactly, of slipping water.

Slipping water! He listened, his head up, and it seemed to him that from beyond the window he caught the stir of water, not running, but rather welling up and up, gurgling with satisfaction as it filled and filled.

He sat up higher in bed, and then saw that down the wallpaper beneath the window water was undoubtedly trickling. He could see it lurch to the projecting wood of the sill, pause and then slip, slither down the incline. The odd thing was that it fell so silently.

Beyond the window there was that odd gurgle, but in the room itself absolute silence. Whence could it come? He saw the line of silver rise and fall as the stream on the window ledge ebbed and flowed.

He must get up and close the window. He drew his legs above the sheets and blankets and looked down.

He shrieked. The floor was covered with a shining film of water. It was rising. As he looked it had covered half the short stumpy legs of the bed. It rose without a wink, a bubble, a break! Over the sill it poured now in a steady flow, but soundless. Fenwick sat up in the bed, the clothes gathered up to his chin, his eyes blinking, the Adam's apple throbbing like a throttle in his throat.

But he must do something, he must stop this. The water was now level with the seats of the chairs, but still was soundless. Could he but reach the door!

He put down his naked foot, then cried again. The water was icy cold. Suddenly, leaning, staring at its dark, unbroken sheen, something seemed to push him forward. He fell. His head, his face was under the icy liquid; it seemed adhesive and, in the heart of its ice, hot like melting wax. He struggled to his feet. The water was breast-high. He screamed again and again. He could see the looking glass, the row of books, the picture of Dürer's *Horse*, aloof, impervious. He beat at the water, and flakes of it seemed to cling to him like scales of fish, clammy to his touch. He struggled, ploughing his way towards the door.

The water now was at his neck. Then something had caught him by the ankle. Something held him. He struggled, crying, 'Let me go! Let me go! I tell you to let me go! I hate you! I hate you! I will not come down to you! I will not –'

The water covered his mouth. He felt that someone

pushed in his eyeballs with bare knuckles. A cold hand reached up and caught his naked thigh.

VIII

In the morning the little maid knocked and, receiving no answer, came in, as was her wont, with his shaving water. What she saw made her scream. She ran for the gardener.

They took the body with its staring, protruding eyes, its tongue sticking out between the clenched teeth, and laid it on the bed.

The only sign of disorder was an overturned water jug. A small pool of water stained the carpet.

It was a lovely morning. A twig of ivy idly, in the little breeze, tapped the pane.

RUTH RENDELL

(1930–)

Ruth Rendell was born in London, of Swedish and English descent. Her elegant crime fiction and thrillers, which focus on the psychological complexities behind seemingly ordinary lives, have been praised by authors from Toni Morrison to Ian Rankin. She has also edited the ghost stories of M. R. James, whom she described as 'the best of all' ghost story writers. During an early job at the *Chigwell Times*, she reported on a house supposedly haunted by the ghost of an old woman; the owners threatened the newspaper with litigation for devaluing their home. She was made a life peer, Baroness Rendell of Babergh, in 1997 and sits in the House of Lords for Labour. 'The Haunting of Shawley Rectory' was first published in *Ellery Queen's Mystery Magazine* in 1972.

THE HAUNTING OF
SHAWLEY RECTORY

I DON'T BELIEVE in the supernatural, but just the same I wouldn't live in Shawley Rectory.

That was what I had been thinking and what Gordon Scott said to me when we heard we were to have a new rector at St Mary's. Our wives gave us quizzical looks.

'Not very logical,' said Eleanor, my wife.

'What I mean is,' said Gordon, 'that however certain you might be that ghosts don't exist, if you lived in a place that was reputedly haunted you wouldn't be able to help wondering every time you heard a stair creak. All the normal sounds of an old house would take on a different significance.'

I agreed with him. It wouldn't be very pleasant feeling uneasy every time one was alone in one's own home at night.

'Personally,' said Patsy Scott, 'I've always believed there are no ghosts in the Rectory that a good central-heating system wouldn't get rid of.'

We laughed at that, but Eleanor said, 'You can't just dismiss it like that. The Cobworths heard and felt things even if they didn't actually see anything. And so did the Bucklands before them. And you won't find anyone more level-headed than Kate Cobworth.'

Patsy shrugged. 'The Loys didn't even hear or feel anything. They'd heard the stories, they *expected* to hear the footsteps and the carriage wheels. Diana Loy told me. And Diana was quite a nervy, highly strung sort of person. But absolutely nothing happened while they were there.'

'Well, maybe the Church of England or whoever's responsible will install central heating for this new person,' I said, 'and we'll see if your theory's right, Patsy.'

Eleanor and I went home after that. We went on foot because our house is only about a quarter of a mile up Shawley Lane. On the way we stopped in front of the Rectory, which is about a hundred yards along. We stood and looked over the gate.

I may as well describe the Rectory to you before I get on with this story. The date of it is around 1760 and it's built of pale dun-coloured brick with plain classical windows and a front door in the middle with a pediment over it. It's a big house with three reception rooms, six bedrooms, two kitchens and two staircases – and one poky little bathroom made by having converted a linen closet. The house is a bit stark to look at, a bit forbidding; it seems to stare straight back at you, but the trees round it are pretty enough and so are the stables on the left-hand side with a clock in their gable and a weathervane on top. Tom Cobworth, the last rector, kept his old Morris in there. The garden is huge, a wilderness that no one could keep tidy these days – eight acres of it including the glebe.

It was years since I had been inside the Rectory. I remember wondering if the interior was as shabby and in need of paint as the outside. The windows had that black, blank, hazy look of windows at which no curtains hang and which no one has cleaned for months or even years.

'Who exactly does it *belong* to?' said Eleanor.

'Lazarus College, Oxford,' I said. 'Tom was a Fellow of Lazarus.'

'And what about this new man?'

'I don't know,' I said. 'I think all that system of livings has changed but I'm pretty vague about it.'

I'm not a churchgoer, not religious at all really. Perhaps that was why I hadn't got to know the Cobworths all that well. I used to feel a bit uneasy in Tom's company, I used to have the feeling he might suddenly round on me and demand to know why he never saw me in church. Eleanor had no such inhibitions with Kate. They were friends, close friends, and Eleanor missed her after Tom died suddenly of a heart attack and she had had to leave the Rectory. She had gone back to her people up north, taking her fifteen-year-old daughter Louise with her.

Kate is a practical down-to-earth Yorkshire woman. She had been a nurse – a ward sister, I believe – before her marriage. When Tom got the living of Shawley she several times met Mrs Buckland, the wife of the retiring incumbent, and from her learned to expect what Mrs Buckland called 'manifestations'.

'I couldn't believe she was actually saying it,' Kate had said to Eleanor. 'I thought I was dreaming and then I thought she was mad. I mean really psychotic, mentally ill.

Ghosts! I ask you – people believing things like that in this day and age. And then we moved in and I heard them too.'

The crunch of carriage wheels on the gravel drive when there was no carriage or any kind of vehicle to be seen. Doors closing softly when no doors had been left open. Footsteps crossing the landing and going downstairs, crossing the hall, then the front door opening softly and closing softly.

'But how could you bear it?' Eleanor said. 'Weren't you afraid? Weren't you terrified?'

'We got used to it. We had to, you see. It wasn't as if we could sell the house and buy another. Besides, I love Shawley – I loved it from the first moment I set foot in the village. After the harshness of the north, Dorset is so gentle and mild and pretty. The doors closing and the footsteps and the wheels on the drive – they didn't do us any harm. And we had each other, we weren't alone. You can get used to anything – to ghosts as much as to damp and woodworm and dry rot. There's all that in the Rectory too and I found it much more trying!'

The Bucklands, apparently, had got used to it too. Thirty years he had been rector of the parish, thirty years they had lived there with the wheels and the footsteps, and had brought up their son and daughter there. No harm had come to them; they slept soundly, and their grown-up children used to joke about their haunted house.

'Nobody ever seems to *see* anything,' I said to Eleanor as we walked home. 'And no one ever comes up with a story, a sort of background to all this walking about and banging and crunching. Is there supposed to be a murder there or some sort of violent death?'

She said she didn't know, Kate had never said. The sound of the wheels, the closing of the doors, always took place at about nine in the evening, followed by the footsteps and the opening and closing of the front door. After that there was silence, and it hadn't happened every evening by any means. The only other thing was that Kate had never cared to use the big drawing room in the evenings. She and Tom and Louise had always stayed in the dining room or the morning room.

They did use the drawing room in the daytime – it was just that in the evenings the room felt strange to her, chilly even in summer and indefinably hostile. Once she had had to go in there at ten-thirty. She needed her reading glasses which she had left in the drawing room during the afternoon. She ran into the room and ran out again. She hadn't looked about her, just rushed in, keeping her eyes fixed on the eyeglass case on the mantelpiece. The icy hostility in that room had really frightened her, and that had been the only time she had felt dislike and fear of Shawley Rectory.

Of course one doesn't have to find explanations for an icy hostility. It's much more easily understood as being the product of tension and fear than aural phenomena are. I didn't have much faith in Kate's feelings about the drawing room. I thought with a kind of admiration of Jack and Diana Loy, that elderly couple who had rented the Rectory for a year after Kate's departure, had been primed with stories of hauntings by Kate, yet had neither heard nor felt a thing. As far as I know, they had used that drawing room constantly. Often, when I had passed the gate in their time,

I had seen lights in the drawing-room windows, at nine, at ten-thirty and even at midnight.

The Loys had been gone three months. When Lazarus had first offered the Rectory for rent, the idea had been that Shawley should do without a clergyman of its own. I think this must have been the Church economising – nothing to do certainly with ghosts. The services at St Mary's were to be undertaken by the vicar of the next parish, Mr Hartley. Whether he found this too much for him in conjunction with the duties of his own parish or whether the powers-that-be in affairs Anglican had second thoughts, I can't say; but on the departure of the Loys it was decided there should be an incumbent to replace Tom.

The first hint of this we had from local gossip; next the facts appeared in our monthly news sheet, the *Shawley Post*. Couched in its customary parish magazine journalese it said, 'Shawley residents all extend a hearty welcome to their new rector, the Reverend Stephen Galton, whose coming to the parish with his charming wife will fill a long-felt need.'

'He's very young,' said Eleanor a few days after our discussion of haunting with the Scotts. 'Under thirty.'

'That won't bother me,' I said. 'I don't intend to be preached at by him. Anyway, why not? Out of the mouths of babes and sucklings,' I said, 'hast Thou ordained strength.'

'Hark at the devil quoting scripture,' said Eleanor. 'They say his wife's only twenty-three.'

I thought she must have met them, she knew so much. But no.

'It's just what's being said. Patsy got it from Judy

Lawrence. Judy said they're moving in next month and her mother's coming with them.'

'Who, Judy's?' I said.

'Don't be silly,' said my wife. 'Mrs Galton's mother, the rector's mother-in-law. She's coming to live with them.'

Move in they did. And out again two days later.

The first we knew that something had gone very wrong for the Galtons was when I was out for my usual evening walk with our Irish setter Liam. We were coming back past the cottage that belongs to Charlie Lawrence (who is by way of being Shawley's squire) and which he keeps for the occupation of his gardener when he is lucky enough to have a gardener. At that time, last June, he hadn't had a gardener for at least six months, and the cottage should have been empty. As I approached, however, I saw a woman's face, young, fair, very pretty, at one of the upstairs windows.

I rounded the hedge and Liam began an insane barking, for just inside the cottage gate, on the drive, peering in under the hood of an aged Wolseley, was a tall young man wearing a tweed sports jacket over one of those black-top things the clergy wear, and a clerical collar.

'Good evening,' I said. 'Shut up, Liam, will you?'

'Good evening,' he said in a quiet, abstracted sort of way.

I told Eleanor. She couldn't account for the Galtons occupying Charlie Lawrence's gardener's cottage instead of Shawley Rectory, their proper abode. But Patsy Scott could. She came round on the following morning with a punnet of strawberries for us. The Scotts grow the best strawberries for miles around.

'They've been driven out by the ghosts,' she said. 'Can you credit it? A clergyman of the Church of England! An educated man! They were in that place not forty-eight hours before they were screaming to Charlie Lawrence to find them somewhere else to go.'

I asked her if she was sure it wasn't just the damp and the dry rot.

'Look, you know me. *I* don't believe the Rectory's haunted or anywhere *can* be haunted, come to that. I'm telling you what Mrs Galton told me. She came to us on Thursday morning and said did I think there was anyone in Shawley had a house or a cottage to rent because they couldn't stick the Rectory another night. I asked her what was wrong. And she said she knew it sounded crazy – it did too, she was right there – she knew it sounded mad, but they'd been terrified out of their lives by what they'd heard and seen since they moved in.'

'*Seen?*' I said. 'She actually claims to have seen something?'

'She said her mother did. She said her mother saw something in the drawing room the first evening they were there. They'd already heard the carriage wheels and the doors closing and the footsteps and all that. The second evening no one dared go in the drawing room. They heard all the sounds again and Mrs Grainger – that's the mother – heard voices in the drawing room, and it was then that they decided they couldn't stand it, that they'd have to get out.'

'I don't believe it!' I said. 'I don't believe any of it. The woman's a psychopath, she's playing some sort of ghastly joke.'

'Just as Kate was and the Bucklands,' said Eleanor quietly.

Patsy ignored her and turned to me. 'I feel just like you. It's awful, but what can you do? These stories grow and they sort of infect people and the more suggestible the people are, the worse the infection. Charlie and Judy are furious, they don't want it getting in the paper that Shawley Rectory is haunted. Think of all the people we shall get coming in cars on Sundays and gawping over the gates. But they had to let them have the cottage in common humanity. Mrs Grainger was hysterical and poor little Mrs Galton wasn't much better. Who told them to expect all those horrors? That's what I'd like to know.'

'What does Gordon say?' I said.

'He's keeping an open mind, but he says he'd like to spend an evening there.'

In spite of the Lawrences' fury, the haunting of Shawley Rectory did get quite a lot of publicity. There was a sensational story about it in one of the popular Sundays and then Stephen Galton's mother-in-law went on television. Western TV interviewed her on a local news programme. I hadn't ever seen Mrs Grainger in the flesh and her youthful appearance rather surprised me. She looked no more than thirty-five, though she must be into her forties.

The interviewer asked her if she had ever heard any stories of ghosts at Shawley Rectory before she went there and she said she hadn't. Did she believe in ghosts? Now she did. What had happened, asked the interviewer, after they had moved in?

It had started at nine o'clock, she said, at nine on their

first evening. She and her daughter were sitting in the bigger of the two kitchens, having a cup of coffee. They had been moving in all day, unpacking, putting things away. They heard two doors close upstairs, then footsteps coming down the main staircase. She had thought it was her son-in-law, except that it couldn't have been because as the footsteps died away he came in through the door from the back kitchen. They couldn't understand what it had been, but they weren't frightened. Not then.

'We were planning on going to bed early,' said Mrs Grainger. She was very articulate, very much at ease in front of the cameras. 'Just about half-past ten I had to go into the big room they call the drawing room. The removal men had put some of our boxes in there and my radio was in one of them. I wanted to listen to my radio in bed. I opened the drawing-room door and put my hand to the light switch. I didn't put the light on. The moon was quite bright that night and it was shining into the room.'

'There were people, two figures, I don't know what to call them, between the windows. One of them, the girl, was lying huddled on the floor. The other figure, an older woman, was bending over her. She stood up when I opened the door and looked at me. I knew I wasn't seeing real people, I don't know how but I knew that. I remember I couldn't move my hand to switch the light on. I was frozen, just staring at that pale tragic face while it stared back at me. I did manage at last to back out and close the door, and I got back to my daughter and my son-in-law in the kitchen and I – well, I collapsed. It was the most terrifying experience of my life.'

Yet you stayed a night and a day and another night in

the Rectory? said the interviewer. Yes, well, her daughter and her son-in-law had persuaded her it had been some sort of hallucination, the consequence of being overtired. Not that she had ever really believed that. The night had been quiet and so had the next day until nine in the evening, when they were all this time in the morning room and they heard a car drive up to the front door. They had all heard it, wheels crunching on the gravel, the sound of the engine, the brakes going on. Then had followed the closing of the doors upstairs and the footsteps, the opening and closing of the front door.

Yes, they had been very frightened, or she and her daughter had. Her son-in-law had made a thorough search of the whole house but found nothing, seen or heard no one. At ten-thirty they had all gone into the hall and listened outside the drawing-room door and she and her daughter had heard voices from inside the room, women's voices. Stephen had wanted to go in, but they had stopped him, they had been so frightened.

Now the interesting thing was that there had been something in the *Sunday Express* account about the Rectory being haunted by the ghosts of two women. The story quoted someone it described as a 'local antiquarian', a man named Joseph Lamb, whom I had heard of but never met. Lamb told the *Express* there was an old tradition that the ghosts were of a mother and daughter and that the mother had killed the daughter in the drawing room.

'I never heard any of that before,' I said to Gordon Scott, 'and I'm sure Kate Cobworth hadn't. Who is this Joseph Lamb?'

'He's a nice chap,' said Gordon. 'And he's supposed to know more of local history than anyone else around. I'll ask him over and you can come and meet him if you like.'

Jospeh Lamb lives in a rather fine Jacobean house in a hamlet – you could hardly call it a village – about a mile to the north of Shawley. I had often admired it without knowing who had lived there. The Scotts asked him and his wife to dinner shortly after Mrs Grainger's appearance on television, and after dinner we got him on to the subject of the hauntings. Lamb wasn't at all unwilling to enlighten us. He's a man of about sixty and he said he first heard the story of the two women from his nurse when he was a little boy. Not a very suitable subject with which to regale a seven-year-old, he said.

'These two are supposed to have lived at the Rectory at one time,' he said. 'The story is that the mother had a lover or a man friend or whatever, and the daughter took him away from her. When the daughter confessed it, the mother killed her in a jealous rage.'

It was Eleanor who objected to this. 'But surely if they lived in the Rectory they must have been the wife and daughter of a rector. I don't really see how in those circumstances the mother could have had a lover or the daughter could steal him away.'

'No, it doesn't much sound like what we've come to think of as the domestic life of the English country parson, does it?' said Lamb. 'And the strange thing is, although my nanny used to swear by the story and I heard it later from someone who worked at the Rectory, I haven't been able to find any trace of these women in the Rectory's history. It's not hard to research, you see, because only the rectors of

Shawley had ever lived there until the Loys rented it, and the rectors' names are all up on that plaque in the church from 1380 onwards. There was another house on the site before this present one, of course, and parts of the older building are incorporated in the newer.

'My nanny used to say that the elder lady hadn't got a husband, he had presumably died. She was supposed to be forty years old and the girl nineteen. Well, I tracked back through the families of the various rectors and I found a good many cases where the rectors had predeceased their wives. But none of them fitted my nanny's story. They were either too old – one was much too young – or their daughters were too old or they had no daughters.'

'It's a pity Mrs Grainger didn't tell us what kind of clothes her ghosts were wearing,' said Patsy with sarcasm. 'You could have pinpointed the date then, couldn't you?'

'You mean that if the lady had had a steeple hat on she'd be medieval or around 1850 if she was wearing a crinoline?'

'Something like that,' said Patsy.

At this point Gordon repeated his wish to spend an evening in the Rectory. 'I think I'll write to the Master of Lazarus and ask permission,' he said.

Very soon after we heard that the Rectory was to be sold. Noticeboards appeared by the front gate and at the corner where the glebe abutted Shawley Lane, announcing that the house would go up for auction on 30 October. Patsy, who always seems to know everything, told us that a reserve price of £60,000 had been put on it.

'Not as much as I'd have expected,' she said. 'It must be the ghosts keeping the price down.'

'Whoever buys it will have to spend another ten thousand on it,' said Eleanor.

'And central heating will be a priority.'

Whatever was keeping the price down – ghosts, cold or dry rot – there were plenty of people anxious to view the house and land with, I supposed, an idea of buying it. I could hardly be at work in my garden or out with Liam without a car stopping and the driver asking me the way to the Rectory. Gordon and Patsy got quite irritated about what they described as 'crowds milling about' in the lane and trippers everywhere, waving orders to view.

The estate agents handling the sale were a firm called Curlew, Pond and Co. Gordon didn't bother with the Master of Lazarus but managed to get the key from Graham Curlew, whom he knew quite well, and permission to spend an evening in the Rectory. Curlew didn't like the idea of anyone staying the night, but Gordon didn't want to do that anyway; no one had ever heard or seen anything after ten-thirty. He asked me if I'd go with him. Patsy wouldn't – she thought it was all too adolescent and stupid.

'Of course I will,' I said. 'As long as you'll agree to our taking some sort of heating arrangement with us and brandy in case of need.'

By then it was the beginning of October and the evenings were turning cool. The day on which we decided to have our vigil happened also to be the one on which Stephen Galton and his wife moved out of Charlie Lawrence's cottage and left Shawley for good. According to the *Shawley Post*, he had got a living in Manchester. Mrs Grainger had gone back to her own home in London, from where she had written an article about the Rectory for *Psychic News*.

Patsy shrieked with laughter to see the two of us setting forth with our oil stove, a dozen candles, two torches and half a bottle of Courvoisier. She did well to laugh, her amusement wasn't misplaced. We crossed the lane and opened the Rectory gate and went up the gravel drive on which those spirit wheels had so often been heard to crunch. It was seven o'clock in the evening and still light. The day had been fine and the sky was red with the aftermath of a spectacular sunset.

I unlocked the front door and in we went.

The first thing I did was put a match to one of the candles, because it wasn't at all light inside. We walked down the passage to the kitchens, I carrying the candle and Gordon shining one of the torches across the walls. The place was a mess. I suppose it hadn't had anything done it, not even a cleaning, since the Loys moved out. It smelled damp and there was even fungus growing in patches on the kitchen walls. And it was extremely cold. There was a kind of deathly chill in the air, far more of a chill than one would have expected on a warm day in October. That kitchen had the feel you get when you open the door of a refrigerator that hasn't been kept too clean and is in need of defrosting.

We put our stuff down on a kitchen table someone had left behind and made our way up the back stairs. All the bedroom doors were open and we closed them. The upstairs had a neglected, dreary feel but it was less cold. We went down the main staircase, a rather fine curving affair with elegant banisters and carved newel posts, and entered the drawing room. It was empty, palely lit by the evening light from two windows. On the mantelpiece was a glass jar with greenish water in it, a half-burnt candle in a saucer and a screwed-up paper table napkin. We had decided not to remain in this room but to open the door and look in at ten-thirty; so accordingly we returned to the kitchen, fetched out candles and torches and brandy, and settled down in the morning room, which was at the front of the house, on the other side of the front door.

Curlew had told Gordon there were a couple of deck-chairs in this room. We found them resting against the wall and we put them up. We lit our oil stove and a second candle, and we set one candle on the windowsill and one on the floor between us. It was still and silent and cold. The dark closed in fairly rapidly, the red fading from the sky, which became a deep blue, then indigo.

We sat and talked. It was about the haunting that we talked, collating the various pieces of evidence, assessing the times this or that was supposed to happen and making sure we both knew the sequence in which things happened. We were both wearing watches and I remember that we constantly checked the time. At half-past eight we again opened the drawing-room door and looked inside. The moon had come up and was shining through the windows as it had shone for Mrs Grainger.

Gordon went upstairs with a torch and checked that all the doors remained closed and then we both looked into the other large downstairs room, the dining room, I suppose. Here a fanlight in one of the windows was open.

That accounted for some of the feeling of cold and damp, Gordon said. The window must have been opened by some prospective buyer, viewing the place. We closed it and went back into the morning room to wait.

The silence was absolute. We didn't talk any more. We waited, watching the candles and the glow of the stove, which had taken some of the chill from the air. Outside it was pitch dark. The hands of our watches slowly approached nine.

At three minutes to nine we heard the noise.

Not wheels or doors closing or a tread on the stairs but a faint, dainty, pattering sound. It was very faint, it was very distant, it was on the ground floor. It was as if made by something less than human, lighter than that, tiptoeing. I had never thought about this moment beyond telling myself that if anything did happen, if there was a manifestation, it would be enormously interesting. It had never occurred to me even once that I should be so dreadfully, so hideously, afraid.

I didn't look at Gordon, I couldn't. I couldn't move either. The pattering feet were less faint now, were coming closer. I felt myself go white, the blood all drawn in from the surface of my skin, as I was gripped by that awful primitive terror that has nothing to do with reason or with knowing what you believe in and what you don't.

Gordon got to his feet and stood there looking at the door. And then I couldn't stand it any more. I jumped up and threw open the door, holding the candle aloft – and looked into a pair of brilliant golden-green eyes, staring steadily back at me about a foot from the ground.

'My God,' said Gordon. 'My God, it's Lawrence's cat. It must have got in through the window.'

He bent down and picked up the cat, a soft, stout, marmalade-coloured creature. I felt sick at the anticlimax. The time was exactly nine o'clock. With the cat draped over his arm, Gordon went back into the morning room and I followed him. We didn't sit down. We stood waiting for the wheels and the closing of the doors.

Nothing happened.

I have no business to keep you in suspense any longer for the fact is that after the business with the cat nothing happened at all. At nine-fifteen we sat down in our deck-chairs. The cat lay on the floor beside the oil stove and went to sleep. Twice we heard a car pass along Shawley Lane, a remotely distant sound, but we heard nothing else.

'Feel like a spot of brandy?' said Gordon.

'Why not?' I said.

So we each had a nip of brandy and at ten we had another look in the drawing room. By then we were both feeling bored and quite sure that since nothing had happened at nine nothing would happen at ten-thirty either. Of course we stayed till ten-thirty and for half an hour after that, and then we decamped. We put the cat over the wall into Lawrence's grounds and went back to Gordon's house, where Patsy awaited us, smiling cynically.

I had had quite enough of the Rectory but that wasn't true of Gordon. He said it was well known that the phenomena didn't take place every night; we had simply struck an off-night and he was going back on his own. He did too, half a dozen times between then and the 30th, even going so far as to have (rather unethically) a key cut from the one Curlew had lent him. Patsy would never go with him, though he tried hard to persuade her.

But in all those visits he never saw or heard anything. And the effect on him was to make him as great a sceptic as Patsy.

'I've a good mind to make an offer for the Rectory myself,' he said. 'It's a fine house and I've got quite attached to it.'

'You're not serious,' I said.

'I'm perfectly serious. I'll go to the auction with a view for buying it if I can get Patsy to agree.'

But Patsy preferred her own house and, very reluctantly, Gordon had to give up the idea. The Rectory was sold for £62,000 to an American woman, a friend of Judy Lawrence. About a month after the sale the builders moved in. Eleanor used to get progress reports from Patsy, how they had rewired and treated the whole place for woodworm and painted and relaid floors. The central-heating engineers came too, much to Patsy's satisfaction.

We met Carol Marcus, the Rectory's new owner, when we were asked round to the Hall for drinks one Sunday morning. She was staying there with the Lawrences until such time as the improvements and decorations to the Rectory were complete. We were introduced by Judy to a very pretty, well-dressed woman in young middle age. I asked her when she expected to move in. April, she hoped, as soon as the builders had finished the two extra bathrooms. She had heard rumours that the Rectory was supposed to be haunted and these had amused her very much. A haunted house in the English countryside! It was too good to be true.

'It's all nonsense, you know,' said Gordon, who had joined us. 'It's all purely imaginary.' And he went on to tell her of his own experiences in the house during October – or his non-experiences, I should say.

'Well, for goodness' sake, I didn't *believe* it!' she said, and she laughed and went on to say how much she loved the house and wanted to make it a real home for her children to come to. She had three, she said, all in their teens, two boys away at school and a girl a bit older.

That was the only time I ever talked to her and I remember thinking she would be a welcome addition to the neighbourhood. A nice woman. Serene is the word that best described her. There was a man friend of hers there too. I didn't catch his surname but she called him Guy. He was staying at one of the locals, to be near her presumably.

'I should think those two would get married, wouldn't you?' said Eleanor on the way home. 'Judy told me she's waiting to get her divorce.'

Later that day I took Liam for a walk along Shawley Lane and when I came to the Rectory I found the gate open. So I walked up the gravel drive and looked through the drawing-room window at the new woodblock floor and ivory-painted walls and radiators. The place was swiftly being transformed. It was no longer sinister or grim. I walked round the back and peered in at the splendidly fitted kitchens, one a laundry now, and wondered what on earth had made sensible women like Mrs Buckland

and Kate spread such vulgar tales, and the Galtons' panic. What had come over them? I could only imagine that they felt a need to direct attention to themselves which they perhaps could do in no other way.

I whistled for Liam and strolled down to the gate and looked back at the Rectory. It stared back at me. Is it hindsight that makes me say this or did I really feel it then? I think I did feel it, that the house stared at me with a kind of steady insolence.

Carol Marcus moved in three weeks ago, on a sunny day in the middle of April. Two nights later, just before eleven, there came a sustained ringing at Gordon's door as if someone were leaning on the bell. Gordon went to the door. Carol Marcus stood outside, absolutely calm but deathly white.

She said to him, 'May I use your phone, please? Mine isn't in yet and I have to call the police. I just shot my daughter.'

She took a step forward and crumpled in a heap on the threshold.

Gordon picked her up and carried her into the house and Patsy gave her brandy, and then he went across the road to the Rectory. There were lights on all over the house; the front door was open and light was streaming out on to the drive and the little Citroën Diane that was parked there.

He walked into the house. The drawing-room door was open and he walked in there and saw a young girl lying on the carpet between the windows. She was dead. There was blood from a bullet wound on the front of the dress, and on a low round table lay the small automatic that Carol Marcus had used.

In the meantime Patsy had been the unwilling listener to a confession. Carol Marcus told her that the girl, who was nineteen, had unexpectedly driven down from London, arriving at the Rectory at nine o'clock. She had had a drink and something to eat and then she had something to tell her mother, that was why she had come down. While in London she was seeing a lot of the man called Guy and now they found that they were in love with each other. She knew it would hurt her mother, but she wanted to tell her at once, she wanted to be honest about it.

Carol Marcus told Patsy she felt nothing, no shock, no hatred or resentment, no jealousy. It was as if she were impelled by some external force to do what she did – take the gun she always kept with her from a drawer in the writing desk and kill her daughter.

At this point Gordon came back and they phoned the police. Within a quarter of an hour the police were at the house. They arrested Carol Marcus and took her away and now she is on remand, awaiting trial on a charge of murder.

So what is the explanation of all this? Or does there, in fact, have to be an explanation? Eleanor and I were so shocked by what had happened, and awed too, that for a while we were somehow wary of talking about it even to each other. Then Eleanor said, 'It's as if all this time the coming event cast its shadow before it.'

I nodded, yet it didn't seem quite that to me. It was more that the Rectory was waiting for the right people to come along, the people who would *fit* its still unplayed scenario, the woman of forty, the daughter of nineteen, the lover. And only to those who approximated these characters could it show shadows and whispers of the drama; the closer the approximation, the clearer the sounds and signs.

The Loys were old and childless, so they saw nothing. Nor did Gordon and I – we were of the wrong sex. But the Bucklands, who had a daughter, heard and felt things, and so did Kate, though she was too old for the tragic leading role and her adolescent girl too young for victim. The Galtons had been nearly right – had Mrs Grainger once hoped the young rector would marry her before he showed his preference for her daughter? – but the women had been a few years too senior for the parts. Even so, they had come closer to participation than those before them.

All this is very fanciful and I haven't mentioned a word of it to Gordon and Patsy. They wouldn't listen if I did. They persist in seeing the events of three weeks ago as no more than a sordid murder, a crime of jealousy committed by someone whose mind was disturbed.

But I haven't been able to keep from asking myself what would have happened if Gordon had bought the Rectory when he talked of doing so. Patsy will be forty this year. I don't think I've mentioned that she has a daughter by her first marriage who is away at the university and going on nineteen now, a girl that they say is extravagantly fond of Gordon.

He is talking once more of buying, since Carol Marcus, whatever may become of her, will hardly keep the place now. The play is played out, but need that mean there will never be a repeat performance … ?

L. P. HARTLEY
(1895–1972)

Leslie Poles Hartley was educated at Harrow and Oxford, where his friends included Aldous Huxley. His university career was interrupted by the First World War, although ill health meant that he was, as he bitterly described it, 'Second-Lieutenant Hartley, only fit for home service'. For much of his later life he lived in Venice (at one point poaching his gondolier from another expat, the composer Cole Porter). However, his time there was not entirely happy. 'The Cotillon' was written after the sudden and traumatic end of a love affair and, like much of Hartley's work, is suffused with a sense of lost or thwarted love and a profound air of pessimism. Hartley also suffered from acute social anxiety; nervously contemplating a dinner with Oswald Sitwell, he wrote to his mother, 'I feel sure my false teeth will fall out.'

THE COTILLON

'BUT,' PROTESTED MARION LANE, 'you don't mean that we've all got to dance the cotillon in masks? Won't that be terribly hot?'

'My dear,' Jane Manning, her friend and hostess, reminded her, 'this is December, not July. Look!' She pointed to the window, their only protection against a soft bombardment of snowflakes.

Marion moved across from the fireplace where they were sitting and looked out. The seasonable snow had just begun to fall, as though in confirmation of Mrs Manning's words. Here and there the gravel still showed black under its powdery coating, and on the wing of the house which faced east the shiny foliage of the magnolia, pitted with pockets of snow, seemed nearly black too. The trees of the park which yesterday, when Marion arrived, were so distinct against the afternoon sky that you could see their twigs, were almost invisible now, agitated shapes dim in the slanting snow. She turned back to the room.

'I think the cotillon's a good idea, and I don't want to

make difficulties,' she said. 'I'm not an obstructionist by nature, am I? Tell me if I am.'

'My dear, of course you're not.'

'Well, I was thinking, wouldn't half the fun of the cotillon be gone if you didn't know who was who? I mean, in those figures when the women powder the men's faces, and rub their reflections off the looking glass, and so on. There doesn't seem much point in powdering a mask.'

'My darling Marion, the mask's only a bit of black silk that covers the top part of one's face; you don't imagine we shan't recognise each other?'

'You may,' said Marion, 'find it difficult to recognise the largest, barest face. I often cut my best friends in the street. They needn't put on a disguise for me not to know them.'

'But you can tell them by their voices.'

'Supposing they won't speak?'

'Then you must ask questions.'

'But I shan't know half the people here.'

'You'll know all of us in the house,' her friend said; 'that's sixteen to start with. And you know the Grays and the Fosters and the Boltons. We shall only be about eighty, if as many.'

'Counting gatecrashers?'

'There won't be any.'

'But how will you be able to tell, if they wear masks?'

'I shall know the exact numbers, for one thing, and for another, at midnight, when the cotillon stops, everyone can take their masks off – must, in fact.'

'I see.'

The room was suddenly filled with light. A servant had come in to draw the curtains. They sat in silence until he had finished the last of the windows; there were five of them in a row.

'I had forgotten how long this room was,' Marion said. 'You'll have the cotillon here, I suppose?'

'It's the only possible place. I wish it were a little longer, then we could have a cushion race. But I'm afraid we shall have to forgo that. It would be over as soon as it began.'

The servant arranged the tea table in front of them and went away.

'Darling,' said Jane suddenly, 'before Jack comes in from shooting with his tired but noisy friends, I want to say what a joy it is to have you here. I'm glad the others aren't coming till Christmas Eve. You'll have time to tell me all about yourself.'

'Myself?' repeated Marion. She stirred in her chair. 'There's nothing to tell.'

'Dearest, I can't believe it! There must be, after all these months. My life is dull, you know – no, not dull, quiet. And yours is always so *mouvementée*.'

'It used to be,' admitted Marion. 'It used to be; but now I –'

There was a sound of footsteps and laughter at the door, and a voice cried, 'Jenny, Jenny, have you some tea for us?'

'You shall have it in a moment,' Mrs Manning called back. Sighing, she turned to her friend.

'We must postpone our little séance.'

*

Five days had gone by – it was the evening of the 27th, the night of the ball. Marion went up to her room to rest. Dinner was at half-past eight, so she had nearly two hours' respite. She lay down on the bed and turned out all the lights except the one near her head. She felt very tired. She had talked so much during the past few days that even her thoughts had become articulate; they would not stay in her mind; they rose automatically to her lips, or it seemed to her that they did. 'I am glad I did not tell Jenny,' she soliloquised; 'it would only have made her think worse of me, and done no good. What a wretched business.' She extinguished the light, but the gramophone within her went on more persistently than ever. It was a familiar record; she knew every word of it: it might have been called 'The Witness for the Defence'. 'He had no reason to take me so seriously,' announced the machine in self-excusatory accents. 'I only wanted to amuse him. It was Hugh Travers who introduced us: he knows what I am like; he must have told Harry; men always talk these things over among themselves. Hugh had a grievance against me, too, once; but he got over it; I have never known a man who didn't.' For a moment Marion's thoughts broke free from their bondage to the turning wheel and hovered over her past life. Yes, more or less, they had all got over it. 'I never made him any promise,' pursued the record, inexorably taking up its tale; 'what right had he to think he could coerce me? Hugh ought not to have let us meet, knowing the kind of man he was – and – and the kind of woman I was. I was very fond of him, of course; but he would have been so exacting, he *was* so exacting. All the same,' continued the record – sliding a moment into the major key only to relapse into the minor – 'left to myself I could have managed it all right, as I always have. It was pure bad luck that he found me that night with the other Harry. That was a dreadful affair.' At this point the record, as always, wobbled and scratched: Marion had to improvise something less painful to bridge over the gap. Her thoughts flew to the other Harry and dwelt on him tenderly; he had been so sweet to her afterwards. 'It was just bad luck,' the record resumed; 'I didn't want to blast his happiness and wreck his life, or whatever he says I did.'

What had he actually said? There was an ominous movement in Marion's mind. The mechanism was being wound up, was going through the whole dreary performance again. Anything rather than that! She turned on the light, jumped off the bed and searched among her letters. The moment she had it in her hand, she realised that she knew it by heart.

Dear Marion,

After what has happened I don't suppose you will want to see me again, and though I want to see you, I think it better for us both that I shouldn't. I know it sounds melodramatic to say it, but you have spoilt my life, you have killed something inside me. I never much valued Truth for its own sake, and I am grateful to Chance for affording me that peep behind the scenes last night. I am more grateful to you for keeping up the disguise as long as you did. But though you have taken away so much, you have left me one flicker of curiosity: before I die (or after, it doesn't much matter!) I should like to see you (forgive the expression) unmasked, so that for a moment I can compare the reality with the illusion I used to cherish. Perhaps I shall. Meanwhile goodbye.

Yours once, and in a sense still yours,

Henry Chichester.

Marion's eyes slid from the letter to the chair beside her where lay mask and domino, ready to put on. She did not feel the irony of their presence; she did not think about them; she was experiencing an immense relief – a relief that always came after reading Harry's letter. When she thought about it it appalled her; when she read it it seemed much less hostile, flattering almost; a testimonial from a wounded and disappointed but still adoring man. She lay down again and in a moment was asleep.

Soon after ten o'clock the gentlemen followed the ladies into the long drawing room; it looked unfamiliar even to Jack Manning, stripped of furniture except for a thin lining of gilt chairs. So far everything had gone off splendidly; dinner, augmented by the presence of half a dozen neighbours, had been a great success; but now everyone, including the host and hostess, was a little uncertain what to do next. The zero hour was approaching; the cotillon was supposed to start at eleven and go on till twelve, when the serious dancing would begin; but guests motoring from a distance might arrive at any time. It would spoil the fun of the thing to let the masked and the unmasked meet before the cotillon started; but how could they be kept apart? To preserve the illusion of secrecy Mrs Manning had asked them to announce themselves at the head of the staircase, in tones sufficiently discreet to be heard by her alone. Knowing how fallible are human plans, she had left in the cloakroom a small supply of masks for those men who, she knew, would forget to bring them. She thought her arrangements were proof against mischance, but she was by no means sure; and as she looked about the room and saw the members of the dinner party stealing furtive glances at the clock, or plunging into frantic and short-lived conversations, she began to share their uneasiness.

'I think,' she said, after one or two unsuccessful efforts to gain the ear of the company, 'I think you had all better go and disguise yourselves, before anyone comes and finds you in your natural state.' The guests tittered nervously at this pleasantry, then with signs of relief upon their faces they began to file out, some by one door, some by the other, according as the direction of their own rooms took them. The long gallery (as it was sometimes magniloquently described) stood empty and expectant.

'There,' breathed Mrs Manning, 'would you have recognised that parlour bandit as Sir Joseph Dickinson?'

'No,' said her husband, 'I wouldn't have believed a mask and a domino could make such a difference. Except for a few of the men, I hardly recognised anyone.'

'You're like Marion; she told me she often cuts her best friends in the street.'

'I dare say that's a gift she's grateful for.'

'Jack! You really mustn't. Didn't she look lovely tonight! What a pity she has to wear a mask, even for an hour!'

Her husband grunted.

'I told Colin Chillingworth she was to be here: you know he's always wanted to see her. He is such a nice old man, so considerate – the manners of the older generation.'

'Why, because he wants to see Marion?'

'No, idiot! But he had asked me if he might bring a guest –'

'Who?'

'I don't remember the man's name, but he has a bilious attack or something, and can't come, and Colin apologised profusely for not letting us know: his telephone is out of order, he said.'

'Very civil of him. How many are we, then, all told?'

'Seventy-eight; we should have been seventy-nine.'

'Anyone else to come?'

'I'll just ask Jackson.'

The butler was standing halfway down the stairs. He confirmed Mrs Manning's estimate. 'That's right, madam; there were twenty-two at dinner and fifty-six have come in since.'

'Good staff-work,' said her husband. 'Now we must dash off and put on our little masks.'

They were hurrying away when Mrs Manning called over her shoulder, 'You'll see that the fires are kept up, Jackson?'

'Oh, yes, madam,' he replied, 'it's very warm in there.'

*

It was. Marion, coming into the ballroom about eleven o'clock, was met by a wave of heat, comforting and sustaining. She moved about among the throng, slightly dazed, it is true, but self-confident and elated. As she expected, she could not put a name to many of the people who kept crossing her restricted line of vision, but she was intensely aware of their eyes – dark, watchful but otherwise expressionless eyes, framed in black. She welcomed their direct regard. On all sides she heard conversation and laughter, especially laughter; little trills and screams of delight at identities disclosed; voices expressing bewilderment and polite despair – 'I'm very stupid, I really cannot imagine who you are,' gruff rumbling voices and high falsetto squeaks, obviously disguised. Marion found herself a little impatient of this childishness. When people recognised her, as they often did (her mask was as much a decoration as a concealment) she smiled with her lips but did not try to identify them in return. She felt faintly scornful of the women who were only interesting provided you did not know who they were. She looked forward to the moment when the real business of the evening would begin.

But now the band in the alcove between the two doors had struck up and a touch on her arm warned her that she was wanted for a figure. Her partner was a raw youth, nice enough in his way, eager, good-natured and jaunty, like a terrier dog. He was not a type she cared for and she longed to give him the slip.

The opportunity came. Standing on a chair, rather

like the Statue of Liberty in New York harbour, she held aloft a lighted candle. Below her seethed a small group of masked males, leaping like salmon, for the first to blow the candle out would have the privilege of dancing with the torch-bearer. Among them was her partner; he jumped higher than the rest, as she feared he would; but each time she saw his Triton-like mouth soaring up she forestalled his agility and moved the candle out of his reach. Her arm began to tire; and the pack, foiled so often, began to relax their efforts. She must do something quickly. Espying her host among the competitors, she shamefacedly brought the candle down to the level of his mouth.

'Nice of you,' he said, when, having danced a few turns, they were sitting side by side. 'I was glad of that bit of exercise.'

'Why, do you feel cold?'

'A little. Don't you?'

Marion considered. 'Perhaps I do.'

'Funny thing,' said her host, 'fires seem to be blazing away all right, and it was too hot ten minutes ago.'

Their eyes travelled enquiringly round the room. 'Why,' exclaimed Manning, 'no wonder we're cold; there's a window open.'

As he spoke, a gust of wind blew the heavy curtains inwards and a drift of snow came after them.

'Excuse me a moment,' he said. 'I'll soon stop that.'

She heard the sash slam and in a few moments he was back at her side.

'Now who on earth can have done it?' he demanded,

still gasping from contact with the cold air. 'The window was wide open!'

'Wide enough to let anyone in?'

'Quite.'

'How many of us ought there to be?' asked Marion. 'I'm sure you don't know.'

'I do – there are –'

'Don't tell me, let's count. I'll race you.'

They were both so absorbed in their calculations that the leaders of the cotillon, coming round armed with favours for the next figure, dropped into their laps a fan and a pocketbook and passed on unnoticed.

'Well, what do you make it?' they cried almost in unison.

'Seventy-nine,' said Marion. 'And you?'

'Seventy-nine, too.'

'And how many ought there to be?'

'Seventy-eight.'

'That's a rum go,' said Manning. 'We can't both be mistaken. I suppose someone came in afterwards. When I get a chance I'll talk to Jackson.'

'It can't be a burglar,' said Marion, 'a burglar wouldn't have chosen that way of getting in.'

'Besides, we should have seen him. No, a hundred to one it was just somebody who was feeling the heat and needed air. I don't blame them, but they needn't have blown us away. Anyhow, if there is a stranger among us he'll soon have to show up, for in half an hour's time we can take off these confounded masks. I wouldn't say it of everyone, but I like you better without yours.'

'Do you?' smiled Marion.

'Meanwhile, we must do something about these favours. The next figure's beginning. I say, a fur rug would be more suitable, but may I give this fan to you?'

'And will you accept this useful pocketbook?'

They smiled and began to dance.

Ten minutes passed; the fires were heaped up, but the rubbing of hands and hunching of shoulders which had followed the inrush of cold air did not cease. Marion, awaiting her turn to hold the looking glass, shivered slightly. She watched her predecessor on the chair. Armed with a handkerchief, she was gazing intently into the mirror while each in his turn the men stole up behind her, filling the glass with their successive reflections; one after another she rubbed the images out. Marion was wondering idly whether she would wait too long and find the candidates exhausted when she jumped up from her chair, handed the looking glass to the leader of the cotillon and danced away with the man of her choice. Marion took the mirror and sat down. A feeling of unreality oppressed her. How was she to choose between these grotesque faces? One after another they loomed up, dream-like, in the glass, their intense, almost hypnotic eyes searching hers. She could not tell whether they were smiling, they gave so little indication of expression. She remembered how the other women had paused, peered into the glass and seemed to consider; rubbing away this one at sight, with affected horror, lingering over that one as though sorely tempted, only erasing him after a show of reluctance. She had fancied that some of the men looked piqued when they were rejected; they walked off with a toss of the head; others had seemed frankly pleased to be chosen. She was not indifferent to the mimic drama of the figure, but she couldn't contribute to it. The chill she still felt numbed her mind and made it drowsy; her gestures seemed automatic, outside the control of her will. Mechanically she rubbed away the reflection of the first candidate, of the second, of the third. But when the fourth presented himself and hung over her chair till his mask was within a few inches of her hair, the onlookers saw her pause; the hand with the handkerchief lay motionless in her lap, her eyes were fixed upon the mirror. So she sat for a full minute, while the man at the back, never shifting his position, drooped over her like an earring.

'She's taking a good look this time,' said a bystander at last, and the remark seemed to pierce her reverie – she turned round slowly and then gave a tremendous start; she was on her feet in a moment. 'I'm so sorry,' someone heard her say as she gave the man her hand, 'I never saw you. I had no idea that anyone was there.'

A few minutes later Jane Manning, who had taken as much share in the proceedings as a hostess can, felt a touch upon her arm. It was Marion.

'Well, my dear,' she said. 'Are you enjoying yourself?'

Marion's voice shook a little. 'Marvellously!' She added in an amused tone, 'Queer fellow I got hold of just now.'

'Queer-looking, do you mean?'

'Really I don't know; he was wearing a sort of

death-mask that covered him almost completely, and he was made up as well, I thought, with French chalk.'

'What else was queer about him?'

'He didn't talk. I couldn't get a word out of him.'

'Perhaps he was deaf.'

'That occurred to me. But he heard the music all right; he danced beautifully.'

'Show him to me.'

Marion's eyes hovered round the room without catching sight of her late partner.

'He doesn't seem to be here.'

'Perhaps he's our uninvited guest,' said Jane, laughing. 'Jack told me there was an extra person who couldn't be accounted for. Now, darling, you mustn't miss this figure: it's the most amusing of them all. After that, there are some favours to be given and then supper. I long for it.'

'But don't we take off our masks first?'

'Yes, of course, I'd forgotten that.'

The figure described by Mrs Manning as being the most amusing of all would have been much more amusing, Marion thought, if they had played it without masks. If the dancers did not recognise each other, it lost a great deal of its point. Its success depended on surprise. A space had been cleared in the middle of the room, an oblong space like a badminton court, divided into two, not by a net but by a large white sheet supported at either end by the leaders of the cotillon and held nearly at arm's length above their heads. On one side were grouped the men, on the other the women, theoretically invisible to each other; but Marion noticed that they moved about and took furtive peeps at each other round the sides, a form of cheating which, in the interludes, the leaders tried to forestall by rushing the sheet across to intercept the view. But most of the time these stolen glimpses went on unchecked, to the accompaniment of a good deal of laughter; for while the figure was in progress the leaders were perforce stationary. One by one the men came up from behind and clasped the top edge of the sheet, so that their gloved fingers, and nothing else, were visible the further side. With becoming hesitation a woman would advance and take these anonymous fingers in her own; then the sheet was suddenly lowered and the dancers stood face to face, or rather mask to mask. Sometimes there were cries of recognition, sometimes silence, the masks were as impenetrable as the sheet had been.

It was Marion's turn. As she walked forward she saw that the gloved hands were not resting on the sheet like the rest; they were clutching it so tightly that the linen was caught up in creases between the fingers and crumpled round their tips. For a moment they did not respond to her touch, then they gripped with surprising force. Down went the leader's arms, down went the corners of the sheet. But Marion's unknown partner did not take his cue. He forgot to release the sheet, and she remained with her arms held immovably aloft, the sheet falling in folds about her and almost covering her head. 'An unrehearsed effect, jolly good, I call it,' said somebody. At last, in response to playful tugs and twitches from the leaders, the man let the sheet go and discovered himself to the humiliated Marion. It was her partner of the previous figure, that uncommunicative man. His hands, that still held hers, felt cold through their kid covering.

'Oh,' she cried, 'I can't understand it – I feel so cold. Let's dance.'

They danced for a little and then sat down. Marion felt chillier than ever, and she heard her neighbours on either side complaining of the temperature. Suddenly she made a decision and rose to her feet.

'Do take me somewhere where it's warmer,' she said. 'I'm perished here.'

The man led the way out of the ballroom, through the anteroom at the end where one or two couples were sitting, across the corridor into a little room where a good fire was burning, throwing every now and then a ruddy gleam on china ornaments and silver photograph frames. It was Mrs Manning's sitting room.

'We don't need a light, do we?' said her companion. 'Let's sit as we are.'

It was the first time he had volunteered a remark. His voice was somehow familiar to Marion, yet she couldn't place it; it had an alien quality that made it unrecognisable, like one's own dress worn by someone else.

'With pleasure,' she said. 'But we mustn't stay long, must we? It's only a few minutes to twelve. Can we hear the music from here?'

They sat in silence, listening. There was no sound.

'Don't think me fussy,' Marion said. 'I'm enjoying this tremendously, but Jenny would be disappointed if we missed the last figure. If you don't mind opening the door, we should hear the music begin.'

As he did not offer to move, she got up to open it herself, but before she reached the door she heard her name called.

'Marion!'

'Who said that, you?' she cried, suddenly very nervous.

'Don't you know who I am?'

'Harry!'

Her voice shook and she sank back into her chair, trembling violently.

'How was it I didn't recognise you? I'm – I'm so glad to see you.'

'You haven't seen me yet,' said he. It was like him to say that, playfully grim. His words reassured her, but his tone left her still in doubt. She did not know how to start the conversation, what effect to aim at, what note to strike; so much depended on divining his mood and playing up to it. If she could have seen his face, if she could even have caught a glimpse of the poise of his head, it would have given her a cue; in the dark like this, hardly certain of his whereabouts in the room, she felt hopelessly at a disadvantage.

'It was nice of you to come and see me – if you did come to see me,' she ventured at last.

'I heard you were to be here.' Again that non-committal tone!

Trying to probe him, she said, 'Would you have come otherwise? It's rather a childish entertainment, isn't it?'

'I should have come,' he answered, 'but it would have been in – in a different spirit.'

She could make nothing of this.

'I didn't know the Mannings were friends of yours,' she told him. 'He's rather a dear, married to a dull woman, if I must be really truthful.'

'I don't know them,' said he.

'Then you gatecrashed?'

'I suppose I did.'

'I take that as a compliment,' said Marion after a pause. 'But – forgive me – I must be very slow – I don't understand. You said you were coming in any case.'

'Some friends of mine called Chillingworth offered to bring me.'

'How lucky I was! So you came with them?'

'Not with them, after them.'

'How odd. Wasn't there room for you in their car? How did you get here so quickly?'

'The dead travel fast.'

His irony baffled her. But her thoughts flew to his letter, in which he accused her of having killed something in him; he must be referring to that.

'Darling Hal,' she said. 'Believe me, I'm sorry to have hurt you. What can I do to – to –'

There was a sound of voices calling, and her attention thus awakened caught the strains of music, muffled and remote.

'They want us for the next figure. We must go,' she cried, thankful that the difficult interview was nearly over. She was colder than ever and could hardly keep her teeth from chattering audibly.

'What is the next figure?' he asked, without appearing to move.

'Oh, you know – we've had it before – we give each other favours, then we unmask ourselves. Hal, we really ought to go! Listen! Isn't that midnight beginning to strike?'

Unable to control her agitation, aggravated by the strain of the encounter, the deadly sensation of cold within her and a presentiment of disaster for which she could not account, she rushed towards the door and her outstretched left hand, finding the switch, flooded the room with light. Mechanically she turned her head to the room; it was empty. Bewildered she looked back over her left shoulder, and there, within a foot of her, stood Harry Chichester, his arms stretched across the door.

'Harry,' she cried, 'don't be silly! Come out or let me out!'

'You must give me a favour first,' he said sombrely.

'Of course I will, but I haven't got one here.'

'I thought you always had favours to give away.'

'Harry, what do you mean?'

'You came unprovided?'

She was silent.

'I did not. I have something here to give you – a small token. Only I must have a *quid pro quo*.'

He's mad, thought Marion. I must humour him as far as I can.

'Very well,' she said, looking around the room. Jenny would forgive her – it was an emergency. 'May I give you this silver pencil?'

He shook his head.

'Or this little vase?'

Still he refused.

'Or this calendar?'

'The flight of time doesn't interest me.'

'Then what can I tempt you with?'

'Something that is really your own – a kiss.'

'My dear,' said Marion, trembling, 'you needn't have asked for it.'

'Thank you,' he said. 'And to prove I don't want something for nothing, here is your favour.'

He felt in his pocket. Marion saw a dark silvery gleam; she held her hand out for the gift.

It was a revolver.

'What am I to do with this?' she asked.

'You are the best judge of that,' he replied. 'Only one cartridge has been used.'

Without taking her eyes from his face she laid down the revolver among the bric-à-brac on the table by her side.

'And now your gift to me.'

'But what about our masks?' said Marion.

'Take yours off,' he commanded.

'Mine doesn't matter,' said Marion, removing as she spoke the silken visor. 'But you are wearing an entirely false face.'

'Do you know why?' he asked, gazing at her fixedly through the slits in the mask.

She didn't answer.

'I was always an empty-headed fellow,' he went on, tapping the waxed covering with his gloved forefinger, so that it gave out a wooden hollow sound – 'there's nothing much behind this. No brains to speak of, I mean. Less than I used to have, in fact.'

Marion stared at him in horror.

'Would you like to see? Would you like to look right into my mind?'

'No! No!' she cried wildly.

'But I think you ought to,' he said, coming a step nearer and raising his hands to his head.

'Have you seen Marion?' said Jane Manning to her husband. 'I've a notion she hasn't been enjoying herself. This was in a sense her party, you know. We made a mistake to give her Tommy Cardew as a partner; he doesn't carry heavy enough guns for her.'

'Why, does she want shooting?' enquired her husband.

'Idiot! But I could see they didn't get on. I wonder where she's got to – I'm afraid she may be bored.'

'Perhaps she's having a quiet talk with a howitzer,' her husband suggested.

Jane ignored him. 'Darling, it's nearly twelve. Run into the anteroom and fetch her; I don't want her to miss the final figure.'

In a few seconds he returned. 'Not there,' he said. 'Not there, my child. Sunk by a twelve-inch shell, probably.'

'She may be sitting out in the corridor.'

'Hardly, after a direct hit.'

'Well, look.'

They went away and returned with blank faces. The guests were standing about talking; the members of the band, their hands ready on their instruments, looked up enquiringly.

'We shall have to begin without her,' Mrs Manning

reluctantly decided. 'We shan't have time to finish as it is.'

The hands of the clock showed five minutes to twelve.

The band played as though inspired, and many said afterwards that the cotillon never got really going, properly warmed up, till those last five minutes. All the fun of the evening seemed to come to a head, as though the spirit of the dance, mistrustful of its latter-day devotees, had withheld its benison till the final moments. Everyone was too excited to notice, as they whirled past, that the butler was standing in one of the doorways with a white and anxious face.

Even Mrs Manning, when at last she saw him, called out cheerfully, almost without pausing for an answer, 'Well, Jackson, everything all right, I hope?'

'Can I speak to you a moment, madam?' he said. 'Or perhaps Mr Manning would be better.'

Mrs Manning's heart sank. Did he want to leave?

'Oh, I expect I shall do, shan't I? I hope it's nothing serious.'

'I'm afraid it is, madam, very serious.'

'All right, I'll come.' She followed him onto the landing.

A minute later her husband saw her threading her way towards him.

'Jack! Just a moment.'

He was dancing and affected not to hear. His partner's eyes looked surprised and almost resentful, Mrs Manning thought; but she persisted nonetheless.

'I know I'm a bore and I'm sorry, but I really can't help myself.'

This brought them to a stand.

'Why, Jane, has the boiler burst?'

'No, it's more serious than that, Jack,' she said, as he disengaged himself from his partner with an apology. 'There's been a dreadful accident or something at the Chillingworths'. That guest of theirs, do you remember, whom they were to have brought and didn't –'

'Yes, he stayed behind with a headache – rotten excuse –'

'Well, he's shot himself.'

'Good God! When?'

'They found him half an hour ago, apparently, but they couldn't telephone because the machine was out of order, and had to send.'

'Is he dead?'

'Yes, he blew his brains out.'

'Do you remember his name?'

'The man told me. He was called Chichester.'

They were standing at the side of the room, partly to avoid the dancers, partly to be out of earshot. The latter consideration need not have troubled them, however. The band, which for some time past had been playing nine-teenth-century waltzes, now burst into the strains of 'John Peel'. There was a tremendous sense of excitement and climax. The dancers galloped by at breakneck speed; the band played fortissimo; the volume of sound was terrific. But above the din – the music, the laughter and the thud of feet – they could just hear the clock striking twelve.

Jack Manning looked doubtfully at his wife. 'Should I

go and tell Chillingworth now? What do you think?'

'Perhaps you'd better – it seems so heartless not to. Break it to him as gently as you can, and don't let the others know if you can help it.'

Jack Manning's task was neither easy nor agreeable, and he was a born bungler. Despairing of making himself heard, he raised his hand and cried out, 'Wait a moment!' Some of the company stood still and, imagining it was a signal to take off their masks, began to do so; others went on dancing; others stopped and stared. He was the centre of attention; and before he had got his message fairly delivered, it had reached other ears than those for which it was intended. An excited whispering went round the room: 'What is it? What is it?' Men and women stood about with their masks in their hands, and faces blanker than before they were uncovered.

Others looked terrified and incredulous. A woman came up to Jane Manning and said, 'What a dreadful thing for Marion Lane.'

'Why?' Jane asked.

'Didn't you know? She and Harry Chichester were the greatest friends. At one time it was thought –'

'I live out of the world, I had no idea,' said Jane quickly. Even in the presence of calamity, she felt a pang that her friend had not confided in her.

Her interlocutor persisted: 'It was talked about a great deal. Some people said – you know how they chatter – that she didn't treat him quite fairly. I hate to make myself a busybody, Mrs Manning, but I do think you ought to tell her; she ought to be prepared.'

'But I don't know where she is!' cried Jane, from whose mind all thought of her friend had been banished. 'Have you seen her?'

'Not since the sheet incident.'

'Nor have I.'

Nor, it seemed, had anyone. Disturbed by this new misadventure far more than its trivial nature seemed to warrant, Jane hastened in turn to such of her guests as might be able to enlighten her as to Marion's whereabouts. Some of them greeted her enquiry with a lift of the eyebrows but none of them could help her in her quest. Nor could she persuade them to take much interest in it. They seemed to have forgotten that they were at a party and owed a duty of responsiveness to their hostess. Their eyes did not light up when she came near. One and all they were discussing the suicide and suggesting its possible motive. The room rustled with their whispering, with the soft hissing sound of 'Chichester' and the succeeding 'Hush!' which was meant to stifle but only multiplied and prolonged it. Jane felt that she must scream.

All at once there was silence. Had she screamed? No, for the noise they had all heard came from somewhere inside the house. The room seemed to hold its breath. There it was again and coming closer; a cry, a shriek, the shrill tones of terror alternating in a dreadful rhythm with a throaty, choking sound like whooping cough. No one could have recognised it as Marion Lane's voice and few could have told for Marion Lane the dishevelled figure, mask in hand, that lurched through the ballroom doorway and with quick stumbling steps, before which the onlookers fell back, zigzagged into the middle of the room.

'Stop him!' she gasped. 'Don't let him do it!'

Jane Manning ran to her. 'Dearest, what is it?'

'It's Harry Chichester,' sobbed Marion, her head rolling about on her shoulders as if it had come loose. 'He's in there. He wants to take his mask off, but I can't bear it! It would be awful! Oh, do take him away!'

'Where is he?' someone asked.

'Oh, I don't know! In Jane's sitting room, I think. He wouldn't let me go. He's so cold, so dreadfully cold.'

'Look after her, Jane,' said Jack Manning. 'Get her out of here. Anyone coming with me?' he asked, looking round. 'I'm going to investigate.'

Marion caught the last words. 'Don't go,' she implored. 'He'll hurt you.' But her voice was drowned in the scurry and stampede of feet. The whole company was following their host. In a few moments the ballroom was empty.

Five minutes later there were voices in the anteroom. It was Manning leading back his troops. 'Barring, of course, the revolver,' he was saying, 'and the few things that had been knocked over, and those scratches on the door, there wasn't a trace. Hello!' he added, crossing the threshold, 'what's this?'

The ballroom window was open again; the curtains fluttered wildly inwards; on the boards lay a patch of nearly melted snow.

Jack Manning walked up to it. Just within the further edge, near the window, was a kind of smear, darker than the toffee-coloured mess around it and roughly oval in shape.

'Do you think that's a footmark?' he asked of the company in general.

No one could say.

M. R. JAMES

(1862–1936)

Montague Rhodes James was an eminent medieval scholar, Provost of King's College, Cambridge, and Eton College, Director of the Fitzwilliam Museum and, according to his biographer Michael Cox, 'an early and adventurous cyclist' who toured France on a two-man tricycle. His ghost stories were first composed on Christmas Eve for his friends in King's College, while later works were tested on the scout troop at Eton. Like many of his best stories, 'The Haunted Dolls' House' combines a fascination with antiquarianism and a virtuoso control of the interplay between the mundane and the terrifying. 'Everyone,' he wrote as a schoolboy at Eton, 'can remember a time when he has searched his curtains and poked in the dark corners of his room. Of course we know there are no such things – but … it's best to be quite sure. People do tell such odd stories.'

THE HAUNTED
DOLLS' HOUSE

'I SUPPOSE YOU GET STUFF of that kind through your hands pretty often?' said Mr Dillet, as he pointed with his stick to an object which shall be described when the time comes: and when he said it, he lied in his throat, and knew that he lied. Not once in twenty years – perhaps not once in a lifetime – could Mr Chittenden, skilled as he was in ferreting out the forgotten treasures of half a dozen counties, expect to handle such a specimen. It was collectors' palaver, and Mr Chittenden recognised it as such.

'Stuff of that kind, Mr Dillet! It's a museum piece, that is.'

'Well, I suppose there are museums that'll take anything.'

'I've seen one, not as good as that, years back,' said Mr Chittenden thoughtfully. 'But that's not likely to come into the market: and I'm told they 'ave some fine ones of the period over the water. No, I'm only telling you the truth, Mr Dillet, when I was to say that if you was to place an unlimited order with me for the very best that could be got – and you know I 'ave facilities for getting to know of such things, and a reputation to maintain – well, all I can say is, I should lead you straight up to that one and say, "I can't do no better for you than that, sir."'

'Hear, hear!' said Mr Dillet, applauding ironically with the end of his stick on the floor of the shop. 'How much are you sticking the innocent American buyer for it, eh?'

'Oh, I shan't be over-hard on the buyer, American or otherwise. You see, it stands this way, Mr Dillet – if I knew just a bit more about the pedigree –'

'Or just a bit less,' Mr Dillet put in.

'Ha, ha! You will have your joke, sir. No, but as I was saying, if I knew just a little more than what I do about the piece – though anyone can see for themselves it's a genuine thing, every last corner of it, and there's not been one of my men allowed to so much as touch it since it came into the shop – there'd be another figure in the price I'm asking.'

'And what's that: five and twenty?'

'Multiply that by three and you've got it, sir. Seventy-five's my price.'

'And fifty's mine,' said Mr Dillet.

The point of agreement was, of course, somewhere between the two, it does not matter exactly where – I think sixty guineas. But half an hour later the object was being packed, and within an hour Mr Dillet had called for it in his car and driven away. Mr Chittenden, holding the cheque in his hand, saw him off from the door with smiles and returned, still smiling, into the parlour, where his wife was making the tea. He stopped at the door.

'It's gone,' he said.

'Thank God for that!' said Mrs Chittenden, putting down the teapot. 'Mr Dillet, was it?'

'Yes, it was.'

'Well, I'd sooner it was him than another.'

'Oh, I don't know; he ain't a bad feller, my dear.'

'Maybe not, but in my opinion he'd be none the worse for a bit of a shake-up.'

'Well, if that's your opinion, it's my opinion he's put himself into the way of getting one. Anyhow, *we* shan't have no more of it, and that's something to be thankful for.'

And so Mr and Mrs Chittenden sat down to tea.

And what of Mr Dillet and his new acquisition? What it was, the title of this story will have told you. What it was like, I shall have to indicate as well as I can.

There was only just enough room for it in the car, and Mr Dillet had to sit with the driver: he had also to go slow, for though the rooms of the dolls' house had all been stuffed carefully with soft cotton wool, jolting was to be avoided, in view of the immense number of small objects which thronged them; and the ten-mile drive was an anxious time for him, in spite of all the precautions he insisted upon. At last his front door was reached, and Collins, the butler, came out.

'Look here, Collins, you must help me with this thing – it's a delicate job. We must get it out upright, see? It's full of little things that mustn't be displaced more than we can help. Let's see, where shall we have it? (After a pause for consideration.) Really, I think I shall have to put it in my own room, to begin with at any rate. On the big table – that's it.'

It was conveyed – with much talking – to Mr Dillet's spacious room on the first floor, looking out on the drive. The sheeting was unwound from it and the front thrown open, and for the next hour or two Mr Dillet was fully occupied in extracting the padding and setting in order the contents of the rooms.

When this thoroughly congenial task was finished, I must say that it would have been difficult to find a more perfect and attractive specimen of a dolls' house in Strawberry Hill Gothic than that which now stood on Mr Dillet's large kneehole table, lighted up by the evening sun which came slanting through three tall sash windows.

It was quite six feet long, including the chapel or oratory which flanked the front on the left as you faced it, and the stable on the right. The main block of the house was, as I have said, in the Gothic manner: that is to say, the windows had pointed arches and were surmounted by what are called ogival hoods, with crockets and finials such as we see on the canopies of tombs built into church walls. At the angles were absurd turrets covered with arched panels. The chapel had pinnacles and buttresses, and a bell in the turret and coloured glass in the windows. When the front of the house was open you saw four large rooms, bedroom, dining room, drawing room and kitchen, each with its appropriate furniture in a very complete state.

The stable on the right was in two storeys, with its proper complement of horses, coaches and grooms, and with its clock and Gothic cupola for the clock bell.

Pages, of course, might be written on the outfit of the mansion – how many frying pans, how many gilt chairs, what pictures, carpets, chandeliers, four-posters, table linen, glass, crockery and plate it possessed; but all this must be left to the imagination. I will only say that the base or plinth on which the house stood (for it was fitted with one of some depth which allowed of a flight of steps to the front door and a terrace, partly balustraded) contained a shallow drawer or drawers in which were neatly stored sets of embroidered curtains, changes of raiment for the inmates and, in short, all the materials for an infinite series of variations and refittings of the most absorbing and delightful kind.

'Quintessence of Horace Walpole, that's what it is: he must have had something to do with the making of it.' Such was Mr Dillet's murmured reflection as he knelt before it in a reverent ecstasy. 'Simply wonderful! This is my day and no mistake. Five hundred pounds coming in this morning for that cabinet which I never cared about, and now this tumbling into my hands for a tenth, at the very most, of what it would fetch in town. Well, well! It almost makes one afraid something'll happen to counter it. Let's have a look at the population, anyhow.'

Accordingly, he set them before him in a row. Again, here is an opportunity, which some would snatch at, of making an inventory of costume: I am incapable of it.

There were a gentleman and lady, in blue satin and brocade respectively. There were two children, a boy and a girl. There was a cook, a nurse, a footman, and there were the stable servants, two postilions, a coachman, two grooms.

'Anyone else? Yes, possibly.'

The curtains of the four-poster in the bedroom were closely drawn round all four sides of it, and he put his finger in between them and felt in the bed. He drew the finger back hastily, for it almost seemed to him as if something had – not stirred, perhaps, but yielded in an odd live way as he pressed it. Then he put back the curtains, which ran on rods in the proper manner, and extracted from the bed a white-haired old gentleman in a long linen nightdress and cap, and laid him down by the rest. The tale was complete.

Dinner time was now near, so Mr Dillet spent but five minutes in putting the lady and children into the drawing room, the gentleman into the dining room, the servants into the kitchen and stables, and the old man back into his bed. He retired into his dressing room next door, and we see and hear no more of him until something like eleven o'clock at night.

His whim was to sleep surrounded by some of the gems of his collection. The big room in which we have seen him contained his bed; bath, wardrobe and all the appliances of dressing were in a commodious room adjoining; but his four-poster, which itself was a valued treasure, stood in the large room where he sometimes wrote, and often sat, and even received visitors. Tonight he repaired to it in a highly complacent frame of mind.

There was no striking clock within earshot – none on the staircase, none in the stable, none in the distant church tower. Yet it is indubitable that Mr Dillet was started out of a very pleasant slumber by a bell tolling one.

He was so much startled that he did not merely lie

breathless with wide-open eyes, but actually sat up in his bed.

He never asked himself, till the morning hours, how it was that, though there was no light at all in the room, the dolls' house on the kneehole table stood out with complete clearness. But it was so. The effect was that of a bright harvest moon shining full on the front of a big white stone mansion – a quarter of a mile away it might be and yet every detail was photographically sharp. There were trees about it, too – trees rising behind the chapel and the house. He seemed to be conscious of the scent of a cool still September night. He thought he could hear an occasional stamp and clink from the stables, as of horses stirring. And with another shock he realised that, above the house, he was looking, not at the wall of his room with its pictures, but into the profound blue of a night sky.

There were lights, more than one, in the windows, and he quickly saw that this was no four-roomed house with a movable front, but one of many rooms and staircases – a real house, but seen as if through the wrong end of a telescope. 'You mean to show me something,' he muttered to himself, and he gazed earnestly on the lighted windows. They would in real life have been shuttered or curtained, no doubt, he thought; but, as it was, there was nothing to intercept his view of what was being transacted inside the rooms.

Two rooms were lighted – one on the ground floor to the right of the door, one upstairs, on the left – the first brightly enough, the other rather dimly. The lower room was the dining room: a table was laid, but the meal was over, and only wine and glasses were left on the table. The man of the blue satin and the woman of the brocade were alone in the room, and they were talking very earnestly, seated close together at the table, their elbows on it: every now and again stopping to listen, as it seemed. Once *he* rose, came to the window and opened it and put his head out and his hand to his ear. There was a lighted taper in a silver candlestick on a sideboard. When the man left the window he seemed to leave the room also; and the lady, taper in hand, remained standing and listening. The expression on her face was that of one striving her utmost to keep down a fear that threatened to master her – and succeeding. It was a hateful face, too; broad, flat and sly. Now the man came back and she took some small thing from him and hurried out of the room. He, too, disappeared, but only for a moment or two. The front door slowly opened and he stepped out and stood on the top of the *perron*, looking this way and that; then turned towards the upper window that was lighted and shook his fist.

It was time to look at that upper window. Through it was seen a four-post bed: a nurse or other servant in an armchair, evidently sound asleep; in the bed an old man lying: awake and, one would say, anxious, from the way in which he shifted about and moved his fingers, beating tunes on the coverlet. Beyond the bed a door opened. Light was seen on the ceiling and the lady came in: she set down her candle on a table, came to the fireside and roused the nurse. In her hand she had an old-fashioned wine bottle, ready uncorked. The nurse took it, poured some of the contents into a little silver saucepan, added some spice and sugar from casters on the table, and set it to warm on the fire. Meanwhile the old man in the bed beckoned feebly to the lady, who came to him, smiling, took his wrist as if to feel his pulse and bit her lip as if in consternation. He looked at her anxiously, and then pointed to the window and spoke. She nodded and did as the man below had done: opened the casement and listened – perhaps rather ostentatiously – then drew in her head and shook it, looking at the old man, who seemed to sigh.

By this time the posset on the fire was steaming, and the nurse poured it into a small two-handled silver bowl and brought it to the bedside. The old man seemed disinclined for it and was waving it away, but the lady and the nurse together bent over him and evidently pressed it upon him. He must have yielded, for they supported him into a sitting position and put it to his lips. He drank most of it, in several draughts, and they laid him down. The lady left the room, smiling goodnight to him, and took the bowl, the bottle and the silver saucepan with her. The nurse returned to the chair and there was an interval of complete quiet.

Suddenly the old man started up in his bed – and he must have uttered some cry, for the nurse started out of her chair and made but one step of it to the bedside. He was a sad and terrible sight – flushed in the face, almost to blackness, the eyes glaring whitely, both hands clutching at his heart, foam at his lips.

For a moment the nurse left him, ran to the door, flung it wide open and, one supposes, screamed aloud for help, then darted back to the bed and seemed to try feverishly

to soothe him – to lay him down – anything. But as the
lady, her husband and several servants rushed into the
room with horrified faces, the old man collapsed under
the nurse's hands and lay back, and his features, contorted
with agony and rage, relaxed slowly into calm.

A few moments later, lights showed out to the left of
the house and a coach with flambeaux drove up to the
door. A white-wigged man in black got nimbly out and
ran up the steps, carrying a small leather trunk-shaped
box. He was met in the doorway by the man and his wife,
she with her handkerchief clutched between her hands, he
with a tragic face, but retaining his self-control. They led
the newcomer into the dining room, where he set his box
of papers on the table and, turning to them, listened with
a face of consternation at what they had to tell. He nodded
his head again and again, threw out his hands slightly,
declined, it seemed, offers of refreshment and lodging for
the night, and within a few minutes came slowly down the
steps, entering the coach and driving off the way he had
come. As the man in blue watched him from the top of the
steps, a smile not pleasant to see stole slowly over his fat
white face. Darkness fell over the whole scene as the lights
of the coach disappeared.

But Mr Dillet remained sitting up in the bed: he had
rightly guessed that there would be a sequel. The house
front glimmered out again before long. But now there
was a difference. The lights were in other windows, one
at the top of the house, the other illuminating the range
of coloured windows of the chapel. How he saw through
these is not quite obvious, but he did. The interior was

as carefully furnished as the rest of the establishment, with its minute red cushions on the desks, its Gothic stall canopies and its western gallery and pinnacled organ with gold pipes. On the centre of the black and white pavement was a bier: four tall candles burned at the corners. On the bier was a coffin covered with a pall of black velvet.

As he looked the folds of the pall stirred. It seemed to rise at one end: it slid downwards: it fell away, exposing the black coffin with its silver handles and nameplate. One of the tall candlesticks swayed and toppled over. Ask no more, but turn, as Mr Dillet hastily did, and look in at the lighted window at the top of the house, where a boy and girl lay in two truckle beds, and a four-poster for the nurse rose above them. The nurse was not visible for the moment; but the father and mother were there, dressed now in mourning, but with very little sign of mourning in their demeanour. Indeed, they were laughing and talking with a good deal of animation, sometimes to each other and sometimes throwing a remark to one or other of the children, and again laughing at the answers. Then the father was seen to go on tiptoe out of the room, taking with him as he went a white garment that hung on a peg near the door. He shut the door after him. A minute or two later it was slowly opened again and a muffled head poked round it. A bent form of sinister shape stepped across to the truckle beds and suddenly stopped, threw up its arms and revealed, of course, the father, laughing. The children were in agonies of terror, the boy with the bedclothes over his head, the girl throwing herself out of bed into her mother's arms. Attempts at consolation followed – the parents took the children on their laps, patted them, picked up the white gown and showed there was no harm in it, and so forth; and at last, putting the children back into bed, left the room with encouraging waves of the hand. As they left it, the nurse came in and soon the light died down.

Still Mr Dillet watched immovable.

A new sort of light – not of lamp or candle – a pale ugly light, began to dawn around the door-case at the back of the room. The door was opening again. The seer does not like to dwell upon what he saw entering the room: he says it might be described as a frog – the size of a man – but it had scanty white hair about its head. It was busy about the truckle beds, but not for long. The sound of cries – faint, as if coming out of a vast distance, but, even so, infinitely appalling – reached the ear.

There were signs of a hideous commotion all over the house: lights moved along and up, and doors opened and shut, and running figures passed within the windows. The clock in the stable turret tolled one, and darkness fell again.

It was only dispelled once more, to show the house front. At the bottom of the steps dark figures were drawn up in two lines, holding flaming torches. More dark figures came down the steps, bearing, first one, then another small coffin. And the lines of torch-bearers with the coffins between them moved silently onward to the left.

The hours of night passed on – never so slowly, Mr Dillet thought. Gradually he sank down from sitting to lying in his bed – but he did not close an eye: and early next morning he sent for the doctor.

The doctor found him in a disquieting state of nerves, and recommended sea air. To a quiet place on the east coast he accordingly repaired by easy stages in his car.

One of the first people he met on the seafront was Mr Chittenden, who, it appeared, had likewise been advised to take his wife away for a bit of a change.

Mr Chittenden looked somewhat askance upon him when they met, and not without cause.

'Well, I don't wonder at you being a bit upset, Mr Dillet. What? Yes, well, I might say 'orrible upset, to be sure, seeing what me and my poor wife went through ourselves. But I put it to you, Mr Dillet, one of two things: was I going to scrap a lovely piece like that on the one 'and, or was I going to tell customers, "I'm selling you a regular picture-palace dramar in reel life of the olden time, billed to perform regular at one o'clock a.m."? Why, what would you 'ave said yourself? And next thing you know, two Justices of the Peace in the back parlour and pore Mr and Mrs Chittenden off in a spring cart to the county asylum and everyone in the street saying, "Ah, I thought it 'ud come to that. Look at the way the man drank!" – and me next door, or next door but one, to a total abstainer, as you know. Well, there was my position. What? Me 'ave it back in the shop? Well, what do *you* think? No, but I'll tell you what I will do. You shall have your money back, bar the ten pound I paid for it, and you make what you can.'

Later in the day, in what is offensively called the 'smoke room' of the hotel, a murmured conversation between the two went on for some time.

'How much do you really know about that thing and where it came from?'

'Honest, Mr Dillet, I don't know the 'ouse. Of course, it came out of the lumber room of a country 'ouse – that anyone could guess. But I'll go as far as say this, that I believe it's not a hundred miles from this place. Which direction and how far I've no notion. I'm only judging by guesswork. The man as I actually paid the cheque to ain't one of my regular men and I've lost sight of him; but I 'ave the idea that this part of the country was his beat, and that's every word I can tell you. But now, Mr Dillet, there's one thing that rather physics me. That old chap – I suppose you saw him drive up to the door – I thought so: now, would he have been the medical man, do you take it? My wife would have it so, but I stuck to it that was the lawyer, because he had papers with him and one he took out was folded up.'

'I agree,' said Mr Dillet. 'Thinking it over, I came to the conclusion that was the old man's will, ready to be signed.'

'Just what I thought,' said Mr Chittenden, 'and I took it that will would have cut out the young people, eh? Well, well! It's been a lesson to me, I know that. I shan't buy no more dolls' houses, nor waste no more money on the pictures – and as to this business of poisonin' grandpa, well, if I know myself, I never 'ad much of a turn for that. Live and let live: that's bin my motto throughout life, and I ain't found it a bad one.'

Filled with these elevated sentiments, Mr Chittenden retired to his lodgings. Mr Dillet next day repaired to the local institute, where he hoped to find some clue to the riddle that absorbed him. He gazed in despair at a long file of the Canterbury and York Society's publications of the parish registers of the district. No print resembling the house of his nightmare was among those that hung on the staircase and in the passages. Disconsolate, he found himself at last in a derelict room, staring at a dusty model of a church in a dusty glass case: *Model of St Stephen's Church, Coxham. Presented by J. Merewether, Esq., of Ilbridge House, 1877. The work of his ancestor James Merewether, d. 1786.* There was something in the fashion of it that reminded him dimly of his horror. He retraced his steps to a wall map he had noticed, and made out that Ilbridge House was in Coxham Parish. Coxham was, as it happened, one of the parishes of which he had retained the name when he glanced over the file of printed registers, and it was not long before he found in them the record of the burial of Roger Milford, aged seventy-six, on 11 September 1757, and of Roger and Elizabeth Merewether, aged nine and seven, on the 19th of the same month. It seemed worthwhile to follow up this clue, frail as it was, and in the afternoon he drove out to Coxham. The east end of the north aisle of the church is a Milford chapel, and on its north wall are tablets to the same persons; Roger, the elder, it seems, was distinguished by all the qualities which adorn 'the Father, the Magistrate and the Man': the memorial was erected by his attached daughter Elizabeth, 'who did not long survive the loss of a parent ever solicitous for her welfare, and of two amiable children'. The last sentence was plainly an addition to the original inscription.

A yet later slab told of James Merewether, husband of Elizabeth, 'who in the dawn of life practised, not without success, those arts which, had he continued their exercise, might in the opinion of the most competent judges have earned for him the name of the British Vitruvius: but who, overwhelmed by the visitation which deprived him of an affectionate partner and a blooming offspring, passed his Prime and Age in a secluded yet elegant Retirement: his grateful Nephew and Heir indulges a pious sorrow by this too brief recital of his excellences'.

The children were more simply commemorated. Both died on the night of 12 September.

Mr Dillet felt sure that in Ilbridge House he had found the scene of his drama. In some old sketchbook, possibly in some old print, he may yet find convincing evidence that he is right. But the Ilbridge House of today is not that which he sought; it is an Elizabethan erection of the forties, in red brick with stone quoins and dressings. A quarter of a mile from it, in a low part of the park, backed by ancient, stag-horned, ivy-strangled trees and thick undergrowth, are marks of a terraced platform overgrown with rough grass. A few stone balusters lie here and there, and a heap or two, covered with nettles and ivy, of wrought stones with badly carved crockets. This, someone told Mr Dillet, was the site of an older house.

As he drove out of the village, the hall clock struck four, and Mr Dillet started up and clapped his hands to his ears. It was not the first time he had heard that bell.

Awaiting an offer from the other side of the Atlantic, the dolls' house still reposes, carefully sheeted, in a loft over Mr Dillet's stables, whither Collins conveyed it on the day when Mr Dillet started for the sea coast.

[It will be said, perhaps, and not unjustly, that this is no more than a variation on a former story of mine called 'The Mezzotint'. I can only hope that there is enough of variation in the setting to make the repetition of the *motif* tolerable.]

EDITH WHARTON
(1862–1937)

Edith Wharton (née Jones) was born into a wealthy New York family, a branch of which inspired the phrase 'keeping up with the Joneses'. Wharton's childhood was not a happy one, however, and she wrote that, as a bookish child, her parents 'regard[ed] me with fear, like some pale predestined child who disappears at night to dance with "the little people"'. This impression may have been enhanced by Wharton's susceptibility to the supernatural; convalescing from an attack of typhoid, she read a 'tale of robbers and ghosts' which affected her so greatly that she relapsed and, when she came to, 'it was to enter a world haunted by formless horrors' which lasted for 'some seven or eight years'. In later life she became one of the greatest novelists of the twentieth century, the first woman to win a Pulitzer Prize, an interior decorator and landscape architect and an intrepid traveller. 'Pomegranate Seeds' refers to the Greek myth of Persephone. Tricked by her abductor Hades, god of the underworld, into consuming three seeds, she was doomed to remain with him for a portion of each year.

Pomegranate Seed

I

Charlotte Ashby paused on her doorstep. Dark had descended on the brilliancy of the March afternoon, and the grinding, rasping street life of the city was at its highest. She turned her back on it, standing for a moment in the old-fashioned, marble-flagged vestibule before she inserted her key in the lock. The sash curtains drawn across the panes of the inner door softened the light within to a warm blur through which no details showed. It was the hour when, in the first months of her marriage to Kenneth Ashby, she had most liked to return to that quiet house in a street long since deserted by business and fashion. The contrast between the soulless roar of New York, its devouring blaze of lights, the oppression of its congested traffic, congested houses, lives and minds, and this veiled sanctuary she called home always stirred her profoundly. In the very heart of the hurricane she had found her tiny islet – or thought she had. And now, in the last months, everything was changed, and she always wavered on the doorstep and had to force herself to enter.

While she stood there she called up the scene within: the hall hung with old prints, the ladder-like stairs and on the left her husband's long shabby library, full of books and pipes and worn armchairs inviting to meditation. How she had loved that room! Then, upstairs, her own drawing room, in which, since the death of Kenneth's first wife, neither furniture nor hangings had been changed, because there had never been money enough, but which Charlotte had made her own by moving furniture about and adding more books, another lamp, a table for the new reviews. Even on the occasion of her only visit to the first Mrs Ashby – a distant, self-centred woman, whom she had known very slightly – she had looked about her with an innocent envy, feeling it to be exactly the drawing room she would have liked for herself; and now for more than a year it had been hers to deal with as she chose – the room to which she hastened back at dusk on winter days, where she sat reading by the fire, or answering notes at the pleasant roomy desk, or going over her stepchildren's copybooks, till she heard her husband's step.

Sometimes friends dropped in; sometimes – oftener – she was alone; and she liked that best, since it was another way of being with Kenneth, thinking over what he had said when they parted in the morning, imagining what he would say when he sprang up the stairs, found her by herself and caught her to him.

Now, instead of this, she thought of one thing only – the letter she might or might not find on the hall table. Until she had made sure whether or not it was there, her mind had no room for anything else. The letter was always the same – a square greyish envelope with 'Kenneth Ashby, Esquire', written on it in bold but faint characters. From the first it had struck Charlotte as peculiar that anyone who wrote such a firm hand should trace the letters so lightly; the address was always written as though there were not enough ink in the pen, or the writer's wrist were too weak to bear upon it. Another curious thing was that, in spite of its masculine curves, the writing was so visibly feminine. Some hands are sexless, some masculine, at first glance; the writing on the grey envelope, for all its strength and assurance, was without doubt a woman's. The envelope never bore anything but the recipient's name; no stamp, no address. The letter was presumably delivered by hand – but by whose? No doubt it was slipped into the letter box, whence the parlourmaid, when she closed the shutters and lit the lights, probably extracted it. At any rate, it was always in the evening, after dark, that Charlotte saw it lying there. She thought of the letter in the singular, as 'it', because, though there had been several since her marriage – seven, to be exact – they were so alike in appearance that they had become merged in one another in her mind, become one letter, become 'it.'

The first had come the day after their return from their honeymoon – a journey prolonged to the West Indies, from which they had returned to New York after an absence of more than two months. Re-entering the house with her husband, late on that first evening – they had dined at his mother's – she had seen, alone on the hall table, the grey envelope. Her eye fell on it before Kenneth's, and her first thought was: 'Why, I've seen that writing before'; but where she could not recall. The memory was just definite enough for her to identify the script whenever it looked up at her faintly from the same pale envelope; but on that first day she would have thought no more of the letter if, when her husband's glance lit on it, she had not chanced to be looking at him. It all happened in a flash – his seeing the letter, putting out his hand for it, raising it to his short-sighted eyes to decipher the faint writing, and then abruptly withdrawing the arm he had slipped through Charlotte's and moving away to the hanging light, his back turned to her. She had waited – waited for a sound, an exclamation; waited for him to open the letter; but he had slipped it into his pocket without a word and followed her into the library. And there they had sat down by the fire and lit their cigarettes, and he had remained silent, his head thrown back broodingly against the armchair, his eyes fixed on the hearth, and presently had passed his hand over his forehead and said, 'Wasn't it unusually hot at my mother's tonight? I've got a splitting head. Mind if I take myself off to bed?'

That was the first time. Since then Charlotte had never been present when he had received the letter. It usually came before he got home from his office, and she had to go upstairs and leave it lying there. But even if she had not seen it, she would have known it had come by the change in his face when he joined her – which, on those evenings, he seldom did before they met for dinner. Evidently, whatever the letter contained, he wanted to be by himself to deal with it; and when he reappeared he looked years older, looked emptied of life and courage, and hardly conscious of her presence. Sometimes he was silent for the rest of the evening; and if he spoke, it was usually to hint some criticism of her household arrangements, suggest some change in the domestic administration, to ask, a little nervously, if she didn't think Joyce's nursery governess was rather young and flighty, or if she herself always saw to it that Peter – whose throat was delicate – was properly wrapped up when he went to school. At such times Charlotte would remember the friendly warnings she had received when she became engaged to Kenneth Ashby: 'Marrying a heartbroken widower! Isn't that rather risky? You know Elsie Ashby absolutely dominated him'; and how she had jokingly replied, 'He may be glad of a little liberty for a change.' And in this respect she had been right. She had needed no one to tell her, during the first months, that her husband was perfectly happy with her. When they came back from their protracted honeymoon the same friends said, 'What have you done to Kenneth? He looks twenty years younger'; and this time she answered with careless joy, 'I suppose I've got him out of his groove.'

But what she noticed after the grey letters began to come was not so much his nervous tentative fault-finding – which always seemed to be uttered against his will – as the look in his eyes when he joined her after receiving one of the letters. The look was not unloving, not even indifferent; it was the look of a man who had been so far away from ordinary events that when he returns to familiar things they seem strange. She minded that more than the fault-finding.

Though she had been sure from the first that the handwriting on the grey envelope was a woman's, it was long before she associated the mysterious letters with any sentimental secret. She was too sure of her husband's love, too confident of filling his life, for such an idea to occur to her. It seemed far more likely that the letters – which certainly did not appear to cause him any sentimental pleasure – were addressed to the busy lawyer than to the private person. Probably they were from some tiresome client – women, he had often told her, were nearly always tiresome as clients – who did not want her letters opened by his secretary and therefore had them carried to his house. Yes, but in that case the unknown female must be unusually troublesome, judging from the effect her letters produced. Then again, though his professional discretion was exemplary, it was odd that he had never uttered an impatient comment, never remarked to Charlotte, in a moment of expansion, that there was a nuisance of a woman who kept badgering him about a case that had gone against her. He had made more than one semi-confidence of the kind – of course without giving names or details; but concerning this mysterious correspondent his lips were sealed.

There was another possibility: what is euphemistically called an 'old entanglement'. Charlotte Ashby was a sophisticated woman. She had few illusions about the intricacies of the human heart; she knew that there were often old entanglements. But when she had married Kenneth Ashby, her friends, instead of hinting at such a possibility, had said, 'You've got your work cut out for you. Marrying a Don Juan is a sinecure to it. Kenneth's never looked at another woman since he first saw Elsie Corder. During all the years of their marriage he was more like an unhappy lover than a comfortably contented husband. He'll never let you move an armchair or change the place of a lamp; and whatever you venture to do, he'll mentally compare with what Elsie would have done in your place.'

Except for an occasional nervous mistrust as to her ability to manage the children – a mistrust gradually dispelled by her good humour and the children's obvious fondness for her – none of these forebodings had come true. The desolate widower, of whom his nearest friends said that only his absorbing professional interests had kept him from suicide after his first wife's death, had fallen in love, two years later, with Charlotte Gorse, and after an impetuous wooing had married her and carried her off on a tropical honeymoon. And ever since he had been as tender and lover-like as during those first radiant weeks. Before asking her to marry him he had spoken to her frankly of his great love for his first wife and his despair after her sudden death; but even then he had assumed no stricken attitude, or implied that life offered no possibility of renewal. He had been perfectly simple and natural, and had confessed to Charlotte that from the beginning he had hoped the future held new gifts for him. And when, after their marriage, they returned to the house where his twelve years with his first wife had been spent, he had told Charlotte at once that he was sorry he couldn't afford to do the place over for her, but that he knew every woman had her own views about furniture and all sorts of household arrangements a man would never notice, and had begged her to make any changes she saw fit without bothering to consult him. As a result, she made as few as possible; but his way of beginning their new life in the old setting was so frank and unembarrassed that it put her immediately at her ease, and she was almost sorry to find that the portrait of Elsie Ashby, which used to hang over the desk in his library, had been transferred in their absence to the children's nursery. Knowing herself to be the indirect cause of this banishment, she spoke of it to her husband; but he answered, 'Oh, I thought they ought to grow up with her looking down on them.' The answer moved Charlotte, and satisfied her; and as time went by she had to confess that she felt more at home in her house, more at ease and in confidence with her husband, since that long, coldly beautiful face on the library wall no longer followed her with guarded eyes. It was as if Kenneth's love had penetrated to the secret she hardly acknowledged to her own heart – her passionate need to feel herself the sovereign even of his past.

With all this stored-up happiness to sustain her, it was curious that she had lately found herself yielding to a nervous apprehension. But there the apprehension was; and on this particular afternoon – perhaps because she was more tired than usual, or because of the trouble of finding a new cook, or for some other ridiculously trivial reason, moral or physical – she found herself unable to react against the feeling. Latchkey in hand, she looked back down the silent street to the whirl and illumination of the great thoroughfare beyond, and up at the sky already aflare with the city's nocturnal life. 'Outside there,' she thought, 'skyscrapers, advertisements, telephones, wireless, airplanes, movies, motors and all the rest of the twentieth century; and on the other side of the door something I can't explain, can't relate to them. Something as old as the world, as mysterious as life … Nonsense! What am I worrying about? There hasn't been a letter for three months now – not since the day we came back from the country after Christmas … Queer that they always seem to come after our holidays! … Why should I imagine there's going to be one tonight!'

No reason why, but that was the worst of it – one of the worst! – that there were days when she would stand there cold and shivering with the premonition of something inexplicable, intolerable, to be faced on the other side of the curtained panes; and when she opened the door and went in, there would be nothing; and on other days when she felt the same premonitory chill, it was justified by the sight of the grey envelope. So that ever since the last had come she had taken to feeling cold and premonitory every evening, because she never opened the door without thinking the letter might be there.

Well, she'd had enough of it: that was certain. She couldn't go on like that. If her husband turned white and had a headache on the days when the letter came, he seemed to recover afterwards; but she couldn't. With her the strain had become chronic, and the reason was not far to seek. Her husband knew from whom the letter came and what was in it; he was prepared beforehand for whatever he had to deal with, and master of the situation, however bad; whereas she was shut out in the dark with her conjectures.

'I can't stand it! I can't stand it another day!' she exclaimed aloud, as she put her key in the lock. She turned the key and went in; and there, on the table, lay the letter.

II

She was almost glad of the sight. It seemed to justify everything, to put a seal of definiteness on the whole blurred business. A letter for her husband; a letter from a woman – no doubt another vulgar case of 'old entanglement'. What a fool she had been ever to doubt it, to rack her brains for less obvious explanations! She took up the envelope with a steady contemptuous hand, looked closely at the faint letters, held it against the light and just discerned the outline of the folded sheet within. She knew that now she would have no peace till she found out what was written on that sheet.

Her husband had not come in; he seldom got back from his office before half-past six or seven, and it was not yet six. She would have time to take the letter up to the drawing room, hold it over the tea kettle, which at that hour always simmered by the fire in expectation of her return, solve the mystery and replace the letter where she had found it. No one would be the wiser and her gnawing uncertainty would be over. The alternative, of course, was to question her husband; but to do that seemed even more difficult. She weighed the letter between thumb and finger, looked at it again under the light, started up the stairs with the envelope – and came down again and laid it on the table.

'No, I evidently can't,' she said, disappointed.

What should she do, then? She couldn't go up alone to that warm, welcoming room, pour out her tea, look over her correspondence, glance at a book or review – not with that letter lying below and the knowledge that in a little while her husband would come in, open it and turn into the library alone, as he always did on the days when the grey envelope came.

Suddenly she decided. She would wait in the library and see for herself; see what happened between him and the letter when they thought themselves unobserved. She wondered the idea had never occurred to her before. By leaving the door ajar and sitting in the corner behind it, she could watch him unseen ... Well, then, she would watch him! She drew a chair into the corner, sat down, her eyes on the crack, and waited.

As far as she could remember, it was the first time she had ever tried to surprise another person's secret, but she was conscious of no compunction. She simply felt as if she were fighting her way through a stifling fog that she must at all costs get out of.

At length she heard Kenneth's latchkey and jumped up. The impulse to rush out and meet him had nearly made her forget why she was there; but she remembered in time and sat down again. From her post she covered the whole range of his movements – saw him enter the hall, draw the key from the door and take off his hat and overcoat. Then he turned to throw his gloves on the hall table and at that moment he saw the envelope. The light was full on his face and what Charlotte first noted there was a look of surprise. Evidently he had not expected the letter – had not thought of the possibility of its being there that day. But though he had not expected it, now that he saw it he knew well enough what it contained. He did not open it immediately, but stood motionless, the colour slowly ebbing from his face. Apparently he could not make up his mind to touch it; but at length he put out his hand, opened the envelope and moved with it to the light. In doing so he turned his back on Charlotte and she saw only his bent head and slightly stooping shoulders. Apparently all the writing was on one page, for he did not turn the sheet but continued to stare at it for so long that he must have reread it a dozen times – or so it seemed to the woman breathlessly watching him. At length she saw him move; he raised the letter still closer to his eyes, as though he had not fully deciphered it. Then he lowered his head and she saw his lips touch the sheet.

'Kenneth!' she exclaimed, and went on out into the hall.

The letter clutched in his hand, her husband turned and looked at her. 'Where were you?' he said in a low, bewildered voice, like a man waked out of his sleep.

'In the library, waiting for you.' She tried to steady her voice. 'What's the matter! What's in that letter? You look ghastly.'

Her agitation seemed to calm him and he instantly put the envelope into his pocket with a slight laugh. 'Ghastly? I'm sorry. I've had a hard day in the office – one or two complicated cases. I look dog tired, I suppose.'

'You didn't look tired when you came in. It was only when you opened that letter –'

He had followed her into the library and they stood gazing at each other. Charlotte noticed how quickly he had regained his self-control; his profession had trained him to rapid mastery of face and voice. She saw at once that she would be at a disadvantage in any attempt to surprise his secret, but at the same moment she lost all desire to manoeuvre, to trick him into betraying anything he wanted to conceal. Her wish was still to penetrate the mystery, but only that she might help him to bear the burden it implied. 'Even if it *is* another woman,' she thought.

'Kenneth,' she said, her heart beating excitedly, 'I waited here on purpose to see you come in. I wanted to watch you while you opened that letter.'

His face, which had paled, turned to dark red; then it paled again. 'That letter? Why especially that letter?'

'Because I've noticed that whenever one of those letters comes it seems to have such a strange effect on you.'

A line of anger she had never seen before came out between his eyes and she said to herself, 'The upper part of his face is too narrow; this is the first time I ever noticed it.'

She heard him continue, in the cool and faintly ironic tone of the prosecuting lawyer making a point: 'Ah, so you're in the habit of watching people open their letters when they don't know you're there?'

'Not in the habit. I never did such a thing before. But I had to find out what she writes to you, at regular intervals, in those grey envelopes.'

He weighed this for a moment; then: 'The intervals have not been regular,' he said.

'Oh, I dare say you've kept a better account of the dates

than I have,' she retorted, her magnanimity vanishing at his tone. 'All I know is that every time that woman writes to you –'

'Why do you assume it's a woman?'

'It's a woman's writing. Do you deny it?'

He smiled. 'No, I don't deny it. I asked only because the writing is generally supposed to look more like a man's.'

Charlotte passed this over impatiently. 'And this woman – what does she write to you about?'

Again he seemed to consider a moment. 'About business.'

'Legal business?'

'In a way, yes. Business in general.'

'You look after her affairs for her?'

'Yes.'

'You've looked after them for a long time?'

'Yes. A very long time.'

'Kenneth, dearest, won't you tell me who she is?'

'No. I can't.' He paused, and brought out, as if with a certain hesitation: 'Professional secrecy.'

The blood rushed from Charlotte's heart to her temples. 'Don't say that – don't!'

'Why not?'

'Because I saw you kiss the letter.'

The effect of the words was so disconcerting that she instantly repented having spoken them. Her husband, who had submitted to her cross-questioning with a sort of contemptuous composure, as though he were humouring an unreasonable child, turned on her a face of terror and distress. For a minute he seemed unable to speak; then, collecting himself, with an effort, he stammered out, 'The writing is very faint; you must have seen me holding the letter close to my eyes to try to decipher it.'

'No, I saw you kissing it.' He was silent. 'Didn't I see you kissing it?'

He sank back into indifference. 'Perhaps.'

'Kenneth! You stand there and say that – to me?'

'What possible difference can it make to you? The letter is on business, as I told you. Do you suppose I'd lie about it? The writer is a very old friend whom I haven't seen for a long time.'

'Men don't kiss business letters, even from women who are very old friends, unless they have been their lovers and still regret them.'

He shrugged his shoulders slightly and turned away, as if he considered the discussion at an end and were faintly disgusted at the turn it had taken.

'Kenneth!' Charlotte moved towards him and caught hold of his arm.

He paused with a look of weariness and laid his hand over hers. 'Won't you believe me?' he asked gently.

'How can I? I've watched these letters come to you – for months now they've been coming. Ever since we came back from the West Indies – one of them greeted me the very day we arrived. And after each one of them I see their mysterious effect on you, I see you disturbed, unhappy, as if someone were trying to estrange you from me.'

'No, dear; not that. Never!'

She drew back and looked at him with passionate entreaty. 'Well, then, prove it to me, darling. It's so easy!'

He forced a smile. 'It's not easy to prove anything to a woman who's once taken an idea into her head.'

'You've only got to show me the letter.'

His hand slipped from hers and he drew back and shook his head.

'You won't?'

'I can't.'

'Then the woman who wrote it is your mistress.'

'No, dear. No.'

'Not now, perhaps. I suppose she's trying to get you back, and you're struggling, out of pity for me. My poor Kenneth!'

'I swear to you she never was my mistress.'

Charlotte felt the tears rushing to her eyes. 'Ah, that's worse, then – that's hopeless! The prudent ones are the kind that keep their hold on a man. We all know that.' She lifted her hands and hid her face in them.

Her husband remained silent; he offered neither consolation nor denial, and at length, wiping away her tears, she raised her eyes almost timidly to his.

'Kenneth, think! We've been married such a short time. Imagine what you're making me suffer. You say you can't show me this letter. You refuse even to explain it.'

'I've told you the letter is on business. I will swear to that too.'

'A man will swear to anything to screen a woman. If you want me to believe you, at least tell me her name. If you'll do that, I promise you I won't ask to see the letter.'

There was a long interval of suspense, during which she felt her heart beating against her ribs in quick admonitory knocks, as if warning her of the danger she was incurring.

'I can't,' he said at length.

'Not even her name?'

'No.'

'You can't tell me anything more?'

'No.'

Again a pause; this time they seemed both to have reached the end of their arguments and to be helplessly facing each other across a baffling waste of incomprehension.

Charlotte stood breathing rapidly, her hands against her breast. She felt as if she had run a hard race and missed the goal. She had meant to move her husband and had succeeded only in irritating him; and this error of reckoning seemed to change him into a stranger, a mysterious incomprehensible being whom no argument or entreaty of hers could reach. The curious thing was that she was aware in him of no hostility or even impatience, but only of a remoteness, an inaccessibility, far more difficult to overcome. She felt herself excluded, ignored, blotted out of his life. But after a moment or two, looking at him more calmly, she saw that he was suffering as much as she was. His distant guarded face was drawn with pain; the coming of the grey envelope, though it always cast a shadow, had never marked him as deeply as this discussion with his wife.

Charlotte took heart; perhaps, after all, she had not spent her last shaft. She drew nearer and once more laid her hand on his arm. 'Poor Kenneth! If you knew how sorry I am for you –'

She thought he winced slightly at this expression of sympathy, but he took her hand and pressed it.

'I can think of nothing worse than to be incapable of

loving long,' she continued, 'to feel the beauty of a great
love and to be too unstable to bear its burden.'

He turned on her a look of wistful reproach. 'Oh, don't
say that of me. Unstable!'

She felt herself at last on the right tack and her voice
trembled with excitement as she went on: 'Then what
about me and this other woman? Haven't you already
forgotten Elsie twice within a year?'

She seldom pronounced his first wife's name; it did not
come naturally to her tongue. She flung it out now as if
she were flinging some dangerous explosive into the open
space between them, and drew back a step, waiting to hear
the mine go off.

Her husband did not move; his expression grew sadder,
but showed no resentment. 'I have never forgotten Elsie,'
he said.

Charlotte could not repress a faint laugh. 'Then, you
poor dear, between the three of us –'

'There are not –' he began; and then broke off and put
his hand to his forehead.

'Not what?'

'I'm sorry; I don't believe I know what I'm saying. I've
got a blinding headache.' He looked wan and furrowed
enough for the statement to be true, but she was exasper-
ated by his evasion.

'Ah, yes; the grey envelope headache!'

She saw the surprise in his eyes. 'I'd forgotten how
closely I've been watched,' he said coldly. 'If you'll excuse
me, I think I'll go up and try an hour in the dark, to see if
I can get rid of this neuralgia.'

She wavered; then she said, with desperate resolution, 'I'm sorry your head aches. But before you go I want to say that sooner or later this question must be settled between us. Someone is trying to separate us, and I don't care what it costs me to find out who it is.' She looked him steadily in the eyes. 'If it costs me your love, I don't care! If I can't have your confidence I don't want anything from you.'

He still looked at her wistfully. 'Give me time.'

'Time for what? It's only a word to say.'

'Time to show you that you haven't lost my love or my confidence.'

'Well, I'm waiting.'

He turned towards the door and then glanced back hesitatingly. 'Oh, do wait, my love,' he said, and went out of the room.

She heard his tired step on the stairs and the closing of his bedroom door above. Then she dropped into a chair and buried her face in her folded arms. Her first movement was one of compunction; she seemed to herself to have been hard, unhuman, unimaginative. 'Think of telling him that I didn't care if my insistence cost me his love! The lying rubbish!' She started up to follow him and unsay the meaningless words. But she was checked by a reflection. He had had his way, after all; he had eluded all attacks on his secret and now he was shut up alone in his room, reading that other woman's letter.

III

She was still reflecting on this when the surprised parlour-maid came in and found her. No, Charlotte said, she wasn't going to dress for dinner; Mr Ashby didn't want to dine. He was very tired and had gone up to his room to rest; later she would have something brought on a tray to the drawing room. She mounted the stairs to her bedroom. Her dinner dress was lying on the bed, and at the sight the quiet routine of her daily life took hold of her and she began to feel as if the strange talk she had just had with her husband must have taken place in another world, between two beings who were not Charlotte Gorse and Kenneth Ashby, but phantoms projected by her fevered imagination. She recalled the year since her marriage – her husband's constant devotion; his persistent, almost too insistent tenderness; the feeling he had given her at times of being too eagerly dependent on her, too searchingly close to her, as if there were not air enough between her soul and his. It seemed preposterous, as she recalled all this, that a few moments ago she should have been accusing him of an intrigue with another woman! But, then, what –

Again she was moved by the impulse to go up to him, beg his pardon and try to laugh away the misunderstanding. But she was restrained by the fear of forcing herself upon his privacy. He was troubled and unhappy, oppressed by some grief or fear; and he had shown her that he wanted to fight out his battle alone. It would be wiser, as well as more generous, to respect his wish. Only, how strange, how unbearable, to be there, in the next room to his, and feel herself at the other end of the world! In her nervous agitation she almost regretted not having had the courage to open the letter and put it back on the hall table before he came in. At least she would have known what his secret was and the bogey might have been laid. For she was beginning now to think of the mystery as something conscious, malevolent: a secret persecution before which he quailed, yet from which he could not free himself. Once or twice in his evasive eyes she thought she had detected a desire for help, an impulse of confession, instantly restrained and suppressed. It was as if he felt she could have helped him if she had known and yet had been unable to tell her!

There flashed through her mind the idea of going to his mother. She was very fond of old Mrs Ashby, a firm-fleshed clear-eyed old lady, with an astringent bluntness of speech which responded to the forthright and simple in Charlotte's own nature. There had been a tacit bond between them ever since the day when Mrs Ashby Senior, coming to lunch for the first time with her new daughter-in-law, had been received by Charlotte downstairs in the library, and glancing up at the empty wall above her son's desk, had remarked laconically, 'Elsie gone, eh?' adding, at Charlotte's murmured explanation, 'Nonsense. Don't have her back. Two's company.' Charlotte, at this reading of her thoughts, could hardly refrain from exchanging a smile of complicity with her mother-in-law; and it seemed to her now that Mrs Ashby's almost uncanny directness might pierce to the core of this new mystery. But here again she hesitated, for the idea almost suggested a betrayal. What right had she to call in anyone, even so close a relation, to surprise a secret which her husband was trying to keep from her? 'Perhaps, by and by, he'll talk to his mother of his own accord,' she thought, and then ended, 'But what does it matter? He and I must settle it between us.'

She was still brooding over the problem when there was a knock on the door and her husband came in. He was dressed for dinner and seemed surprised to see her sitting there, with her evening dress lying unheeded on the bed.

'Aren't you coming down?'

'I thought you were not well and had gone to bed,' she faltered.

He forced a smile. 'I'm not particularly well, but we'd better go down.' His face, though still drawn, looked calmer than when he had fled upstairs an hour earlier.

'There it is; he knows what's in the letter and has fought his battle out again, whatever it is,' she reflected, 'while I'm still in darkness.' She rang and gave a hurried order that dinner should be served as soon as possible – just a short meal, whatever could be got ready quickly, as both she and Mr Ashby were rather tired and not very hungry.

Dinner was announced and they sat down to it. At first neither seemed able to find a word to say; then Ashby began to make conversation with an assumption of ease that was more oppressive than his silence. 'How tired he is! How terribly overtired!' Charlotte said to herself, pursuing her own thoughts while he rambled on about municipal politics, aviation, an exhibition of modern French painting, the health of an old aunt and the installing of the automatic telephone. 'Good heavens, how tired he is!'

When they dined alone they usually went into the library after dinner, and Charlotte curled herself up on the divan with her knitting while he settled down in his armchair under the lamp and lit a pipe. But this evening, by tacit agreement, they avoided the room in which their strange talk had taken place and went up to Charlotte's drawing room.

They sat down near the fire and Charlotte said, 'Your pipe?' after he had put down his hardly tasted coffee.

He shook his head. 'No, not tonight.'

'You must go to bed early; you look terribly tired. I'm sure they overwork you at the office.'

'I suppose we all overwork at times.'

She rose and stood before him with sudden resolution. 'Well, I'm not going to have you use up your strength slaving in that way. It's absurd. I can see you're ill.' She bent over him and laid her hand on his forehead. 'My poor old Kenneth. Prepare to be taken away soon on a long holiday.'

He looked up at her, startled. 'A holiday?'

'Certainly. Didn't you know I was going to carry you off at Easter? We're going to start in a fortnight on a month's voyage to somewhere or other. On any one of the big cruising steamers.' She paused and bent closer, touching his forehead with her lips. 'I'm tired, too, Kenneth.'

He seemed to pay no heed to her last words, but sat, his hands on his knees, his head drawn back a little from her caress, and looked up at her with a stare of apprehension. 'Again? My dear, we can't; I can't possibly go away.'

'I don't know why you say "again", Kenneth; we haven't taken a real holiday this year.'

'At Christmas we spent a week with the children in the country.'

'Yes, but this time I mean away from the children, from servants, from the house. From everything that's familiar and fatiguing. Your mother will love to have Joyce and Peter with her.'

He frowned and slowly shook his head. 'No, dear; I can't leave them with my mother.'

'Why, Kenneth, how absurd! She adores them. You didn't hesitate to leave them with her for over two months when we went to the West Indies.'

He drew a deep breath and stood up uneasily. 'That was different.'

'Different? Why?'

'I mean, at that time I didn't realise –' He broke off as if to choose his words and then went on: 'My mother adores the children, as you say. But she isn't always very judicious. Grandmothers always spoil children. And sometimes she talks before them without thinking.' He turned to his wife with an almost pitiful gesture of entreaty. 'Don't ask me to, dear.'

Charlotte mused. It was true that the elder Mrs Ashby had a fearless tongue, but she was the last woman in the world to say or hint anything before her grandchildren at which the most scrupulous parent could take offence. Charlotte looked at her husband in perplexity.

'I don't understand.'

He continued to turn on her the same troubled and entreating gaze. 'Don't try to,' he muttered.

'Not try to?'

'Not now – not yet.' He put up his hands and pressed them against his temples. 'Can't you see that there's no use in insisting? I can't go away, no matter how much I might want to.'

Charlotte still scrutinised him gravely. 'The question is, *do* you want to?'

He returned her gaze for a moment; then his lips began to tremble and he said, hardly above his breath, 'I want – anything you want.'

'And yet –'

'Don't ask me. I can't leave – I can't!'

'You mean that you can't go away out of reach of those letters!'

Her husband had been standing before her in an uneasy half-hesitating attitude; now he turned abruptly away and walked once or twice up and down the length of the room, his head bent, his eyes fixed on the carpet.

Charlotte felt her resentfulness rising with her fears. 'It's that,' she persisted. 'Why not admit it? You can't live without them.'

He continued his troubled pacing of the room; then he stopped short, dropped into a chair and covered his face with his hands. From the shaking of his shoulders, Charlotte saw that he was weeping. She had never seen a man cry, except her father after her mother's death, when she was a little girl; and she remembered still how the sight had frightened her. She was frightened now; she felt that her husband was being dragged away from her into some mysterious bondage, and that she must use up her last atom of strength in the struggle for his freedom, and for hers.

'Kenneth – Kenneth!' she pleaded, kneeling down beside him. 'Won't you listen to me? Won't you try to see what I'm suffering? I'm not unreasonable, darling, really not. I don't suppose I should ever have noticed the letters if it hadn't been for their effect on you. It's not my way to pry into other people's affairs; and even if the effect had been different – yes, yes, listen to me – if I'd seen that the letters made you happy, that you were watching eagerly for them, counting the days between their coming, that you wanted them, that they gave you something I haven't known how to give – why, Kenneth, I don't say I shouldn't have suffered from that, too; but it would have been in a different way, and I should have had the courage to hide what I felt, and the hope that some day you'd come to feel about me as you did about the writer of the letters. But what I can't bear is to see how you dread them, how they make you suffer, and yet how you can't live without them and won't go away lest you should miss one during your absence. Or perhaps,' she added, her voice breaking into a cry of accusation – 'perhaps it's because she's actually forbidden you to leave. Kenneth, you must answer me! Is that the reason? Is it because she's forbidden you that you won't go away with me?'

She continued to kneel at his side, and raising her hands, she drew his gently down. She was ashamed of her persistence, ashamed of uncovering that baffled disordered face, yet resolved that no such scruples should arrest her. His eyes were lowered, the muscles of his face quivered; she was making him suffer even more than she suffered herself. Yet this no longer restrained her.

'Kenneth, is it that? She won't let us go away together?'

Still he did not speak or turn his eyes to her; and a sense of defeat swept over her. After all, she thought, the struggle was a losing one. 'You needn't answer. I see I'm right,' she said.

Suddenly, as she rose, he turned and drew her down again. His hands caught hers and pressed them so tightly that she felt her rings cutting into her flesh. There was something frightened, convulsive in his hold; it was the clutch of a man who felt himself slipping over a precipice. He was staring up at her now as if salvation lay in the face she bent above him. 'Of course we'll go away together. We'll go wherever you want,' he said in a low, confused voice; and putting his arm about her, he drew her close and pressed his lips on hers.

IV

Charlotte had said to herself, 'I shall sleep tonight', but instead she sat before her fire into the small hours, listening for any sound that came from her husband's room. But he, at any rate, seemed to be resting after the tumult of the evening. Once or twice she stole to the door and in the faint light that came in from the street through his open window she saw him stretched out in heavy sleep – the sleep of weakness and exhaustion. 'He's ill,' she thought, 'he's undoubtedly ill. And it's not overwork; it's this mysterious persecution.'

She drew a breath of relief. She had fought through

the weary fight and the victory was hers – at least for the moment. If only they could have started at once – started for anywhere! She knew it would be useless to ask him to leave before the holidays; and meanwhile the secret influence – as to which she was still so completely in the dark – would continue to work against her, and she would have to renew the struggle day after day till they started on their journey. But after that everything would be different. If once she could get her husband away under other skies, and all to herself, she never doubted her power to release him from the evil spell he was under. Lulled to quiet by the thought, she too slept at last.

When she woke, it was long past her usual hour, and she sat up in bed surprised and vexed at having overslept herself. She always liked to be down to share her husband's breakfast by the library fire; but a glance at the clock made it clear that he must have started long since for his office. To make sure, she jumped out of bed and went into his room, but it was empty. No doubt he had looked in on her before leaving, seen that she still slept and gone downstairs without disturbing her; and their relations were sufficiently lover-like for her to regret having missed their morning hour.

She rang and asked if Mr Ashby had already gone. Yes, nearly an hour ago, the maid said. He had given orders that Mrs Ashby should not be waked and that the children should not come to her till she sent for them ... Yes, he had gone up to the nursery himself to give the order. All this sounded usual enough, and Charlotte hardly knew why she asked, 'And did Mr Ashby leave no other message?'

Yes, the maid said, he did; she was so sorry she'd forgotten. He'd told her, just as he was leaving, to say to Mrs Ashby that he was going to see about their passages, and would she please be ready to sail tomorrow?

Charlotte echoed the woman's 'tomorrow', and sat staring at her incredulously. 'Tomorrow – you're sure he said to sail tomorrow?'

'Oh, ever so sure, ma'am. I don't know how I could have forgotten to mention it.'

'Well, it doesn't matter. Draw my bath, please.' Charlotte sprang up, dashed through her dressing and caught herself singing at her image in the glass as she sat brushing her hair. It made her feel young again to have scored such a victory. The other woman vanished to a speck on the horizon, as this one, who ruled the foreground, smiled back at the reflection of her lips and eyes. He loved her, then – he loved her as passionately as ever. He had divined what she had suffered, had understood that their happiness depended on their getting away at once and finding each other again after yesterday's desperate groping in the fog. The nature of the influence that had come between them did not much matter to Charlotte now; she had faced the phantom and dispelled it. 'Courage – that's the secret! If only people who are in love weren't always so afraid of risking their happiness by looking it in the eyes.' As she brushed back her light abundant hair it waved electrically above her head, like the palms of victory. Ah, well, some women knew how to manage men and some didn't – and only the fair – she gaily paraphrased – deserve the brave! Certainly she was looking very pretty.

The morning danced along like a cockleshell on a bright sea – such a sea as they would soon be speeding over. She ordered a particularly good dinner, saw the children off to their classes, had her trunks brought down, consulted with the maid about getting out summer clothes – for of course they would be heading for heat and sunshine – and wondered if she oughtn't to take Kenneth's flannel suits out of camphor. 'But how absurd,' she reflected, 'that I don't yet know where we're going!' She looked at the clock, saw that it was close on noon and decided to call him up at his office. There was a slight delay; then she heard his secretary's voice saying that Mr Ashby had looked in for a moment early and left again almost immediately ... Oh, very well; Charlotte would ring up later. How soon was he likely to be back? The secretary answered that she couldn't tell; all they knew in the office was that when he left he had said he was in a hurry because he had to go out of town.

Out of town! Charlotte hung up the receiver and sat blankly gazing into new darkness. Why had he gone out of town? And where had he gone? And of all days, why should he have chosen the eve of their suddenly planned departure? She felt a faint shiver of apprehension. Of course he had gone to see that woman – no doubt to get her permission to leave. He was as completely in bondage as that; and Charlotte had been fatuous enough to see the palms of victory on her forehead. She burst into a laugh and, walking across the room, sat down again before her mirror. What a different face she saw! The smile on her pale lips seemed to mock the rosy vision of the other Charlotte. But gradually her colour crept back. After all, she had a right to claim the victory, since her husband was doing what she wanted, not what the other woman exacted of him. It was natural enough, in view of his abrupt decision to leave the next day, that he should have arrangements to make, business matters to wind up; it was not even necessary to suppose that his mysterious trip was a visit to the writer of the letters. He might simply have gone to see a client who lived out of town. Of course they would not tell Charlotte at the office; the secretary had hesitated before imparting even such meagre information as the fact of Mr Ashby's absence. Meanwhile she would go on with her joyful preparations, content to learn later in the day to what particular island of the blest she was to be carried.

The hours wore on, or rather were swept forward on a rush of eager preparations. At last the entrance of the maid who came to draw the curtains roused Charlotte from her labours and she saw to her surprise that the clock marked five. And she did not yet know where they were going the next day! She rang up her husband's office and was told that Mr Ashby had not been there since the early morning. She asked for his partner, but the partner could add nothing to her information, for he himself, his suburban train having been behind time, had reached the office after Ashby had come and gone. Charlotte stood perplexed; then she decided to telephone to her mother-in-law. Of course Kenneth, on the eve of a month's absence, must have gone to see his mother. The mere fact that the children – in spite of his vague objections – would certainly have to be left with old Mrs Ashby made it obvious that he would have all sorts of matters to decide with her. At another time Charlotte might have felt a little hurt at being excluded from their conference, but nothing mattered now but that she had won the day, that her husband was still hers and not another woman's. Gaily she called up Mrs Ashby, heard her friendly voice and began, 'Well, did Kenneth's news surprise you? What do you think of our elopement?'

Almost instantly, before Mrs Ashby could answer, Charlotte knew what her reply would be. Mrs Ashby had not seen her son, she had had no word from him and did not know what her daughter-in-law meant. Charlotte stood silent in the intensity of her surprise. 'But then, where *has* he been?' she thought. Then, recovering herself, she explained their sudden decision to Mrs Ashby, and in doing so, gradually regained her own self-confidence, her conviction that nothing could ever again come between Kenneth and herself. Mrs Ashby took the news calmly and approvingly. She, too, had thought that Kenneth looked worried and overtired, and she agreed with her daughter-in-law that in such cases change was the surest remedy. 'I'm always so glad when he gets away. Elsie hated travelling; she was always finding pretexts to prevent his going anywhere. With you, thank goodness, it's different.' Nor was Mrs Ashby surprised at his not having had time to let her know of his departure. He must have been in a rush from the moment the decision was taken; but no doubt he'd drop in before dinner. Five minutes' talk was really all they needed. 'I hope you'll gradually cure Kenneth of his mania for going over and over a question that could be settled in a dozen words. He never used to be like that, and if he carried the habit into his professional work he'd soon lose all his clients … Yes, do come in for a minute, dear, if you have time; no doubt he'll turn up while you're here.' The tonic ring of Mrs Ashby's voice echoed on reassuringly in the silent room while Charlotte continued her preparations.

Towards seven the telephone rang and she darted to it. Now she would know! But it was only from the conscientious secretary, to say that Mr Ashby hadn't been back, or sent any word, and before the office closed she thought she ought to let Mrs Ashby know. 'Oh, that's all right. Thanks a lot!' Charlotte called out cheerfully, and hung up the receiver with a trembling hand. But perhaps by this time, she reflected, he was at his mother's. She shut her drawers and cupboards, put on her hat and coat and called up to the nursery that she was going out for a minute to see the children's grandmother.

Mrs Ashby lived nearby and during her brief walk through the cold spring dusk Charlotte imagined that every advancing figure was her husband's. But she did not meet him on the way and when she entered the house she found her mother-in-law alone. Kenneth had neither telephoned nor come. Old Mrs Ashby sat by her bright fire, her knitting needles flashing steadily through her active old hands, and her mere bodily presence gave reassurance to Charlotte. Yes, it was certainly odd that Kenneth had gone off for the whole day without letting any of them know; but, after all, it was to be expected. A busy lawyer held so many threads in his hands that any sudden change of plan would oblige him to make all sorts of unforeseen arrangements and adjustments. He might have gone to see some client in the suburbs and been detained there; his mother remembered his telling her that he had charge of the legal business of a queer old recluse somewhere in New Jersey, who was immensely rich but too mean to have a telephone. Very likely Kenneth had been stranded there.

But Charlotte felt her nervousness gaining on her. When Mrs Ashby asked her at what hour they were sailing the next day and she had to say she didn't know – that Kenneth had simply sent her word he was going to take their passages – the uttering of the words again brought home to her the strangeness of the situation. Even Mrs Ashby conceded that it was odd; but she immediately added that it only showed what a rush he was in.

'But, mother, it's nearly eight o'clock! He must realise that I've got to know when we're starting tomorrow.'

'Oh, the boat probably doesn't sail till evening. Sometimes they have to wait till midnight for the tide. Kenneth's probably counting on that. After all, he has a level head.'

Charlotte stood up. 'It's not that. Something has happened to him.'

Mrs Ashby took off her spectacles and rolled up her knitting. 'If you begin to let yourself imagine things –'

'Aren't you in the least anxious?'

'I never am till I have to be. I wish you'd ring for dinner, my dear. You'll stay and dine? He's sure to drop in here on his way home.'

Charlotte called up her own house. No, the maid said, Mr Ashby hadn't come in and hadn't telephoned. She would tell him as soon as he came that Mrs Ashby was dining at his mother's. Charlotte followed her mother-in-law into the dining room and sat with parched throat before her empty plate, while Mrs Ashby dealt calmly and efficiently with a short but carefully prepared repast. 'You'd better eat something, child, or you'll be as bad as Kenneth ... Yes, a little more asparagus, please, Jane.'

She insisted on Charlotte's drinking a glass of sherry and nibbling a bit of toast; then they returned to the drawing room, where the fire had been made up and the cushions in Mrs Ashby's armchair shaken out and smoothed. How safe and familiar it all looked; and out there, somewhere in the uncertainty and mystery of the night, lurked the answer to the two women's conjectures, like an indistinguishable figure prowling on the threshold.

At last Charlotte got up and said, 'I'd better go back. At this hour Kenneth will certainly go straight home.'

Mrs Ashby smiled indulgently. 'It's not very late, my dear. It doesn't take two sparrows long to dine.'

'It's after nine.' Charlotte bent down to kiss her. 'The fact is, I can't keep still.'

Mrs Ashby pushed aside her work and rested her two hands on the arms of her chair. 'I'm going with you,' she said, helping herself up.

Charlotte protested that it was too late, that it was not necessary, that she would call up as soon as Kenneth came in, but Mrs Ashby had already rung for her maid. She was slightly lame and stood resting on her stick while her wraps were brought. 'If Mr Kenneth turns up, tell him he'll find me at his own house,' she instructed the maid as the two women got into the taxi which had been summoned. During the short drive Charlotte gave thanks that she was not returning home alone. There was something warm and substantial in the mere fact of Mrs Ashby's nearness, something that corresponded with the clearness of her eyes and the texture of her fresh, firm complexion. As the taxi drew up she laid her hand encouragingly on Charlotte's. 'You'll see; there'll be a message.'

The door opened at Charlotte's ring and the two entered. Charlotte's heart beat excitedly; the stimulus of her mother-in-law's confidence was beginning to flow through her veins.

'You'll see – you'll see,' Mrs Ashby repeated.

The maid who opened the door said no, Mr Ashby had not come in, and there had been no message from him.

'You're sure the telephone's not out of order?' his mother suggested; and the maid said, well, it certainly wasn't half an hour ago; but she'd just go and ring up to make sure. She disappeared, and Charlotte turned to take off her hat and cloak. As she did so her eyes lit on the hall table, and there lay a grey envelope, her husband's name faintly traced on it. 'Oh!' she cried out, suddenly aware that for the first time in months she had entered her house without wondering if one of the grey letters would be there.

'What is it, my dear?' Mrs Ashby asked with a glance of surprise.

Charlotte did not answer. She took up the envelope and stood staring at it as if she could force her gaze to penetrate to what was within. Then an idea occurred to her. She turned and held out the envelope to her mother-in-law.

'Do you know that writing?' she asked.

Mrs Ashby took the letter. She had to feel with her other hand for her eyeglasses, and when she had adjusted them she lifted the envelope to the light. 'Why!' she exclaimed; and then stopped. Charlotte noticed that the letter shook in her usually firm hand. 'But this is addressed to Kenneth,' Mrs Ashby said at length, in a low voice. Her tone seemed to imply that she felt her daughter-in-law's question to be slightly indiscreet.

'Yes, but no matter,' Charlotte spoke with sudden decision. 'I want to know – do you know the writing?'

Mrs Ashby handed back the letter. 'No,' she said distinctly.

The two women had turned into the library. Charlotte switched on the electric light and shut the door. She still held the envelope in her hand.

'I'm going to open it,' she announced.

She caught her mother-in-law's startled glance. 'But, dearest – a letter not addressed to you? My dear, you can't!'

'As if I cared about that – now!' She continued to look intently at Mrs Ashby. 'This letter may tell me where Kenneth is.'

Mrs Ashby's glossy bloom was effaced by a quick pallor; her firm cheeks seemed to shrink and wither. 'Why should it? What makes you believe – it can't possibly –'

Charlotte held her eyes steadily on that altered face. 'Ah, then you *do* know the writing?' she flashed back.

'Know the writing? How should I? With all my son's correspondents … What I do know is –' Mrs Ashby broke off and looked at her daughter-in-law entreatingly, almost timidly.

Charlotte caught her by the wrist. 'Mother! What do you know? Tell me! You must!'

'That I don't believe any good ever came of a woman's opening her husband's letters behind his back.'

The words sounded to Charlotte's irritated ears as flat as a phrase culled from a book of moral axioms. She laughed impatiently and dropped her mother-in-law's wrist. 'Is that all? No good can come of this letter, opened or unopened. I know that well enough. But whatever ill comes, I mean to find out what's in it.' Her hands had been trembling as they held the envelope, but now they grew firm, and her voice also. She still gazed intently at Mrs Ashby. 'This is the ninth letter addressed in the same hand that has come for Kenneth since we've been married. Always these same grey envelopes. I've kept count of them because after each one he has been like a man who has had some dreadful shock. It takes him hours to shake off their effect. I've told him so. I've told him I must know from whom they come, because I can see they're killing him. He won't answer my questions; he says he can't tell me anything about the letters; but last night he promised to go away with me – to get away from them.'

Mrs Ashby, with shaking steps, had gone to one of the armchairs and sat down in it, her head drooping forward on her breast. 'Ah,' she murmured.

'So now you understand –'

'Did he tell you it was to get away from them?'

'He said, to get away – to get away. He was sobbing so that he could hardly speak. But I told him I knew that was why.'

'And what did he say?'

'He took me in his arms and said he'd go wherever I wanted.'

'Ah, thank God!' said Mrs Ashby. There was a silence, during which she continued to sit with bowed head and eyes averted from her daughter-in-law. At last she looked up and spoke. 'Are you sure there have been as many as nine?'

'Perfectly. This is the ninth. I've kept count.'

'And he has absolutely refused to explain?'

'Absolutely.'

Mrs Ashby spoke through pale, contracted lips. 'When did they begin to come? Do you remember?'

Charlotte laughed again. 'Remember? The first one came the night we got back from our honeymoon.'

'All that time?' Mrs Ashby lifted her head and spoke with sudden energy. 'Then – yes, open it.'

The words were so unexpected that Charlotte felt the blood in her temples, and her hands began to tremble again. She tried to slip her finger under the flap of the envelope, but it was so tightly stuck that she had to hunt on her husband's writing table for his ivory letter opener. As she pushed about the familiar objects his own hands had so lately touched, they sent through her the icy chill emanating from the little personal effects of someone newly dead. In the deep silence of the room the tearing of the paper as she slit the envelope sounded like a human cry. She drew out the sheet and carried it to the lamp.

'Well?' Mrs Ashby asked below her breath.

Charlotte did not move or answer. She was bending

over the page with wrinkled brows, holding it nearer and nearer to the light. Her sight must be blurred, or else dazzled by the reflection of the lamplight on the smooth surface of the paper, for, strain her eyes as she would, she could discern only a few faint strokes, so faint and faltering as to be nearly undecipherable.

'I can't make it out,' she said.

'What do you mean, dear?'

'The writing's too indistinct … Wait.'

She went back to the table and, sitting down close to Kenneth's reading lamp, slipped the letter under a magnifying glass. All this time she was aware that her mother-in-law was watching her intently.

'Well?' Mrs Ashby breathed.

'Well, it's no clearer. I can't read it.'

'You mean the paper is an absolute blank?'

'No, not quite. There is writing on it. I can make out something like "mine" – oh, and "come". It might be "come".'

Mrs Ashby stood up abruptly. Her face was even paler than before. She advanced to the table and, resting her two hands on it, drew a deep breath. 'Let me see,' she said, as if forcing herself to a hateful effort.

Charlotte felt the contagion of her whiteness. 'She knows,' she thought. She pushed the letter across the table. Her mother-in-law lowered her head over it in silence, but without touching it with her pale wrinkled hands.

Charlotte stood watching her as she herself, when she had tried to read the letter, had been watched by Mrs Ashby. The latter fumbled for her glasses, held them to her eyes and bent still closer to the outspread page, in order, as it seemed, to avoid touching it. The light of the lamp fell directly on her old face, and Charlotte reflected what depths of the unknown may lurk under the clearest and most candid lineaments. She had never seen her mother-in-law's features express any but simple and sound emotions – cordiality, amusement, a kindly sympathy; now and again a flash of wholesome anger. Now they seemed to wear a look of fear and hatred, of incredulous dismay and almost cringing defiance. It was as if the spirits warring within her had distorted her face to their own likeness. At length she raised her head. 'I can't – I can't,' she said in a voice of childish distress.

'You can't make it out either?'

She shook her head, and Charlotte saw two tears roll down her cheeks.

'Familiar as the writing is to you?' Charlotte insisted with twitching lips.

Mrs Ashby did not take up the challenge. 'I can make out nothing – nothing.'

'But you do know the writing?'

Mrs Ashby lifted her head timidly; her anxious eyes stole with a glance of apprehension around the quiet familiar room. 'How can I tell? I was startled at first ...'

'Startled by the resemblance?'

'Well, I thought –'

'You'd better say it out, mother! You knew at once it was *her* writing?'

'Oh, wait, my dear – wait.'

'Wait for what?'

Mrs Ashby looked up; her eyes, travelling slowly past

Charlotte, were lifted to the blank wall behind her son's writing table.

Charlotte, following the glance, burst into a shrill laugh of accusation. 'I needn't wait any longer! You've answered me now! You're looking straight at the wall where her picture used to hang!'

Mrs Ashby lifted her hand with a murmur of warning. 'Sh-h.'

'Oh, you needn't imagine that anything can ever frighten me again!' Charlotte cried.

Her mother-in-law still leaned against the table. Her lips moved plaintively. 'But we're going mad – we're both going mad. We both know such things are impossible.'

Her daughter-in-law looked at her with a pitying stare. 'I've known for a long time now that everything was possible.'

'Even this?'

'Yes, exactly this.'

'But this letter – after all, there's nothing in this letter –'

'Perhaps there would be to him. How can I tell? I remember his saying to me once that if you were used to a handwriting the faintest stroke of it became legible. Now I see what he meant. He *was* used to it.'

'But the few strokes that I can make out are so pale. No one could possibly read that letter.'

Charlotte laughed again. 'I suppose everything's pale about a ghost,' she said stridently.

'Oh, my child – my child – don't say it!'

'Why shouldn't I say it, when even the bare walls cry it out? What difference does it make if her letters are illegible to you and me? If even you can see her face on that blank wall, why shouldn't he read her writing on this blank paper? Don't you see that she's everywhere in this house, and the closer to him because to everyone else she's become invisible?' Charlotte dropped into a chair and covered her face with her hands. A turmoil of sobbing shook her from head to foot. At length a touch on her shoulder made her look up and she saw her mother-in-law bending over her. Mrs Ashby's face seemed to have grown still smaller and more wasted, but it had resumed its usual quiet look. Through all her tossing anguish, Charlotte felt the impact of that resolute spirit.

'Tomorrow – tomorrow. You'll see. There'll be some explanation tomorrow.'

Charlotte cut her short. 'An explanation? Who's going to give it, I wonder?'

Mrs Ashby drew back and straightened herself hero-ically. 'Kenneth himself will,' she cried out in a strong voice. Charlotte said nothing and the old woman went on: 'But meanwhile we must act; we must notify the police. Now, without a moment's delay. We must do everything – everything.'

Charlotte stood up slowly and stiffly; her joints felt as cramped as an old woman's. 'Exactly as if we thought it could do any good to do anything?'

Resolutely Mrs Ashby cried, 'Yes!' and Charlotte went up to the telephone and unhooked the receiver.

RUDYARD KIPLING
(1865–1936)

Rudyard Kipling was born in India; his first memories were of 'light and colour and golden and purple fruits' in the Bombay fruit market. Educated in England, he returned to India at the age of sixteen to become 'fifty per cent of the staff' of the *Civil and Military Gazette* in Fort Lahore. He sweated away several intolerable summers in the city, a fever-struck 'mausoleum of ghosts' where 'my world was full of boys but a few years older than I, who ... died mostly at the regulation age of twenty-two'. 'The Phantom 'Rickshaw', a characteristically clear-eyed view of the claustrophobic Anglo-Indian society in which 'every circumstance and relation of a man's life is "public property"', was written after a promotion to the Allahabad *Pioneer*. When Kipling decided that London offered greater scope for his literary ambitions, he received some salutary advice with his last pay packet: 'Take it from me,' the *Pioneer*'s managing director confided, 'you'll never be worth more than four hundred rupees a month to anyone.' Kipling noted that 'at that time I was drawing seven hundred a month'.

THE PHANTOM
'RICKSHAW

May no ill dreams disturb my rest,
Nor Powers of Darkness me molest.

Evening Hymn

O NE OF THE FEW ADVANTAGES that India
has over England is a great knowability. After five
years' service a man is directly or indirectly acquainted
with the two or three hundred civilians in his province,
all the Messes of ten or twelve regiments and batteries,
and some fifteen hundred other people of the non-official
caste. In ten years his knowledge should be doubled, and
at the end of twenty he knows, or knows something about,
every Englishman in the Empire, and may travel anywhere
and everywhere without paying hotel bills.

Globetrotters who expect entertainment as a right have,
even within my memory, blunted this open-heartedness,
but nonetheless today, if you belong to the inner circle and
are neither a bear nor a black sheep, all houses are open to
you and our small world is very kind and helpful.

Rickett of Kamartha stayed with Polder of Kumaon some fifteen years ago. He meant to stay two nights, but was knocked down by rheumatic fever, and for six weeks disorganised Polder's establishment, stopped Polder's work and nearly died in Polder's bedroom. Polder behaves as though he had been placed under eternal obligation by Rickett, and yearly sends the little Ricketts a box of presents and toys. It is the same everywhere. The men who do not take the trouble to conceal from you their opinion that you are an incompetent ass, and the women who blacken your character and misunderstand your wife's amusements, will work themselves to the bone on your behalf if you fall sick or into serious trouble.

Heatherlegh, the doctor, kept, in addition to his regular practice, a hospital on his private account – an arrangement of loose boxes for incurables, his friends called it – but it was really a sort of fitting-up shed for craft that had been damaged by stress of weather. The weather in India is often sultry, and since the tale of bricks is a fixed quantity, and the only liberty allowed is permission to work overtime and get no thanks, men occasionally break down and become as mixed as the metaphors in this sentence.

Heatherlegh is the nicest doctor that ever was, and his invariable prescription to all his patients is, 'Lie low, go slow and keep cool.' He says that more men are killed by overwork than the importance of this world justifies. He maintains that overwork slew Pansay, who died under his hands about three years ago. He has, of course, the right to speak authoritatively, and he laughs at my theory that there was a crack in Pansay's head and a little bit of the Dark World came through and pressed him to death. 'Pansay went off the handle,' says Heatherlegh, 'after the stimulus of long leave at home. He may or he may not have behaved like a blackguard to Mrs Keith-Wessington. My notion is that the work of the Katabundi Settlement ran him off his legs, and that he took to brooding and making much of an ordinary P&O flirtation. He certainly was engaged to Miss Mannering and she certainly broke off the engagement. Then he took a feverish chill and all that nonsense about ghosts developed. Overwork started his illness, kept it alight and killed him, poor devil. Write him off to the system – one man to do the work of two and a half men.'

I do not believe this. I used to sit up with Pansay sometimes when Heatherlegh was called out to visit patients and I happened to be within claim. The man would make me most unhappy by describing in a low, even voice the procession of men, women, children and devils that was always passing at the bottom of his bed. He had a sick man's command of language. When he recovered I suggested that he should write out the whole affair from beginning to end, knowing that ink might assist him to ease his mind. When little boys have learned a new bad word they are never happy till they have chalked it up on a door. And this also is literature.

He was in a high fever while he was writing, and the blood-and-thunder magazine style he adopted did not calm him. Two months afterwards he was reported fit for duty, but, in spite of the fact that he was urgently needed to help an undermanned commission stagger through a deficit, he preferred to die; vowing at the last that he was hag-ridden. I got his manuscript before he died and this is his version of the affair, dated 1885:

My doctor tells me that I need rest and change of air. It is not improbable that I shall get both ere long – rest that neither the red-coated orderly nor the midday gun can break, and change of air far beyond that which any homeward-bound steamer can give me. In the meantime I am resolved to stay where I am; and, in flat defiance of my doctor's orders, to take all the world into my confidence. You shall learn for yourselves the precise nature of my malady; and shall, too, judge for yourselves whether any man born of woman on this weary earth was ever so tormented as I.

Speaking now as a condemned criminal might speak ere the drop-bolts are drawn, my story, wild and hideously improbable as it may appear, demands at least attention. That it will ever receive credence I utterly disbelieve. Two months ago I should have scouted as mad or drunk the man who had dared tell me the like. Two months ago I was the happiest man in India. Today, from Peshawar to the sea, there is no one more wretched. My doctor and I are the only two who know this. His explanation is that my brain, digestion and eyesight are all slightly affected; giving rise to my frequent and persistent 'delusions'. Delusions, indeed! I call him a fool; but he attends me still with the same unwearied smile, the same bland professional manner, the same neatly trimmed red whiskers, till I begin to suspect that I am an ungrateful, evil-tempered invalid. But you shall judge for yourselves.

Three years ago it was my fortune – my great misfortune – to sail from Gravesend to Bombay, on return from long leave, with one Agnes Keith-Wessington, wife of an officer on the Bombay side. It does not in the least concern you to know what manner of woman she was. Be content with the knowledge that, ere the voyage had ended, both she and I were desperately and unreasoningly in love with one another. Heaven knows that I can make the admission now without one particle of vanity. In matters of this sort there is always one who gives and another who accepts. From the first day of our ill-omened attachment, I was conscious that Agnes's passion was a stronger, a more dominant and – if I may use the expression – a purer sentiment than mine. Whether she recognised the fact then, I do not know. Afterwards it was bitterly plain to both of us.

Arrived at Bombay in the spring of the year, we went our respective ways, to meet no more for the next three or four months, when my leave and her love took us both to Simla. There we spent the season together; and there my fire of straw burned itself out to a pitiful end with the closing year. I attempt no excuse. I make no apology. Mrs Wessington had given up much for my sake, and was prepared to give up all. From my own lips, in August 1882, she learned that I was sick of her presence, tired of her company and weary of the sound of her voice. Ninety-nine women out of a hundred would have wearied of me as I wearied of them; seventy-five of that number would have promptly avenged themselves by active and obtrusive flirtation with other men. Mrs Wessington was the hundredth. On her neither my openly expressed aversion nor the cutting brutalities with which I garnished our interviews had the least effect.

'Jack, darling!' was her one eternal cuckoo-cry. 'I'm sure it's all a mistake – a hideous mistake; and we'll be good friends again some day. *Please* forgive me, Jack, dear.'

I was the offender, and I knew it. That knowledge transformed my pity into passive endurance and, eventually, into blind hate – the same instinct, I suppose, which prompts a man to savagely stamp on the spider he has but half killed. And with this hate in my bosom the season of 1882 came to an end.

Next year we met again at Simla – she with her monotonous face and timid attempts at reconciliation, and I with loathing of her in every fibre of my frame. Several times I could not avoid meeting her alone; and on each occasion her words were identically the same. Still the unreasoning wail that it was all a 'mistake'; and still the hope of eventually 'making friends'. I might have seen, had I cared to look, that that hope only was keeping her alive. She grew more wan and thin month by month. You will agree with me, at least, that such conduct would have driven anyone to despair. It was uncalled for, childish, unwomanly. I maintain that she was much to blame. And again, sometimes, in the black, fever-stricken night watches, I have begun to think that I might have been a little kinder to her. But that really *is* a 'delusion'. I could not have continued pretending to love her when I didn't; could I? It would have been unfair to us both.

Last year we met again – on the same terms as before. The same weary appeals and the same curt answers from my lips. At least I would make her see how wholly wrong and hopeless were her attempts at resuming the old relationship. As the season wore on, we fell apart – that is to say, she found it difficult to meet me, for I had other and more absorbing interests to attend to. When I think it over quietly in my sickroom, the season of 1884 seems a confused nightmare wherein light and shade were fantastically intermingled – my courtship of little Kitty Mannering; my hopes, doubts and fears; our long rides together; my trembling avowal of attachment; her reply; and now and again a vision of a white face flitting by in the 'rickshaw with the black and white liveries I once watched for so earnestly; the wave of Mrs Wessington's gloved hand; and, when she met me alone, which was but seldom, the irksome monotony of her appeal. I loved Kitty Mannering; honestly, heartily loved her, and with my love for her grew my hatred for Agnes. In August Kitty and I were engaged. The next day I met those accursed 'magpie' *jhampanies* at the back of Jakko, and, moved by some passing sentiment of pity, stopped to tell Mrs Wessington everything. She knew it already.

'So I hear you're engaged, Jack, dear.' Then, without a moment's pause: 'I'm sure it's all a mistake – a hideous mistake. We shall be as good friends some day, Jack, as we ever were.'

My answer might have made even a man wince. It cut the dying woman before me like the blow of a whip. 'Please forgive me, Jack; I didn't mean to make you angry; but it's true, it's true!'

And Mrs Wessington broke down completely. I turned

away and left her to finish her journey in peace, feeling, but only for a moment or two, that I had been an unutterably mean hound. I looked back and saw that she had turned her 'rickshaw with the idea, I suppose, of overtaking me.

The scene and its surroundings were photographed on my memory. The rain-swept sky (we were at the end of the wet weather), the sodden, dingy pines, the muddy road and the black powder-riven cliffs formed a gloomy background against which the black and white liveries of the *jhampanies*, the yellow-panelled 'rickshaw and Mrs Wessington's down-bowed golden head stood out clearly. She was holding her handkerchief in her left hand and was leaning back exhausted against the 'rickshaw cushions. I turned my horse up a bypath near the Sanjowlie Reservoir and literally ran away. Once I fancied I heard a faint call of 'Jack!' This may have been imagination. I never stopped to verify it. Ten minutes later I came across Kitty on horseback; and, in the delight of a long ride with her, forgot all about the interview.

A week later Mrs Wessington died, and the inexpressible burden of her existence was removed from my life. I went Plainsward perfectly happy. Before three months were over I had forgotten all about her, except that at times the discovery of some of her old letters reminded me unpleasantly of our bygone relationship. By January I had disinterred what was left of our correspondence from among my scattered belongings and had burned it. At the beginning of April of this year, 1885, I was at Simla – semi-deserted Simla – once more, and was deep in lover's talks and walks with Kitty. It was decided that we should be married at the end of June. You will understand, therefore, that, loving Kitty as I did, I am not saying too much when I pronounce myself to have been, at that time, the happiest man in India.

Fourteen delightful days passed almost before I noticed their flight. Then, aroused to the sense of what was proper among mortals circumstanced as we were, I pointed out to Kitty that an engagement ring was the outward and visible sign of her dignity as an engaged girl; and that she must forthwith come to Hamilton's to be measured for one. Up to that moment, I give you my word, we had completely forgotten so trivial a matter. To Hamilton's we accordingly went on 15 April 1885. Remember that – whatever my doctor may say to the contrary – I was then in perfect health, enjoying a well-balanced mind and an absolutely tranquil spirit. Kitty and I entered Hamilton's shop together and there, regardless of the order of affairs, I measured Kitty for the ring in the presence of the amused assistant. The ring was a sapphire with two diamonds. We then rode out down the slope that leads to the Combermere Bridge and Peliti's shop.

While my Waler was cautiously feeling his way over the loose shale, and Kitty was laughing and chattering at my side – while all Simla, that is to say as much of it as had then come from the Plains, was grouped round the reading room and Peliti's veranda, – I was aware that someone, apparently at a vast distance, was calling me by my Christian name. It struck me that I had heard the voice before, but when and where I could not at once determine. In the short space it took to cover the road between the path from Hamilton's shop and the first plank of the Combermere Bridge I had thought over half a dozen people who might have committed such a solecism, and had eventually decided that it must have been singing in my ears. Immediately opposite Peliti's shop my eye was arrested by the sight of four *jhampanies* in black and white livery, pulling a yellow-panelled, cheap, bazaar 'rickshaw. In a moment my mind flew back to the previous season and Mrs Wessington with a sense of irritation and disgust. Was it not enough that the woman was dead and done with, without her black and white servitors reappearing to spoil the day's happiness? Whoever employed them now I thought I would call upon, and ask as a personal favour to change her *jhampanies'* livery. I would hire the men myself and, if necessary, buy their coats from off their backs. It is impossible to say here what a flood of undesirable memories their presence evoked.

'Kitty,' I cried, 'there are poor Mrs Wessington's *jhampanies* turned up again! I wonder who has them now?'

Kitty had known Mrs Wessington slightly last season and had always been interested in the sickly woman.

'What? Where?' she asked. 'I can't see them anywhere.'

Even as she spoke her horse, swerving from a laden mule, threw himself directly in front of the advancing 'rickshaw. I had scarcely time to utter a word of warning when, to my unutterable horror, horse and rider passed *through* men and carriage as if they had been thin air.

'What's the matter?' cried Kitty; 'what made you call out so foolishly, Jack? If I *am* engaged I don't want all creation to know about it. There was lots of space between

the mule and the veranda; and, if you think I can't ride
– there!'

Whereupon wilful Kitty set off, her dainty little head in
the air, at a hand-gallop in the direction of the bandstand;
fully expecting, as she herself afterwards told me, that I
should follow her. What was the matter? Nothing indeed.
Either that I was mad or drunk, or that Simla was haunted
with devils. I reined in my impatient cob and turned round.
The 'rickshaw had turned, too, and now stood immediately
facing me, near the left railing of the Combermere Bridge.

'Jack! Jack, darling.' (There was no mistake about the
words this time: they rang through my brain as if they had
been shouted in my ear.) 'It's some hideous mistake, I'm
sure. *Please* forgive me, Jack, and let's be friends again.'

The 'rickshaw hood had fallen back and inside, as I
hope and pray daily for the death I dread by night, sat Mrs
Keith-Wessington, handkerchief in hand and golden head
bowed on her breast.

How long I stared motionless I do not know. Finally,
I was aroused by my groom taking the Waler's bridle
and asking whether I was ill. I tumbled off my horse and
dashed, half fainting, into Peliti's for a glass of cherry
brandy. There two or three couples were gathered round
the coffee tables discussing the gossip of the day. Their
trivialities were more comforting to me just then than the
consolations of religion could have been. I plunged into the
midst of the conversation at once; chatted, laughed and
jested with a face (when I caught a glimpse of it in a mirror)
as white and drawn as that of a corpse. Three or four men
noticed my condition; and, evidently setting it down to the

results of over-many pegs, charitably endeavoured to draw
me apart from the rest of the loungers. But I refused to be
led away. I wanted the company of my kind – as a child
rushes into the midst of the dinner party after a fright in
the dark. I must have talked for about ten minutes or so,
though it seemed an eternity to me, when I heard Kitty's
clear voice outside enquiring for me. In another minute
she had entered the shop, prepared to roundly upbraid me
for failing so signally in my duties. Something in my face
stopped her.

'Why, Jack,' she cried, 'what *have* you been doing? What
has happened? Are you ill?' Thus driven into a direct lie, I
said that the sun had been a little too much for me. It was
close upon five o'clock of a cloudy April afternoon, and the
sun had been hidden all day. I saw my mistake as soon as
the words were out of my mouth; attempted to recover it;
blundered hopelessly and followed Kitty, in a regal rage,
out of doors, amid the smiles of my acquaintances. I made
some excuse (I have forgotten what) on the score of my
feeling faint; and cantered away to my hotel, leaving Kitty
to finish the ride by herself.

In my room I sat down and tried calmly to reason
out the matter. Here was I, Theobald Jack Pansay, a
well-educated Bengal civilian in the year of grace 1885,
presumably sane, certainly healthy, driven in terror from
my sweetheart's side by the apparition of a woman who
had been dead and buried eight months ago. These were
facts that I could not blink. Nothing was further from my
thought than any memory of Mrs Wessington when Kitty
and I left Hamilton's shop. Nothing was more utterly

commonplace than the stretch of wall opposite Peliti's. It was broad daylight. The road was full of people; and yet here, look you, in defiance of every law of probability, in direct outrage of Nature's ordinance, there had appeared to me a face from the grave.

Kitty's Arab had gone *through* the 'rickshaw; so that my first hope that some woman marvellously like Mrs Wessington had hired the carriage and the coolies with their old livery was lost. Again and again I went round this treadmill of thought; and again and again gave up baffled and in despair. The voice was as inexplicable as the apparition. I had originally some wild notion of confiding it all to Kitty; of begging her to marry me at once; and in her arms defying the ghostly occupant of the 'rickshaw. 'After all,' I argued, 'the presence of the 'rickshaw is in itself enough to prove the existence of a spectral illusion. One may see ghosts of men and women, but surely never of coolies and carriages. The whole thing is absurd. Fancy the ghost of a hill-man!'

Next morning I sent a penitent note to Kitty, imploring her to overlook my strange conduct of the previous afternoon. My divinity was still very wroth and a personal apology was necessary. I explained, with a fluency born of night-long pondering over a falsehood, that I had been attacked with sudden palpitation of the heart – the result of indigestion. This eminently practical solution had its effect; and Kitty and I rode out that afternoon with the shadow of my first lie dividing us.

Nothing would please her save a canter round Jakko. With my nerves still unstrung from the previous night I feebly protested against the notion, suggesting Observatory Hill, Jutogh, the Boileaugunge road – anything rather than the Jakko round. Kitty was angry and a little hurt, so I yielded from fear of provoking further misunderstanding, and we set out together towards Chota Simla. We walked a greater part of the way, and, according to our custom, cantered from a mile or so below the convent to the stretch of level road by the Sanjowlie Reservoir. The wretched horses appeared to fly, and my heart beat quicker and quicker as we neared the crest of the ascent. My mind had been full of Mrs Wessington all the afternoon; and every inch of the Jakko road bore witness to our old-time walks and talks. The boulders were full of it; the pines sang it aloud overhead; the rain-fed torrents giggled and chuckled unseen over the shameful story; and the wind in my ears chanted the iniquity aloud.

As a fitting climax, in the middle of the level men call the Ladies' Mile the Horror was awaiting me. No other 'rickshaw was in sight – only the four black and white *jhampanies*, the yellow-panelled carriage and the golden head of the woman within – all apparently just as I had left them eight months and one fortnight ago! For an instant I fancied that Kitty *must* see what I saw – we were so marvellously sympathetic in all things. Her next words undeceived me – 'Not a soul in sight! Come along, Jack, and I'll race you to the reservoir buildings!' Her wiry little Arab was off like a bird, my Waler following close behind, and in this order we dashed under the cliffs. Half a minute brought us within fifty yards of the 'rickshaw. I pulled my Waler and fell back a little. The 'rickshaw was directly in the middle of the road: and once more the Arab passed through it, my horse following. 'Jack! Jack, dear! *Please* forgive me,' rang with a wail in my ears, and, after an interval, 'It's a mistake, a hideous mistake!'

I spurred my horse like a man possessed. When I turned my head at the reservoir works, the black and white liveries were still waiting – patiently waiting – under the grey hillside, and the wind brought me a mocking echo of the words I had just heard. Kitty bantered me a good deal on my silence throughout the remainder of the ride. I had been talking up till then wildly and at random. To save my life I could not speak afterwards naturally, and from Sanjowlie to the church wisely held my tongue.

I was to dine with the Mannerings that night and had barely time to canter home to dress. On the road to Elysium Hill I overheard two men talking together in the dusk. – 'It's a curious thing,' said one, 'how completely all trace of it disappeared. You know my wife was insanely fond of the woman (never could see anything in her myself) and wanted me to pick up her old 'rickshaw and coolies if they were to be got for love or money. Morbid sort of fancy I call it, but I've got to do what the *Memsahib* tells me. Would you believe that the man she hired it from tells me that all four of the men, they were brothers, died of cholera, on the way to Hardwar, poor devils; and the 'rickshaw has been broken up by the man himself. Told me he never used a dead *Memsahib*'s 'rickshaw. Spoilt his luck. Queer notion, wasn't it? Fancy poor little Mrs Wessington spoiling any one's luck except her own!' I laughed aloud at this point; and my laugh jarred on me as I uttered it. So there *were* ghosts of 'rickshaws after all, and ghostly employments in the other world! How much did Mrs Wessington give her men? What were their hours? Where did they go?

And for visible answer to my last question I saw the infernal thing blocking my path in the twilight. The dead travel fast and by short cuts unknown to ordinary coolies. I laughed aloud a second time and checked my laughter suddenly, for I was afraid I was going mad. Mad to a certain extent I must have been, for I recollect that I reined in my horse at the head of the 'rickshaw and politely wished Mrs Wessington 'good evening'. Her answer was one I knew only too well. I listened to the end; and replied that I had heard it all before, but should be delighted if she had anything further to say. Some malignant devil stronger than I must have entered into me that evening, for I have a dim recollection of talking the commonplaces of the day for five minutes to the thing in front of me.

'Mad as a hatter, poor devil – or drunk. Max, try and get him to come home.'

Surely *that* was not Mrs Wessington's voice! The two men had overheard me speaking to the empty air and had returned to look after me. They were very kind and considerate, and from their words evidently gathered that I was extremely drunk. I thanked them confusedly and cantered away to my hotel, there changed, and arrived at the Mannerings' ten minutes late. I pleaded the darkness of the night as an excuse; was rebuked by Kitty for my unlover-like tardiness; and sat down.

The conversation had already become general; and under cover of it, I was addressing some tender small talk to my sweetheart when I was aware that at the further end of the table a short red-whiskered man was describing, with much broidery, his encounter with a mad unknown that evening. A few sentences convinced me that he was repeating the incident of half an hour ago. In the middle of the story he looked round for applause, as professional storytellers do, caught my eye and straight away collapsed. There was a moment's awkward silence, and the red-whiskered man muttered something to the effect that he had 'forgotten the rest', thereby sacrificing a reputation as a good storyteller which he had built up for six seasons past. I blessed him from the bottom of my heart, and – went on with my fish.

In the fullness of time that dinner came to an end; and with genuine regret I tore myself away from Kitty – as certain as I was of my own existence that It would be waiting for me outside the door. The red-whiskered man, who had been introduced to me as Dr Heatherlegh of Simla, volunteered to bear me company as far as our roads lay together. I accepted his offer with gratitude.

My instinct had not deceived me. It lay in readiness in the Mall, and, in what seemed devilish mockery of our ways, with a lighted headlamp. The red-whiskered man went to the point at once, in a manner that showed he had been thinking over it all dinner time.

'I say, Pansay, what the deuce was the matter with you this evening on the Elysium road?' The suddenness of the question wrenched an answer from me before I was aware.

'That!' said I, pointing to It.

'*That* may be either DT or eyes for aught I know. Now

you don't liquor. I saw as much at dinner, so it can't be DT. There's nothing whatever where you're pointing, though you're sweating and trembling with fright like a scared pony. Therefore, I conclude that it's eyes. And I ought to understand all about them. Come along home with me. I'm on the Blessington lower road.'

To my intense delight the 'rickshaw instead of waiting for us kept about twenty yards ahead – and this, too whether we walked, trotted or cantered. In the course of that long night ride I had told my companion almost as much as I have told you here.

'Well, you've spoilt one of the best tales I've ever laid tongue to,' said he, 'but I'll forgive you for the sake of what you've gone through. Now come home and do what I tell you; and when I've cured you, young man, let this be a lesson to you to steer clear of women and indigestible food till the day of your death.'

The 'rickshaw kept steady in front; and my red-whiskered friend seemed to derive great pleasure from my account of its exact whereabouts.

'Eyes, Pansay – all eyes, brain and stomach; and the greatest of these three is stomach. You've too much conceited brain, too little stomach and thoroughly unhealthy eyes. Get your stomach straight and the rest follows. And all that's French for a liver pill. I'll take sole medical charge of you from this hour; for you're too interesting a phenomenon to be passed over.'

By this time we were deep in the shadow of the Blessington lower road and the 'rickshaw came to a dead stop under a pine-clad, over-hanging shale cliff. Instinctively I halted too, giving my reason. Heatherlegh rapped out an oath.

'Now, if you think I'm going to spend a cold night on the hillside for the sake of a stomach-cum-brain-cum-eye illusion … Lord ha' mercy! What's that?'

There was a muffled report, a blinding smother of dust just in front of us, a crack, the noise of rent boughs, and about ten yards of the cliffside – pines, undergrowth and all – slid down into the road below, completely blocking it up. The uprooted trees swayed and tottered for a moment like drunken giants in the gloom, and then fell prone among their fellows with a thunderous crash. Our two horses stood motionless and sweating with fear. As soon as the rattle of falling earth and stone had subsided, my companion muttered, 'Man, if we'd gone forward we should have been ten feet deep in our graves by now! "There are more things in heaven and earth" … Come home, Pansay, and thank God. I want a peg badly.'

We retraced our way over the Church Ridge and I arrived at Dr Heatherlegh's house shortly after midnight.

His attempts towards my cure commenced almost immediately and for a week I never left his sight. Many a time in the course of that week did I bless the good fortune which had thrown me in contact with Simla's best and kindest doctor. Day by day my spirits grew lighter and more equable. Day by day, too, I became more and more inclined to fall in with Heatherlegh's 'spectral illusion' theory, implicating eyes, brain and stomach. I wrote to Kitty, telling her that a slight sprain caused by a fall from my horse kept me indoors for a few days; and that I should be recovered before she had time to regret my absence.

Heatherlegh's treatment was simple to a degree. It consisted of liver pills, cold-water baths and strong exercise, taken in the dusk or at early dawn – for, as he sagely observed, 'A man with a sprained ankle doesn't walk a dozen miles a day and your young woman might be wondering if she saw you.'

At the end of the week, after much examination of pupil and pulse, and strict injunctions as to diet and pedestrianism, Heatherlegh dismissed me as brusquely as he had taken charge of me. Here is his parting benediction: 'Man, I can certify to your mental cure, and that's as much as to say I've cured most of your bodily ailments. Now, get your traps out of this as soon as you can; and be off to make love to Miss Kitty.'

I was endeavouring to express my thanks for his kindness. He cut me short.

'Don't think I did this because I like you. I gather that you've behaved like a blackguard all through. But, all the same, you're a phenomenon, and as queer a phenomenon as you are a blackguard. Now, go out and see if you can find the eyes-brain-and-stomach business again. I'll give you a lakh for each time you see it.'

Half an hour later I was in the Mannerings' drawing room with Kitty – drunk with the intoxication of present happiness and the foreknowledge that I should never more be troubled with Its hideous presence. Strong in the sense of my newfound security, I proposed a ride at once; and, by preference, a canter round Jakko.

Never have I felt so well, so overladen with vitality and mere animal spirits, as I did on the afternoon of 30 April. Kitty was delighted at the change in my appearance and complimented me on it in her delightfully frank and outspoken manner. We left the Mannerings' house together, laughing and talking, and cantered along the Chota Simla road as of old.

I was in haste to reach the Sanjowlie Reservoir and there make my assurance doubly sure. The horses did their best, but seemed all too slow to my impatient mind. Kitty was astonished at my boisterousness. 'Why, Jack!' she cried at last, 'you are behaving like a child! What are you doing?'

We were just below the convent and from sheer wantonness I was making my Waler plunge and curvet across the road as I tickled it with the loop of my riding whip.

'Doing?' I answered; 'nothing, dear. That's just it. If you'd been doing nothing for a week except lie up, you'd be as riotous as I.'

> Singing and murmuring in your feastful mirth,
> Joying to feel yourself alive;
> Lord over Nature, Lord of the visible Earth,
> Lord of the senses five.

My quotation was hardly out of my lips before we had rounded the corner above the convent; and a few yards further on could see across to Sanjowlie. In the centre of the level road stood the black and white liveries, the yellow-panelled 'rickshaw and Mrs Keith-Wessington. I pulled up, looked, rubbed my eyes and, I believe, must have said something. The next thing I knew was that I was lying face downward on the road with Kitty kneeling above me in tears.

'Has it gone, child?' I gasped.

Kitty only wept more bitterly.

'Has what gone? Jack, dear: what does it all mean? There must be a mistake somewhere, Jack. A hideous mistake.' Her last words brought me to my feet – mad – raving for the time being.

'Yes, there *is* a mistake somewhere,' I repeated, 'a hideous mistake. Come and look at It.'

I have an indistinct idea that I dragged Kitty by the wrist along the road up to where It stood, and implored her for pity's sake to speak to It; to tell It that we were betrothed; that neither Death nor Hell could break the tie between us; and Kitty only knows how much more to the same effect. Now and again I appealed passionately to the Terror in the 'rickshaw to bear witness to all I had said, and to release me from a torture that was killing me. As I talked I suppose I must have told Kitty of my old relations with Mrs Wessington, for I saw her listen intently with white face and blazing eyes.

'Thank you, Mr Pansay,' she said, 'that's *quite* enough. Bring my horse.'

The grooms, impassive as Orientals always are, had come up with the recaptured horses; and as Kitty sprang into her saddle I caught hold of the bridle, entreating her to hear me out and forgive. My answer was the cut of her riding whip across my face from mouth to eye, and a word or two of farewell that even now I cannot write down. So I judged, and judged rightly, that Kitty knew all; and I staggered back to the side of the 'rickshaw. My face was cut and bleeding, and the blow of the riding whip had raised a livid blue weal on it. I had no self-respect. Just then, Heatherlegh, who must have been following Kitty and me at a distance, cantered up.

'Doctor,' I said, pointing to my face, 'here's Miss Mannering's signature to my order of dismissal and … I'll thank you for that lakh as soon as convenient.'

Heatherlegh's face, even in my abject misery, moved me to laughter.

'I'll stake my professional reputation,' he began.

'Don't be a fool,' I whispered. 'I've lost my life's happiness and you'd better take me home.'

As I spoke the 'rickshaw was gone. Then I lost all knowledge of what was passing. The crest of Jakko seemed to heave and roll like the crest of a cloud and fall in upon me.

Seven days later (on 7 May, that is to say) I was aware that I was lying in Heatherlegh's room as weak as a little child. Heatherlegh was watching me intently from behind the papers on his writing table. His first words were not encouraging; but I was too far spent to be much moved by them.

'Here's Miss Kitty has sent back your letters. You corresponded a good deal, you young people. Here's a packet that looks like a ring, and a cheerful sort of a note from Mannering Papa, which I've taken the liberty of reading and burning. The old gentleman's not pleased with you.'

'And Kitty?' I asked, dully.

'Rather more drawn than her father from what she says. By the same token you must have been letting out any number of queer reminiscences just before I met you. Says that a man who would have behaved to a woman as you did to Mrs Wessington ought to kill himself out of sheer pity for his kind. She's a hot-headed little virago, your girl. Will have it too that you were suffering from DT when that row on the Jakko road turned up. Says she'll die before she ever speaks to you again.'

I groaned and turned over to the other side.

'Now you've got your choice, my friend. This engagement has to be broken off; and the Mannerings don't want to be too hard on you. Was it broken through DT or epileptic fits? Sorry I can't offer you a better exchange unless you'd prefer hereditary insanity. Say the word and I'll tell 'em it's fits. All Simla knows about that scene on the Ladies' Mile. Come! I'll give you five minutes to think over it.'

During those five minutes I believe that I explored thoroughly the lowest circles of the Inferno which it is permitted man to tread on earth. And at the same time I myself was watching myself faltering through the dark labyrinths of doubt, misery and utter despair. I wondered, as Heatherlegh in his chair might have wondered, which dreadful alternative I should adopt.

Presently I heard myself answering in a voice that I hardly recognised, 'They're confoundedly particular about morality in these parts. Give 'em fits, Heatherlegh, and my love. Now let me sleep a bit longer.'

Then my two selves joined, and it was only I (half

crazed, devil-driven I) that tossed in my bed, tracing step by step the history of the past month.

'But I am in Simla,' I kept repeating to myself. 'I, Jack Pansay, am in Simla, and there are no ghosts here. It's unreasonable of that woman to pretend there are. Why couldn't Agnes have left me alone? I never did her any harm. It might just as well have been me as Agnes. Only I'd never have come back on purpose to kill *her*. Why can't I be left alone – left alone and happy?'

It was high noon when I first awoke; and the sun was low in the sky before I slept – slept as the tortured criminal sleeps on his rack, too worn to feel further pain.

Next day I could not leave my bed. Heatherlegh told me in the morning that he had received an answer from Mr Mannering, and that, thanks to his (Heatherlegh's) friendly offices, the story of my affliction had travelled through the length and breadth of Simla, where I was on all sides much pitied.

'And that's rather more than you deserve,' he concluded pleasantly, 'though the Lord knows you've been going through a pretty severe mill. Never mind; we'll cure you yet, you perverse phenomenon.'

I declined firmly to be cured. 'You've been much too good to me already, old man,' said I; 'but I don't think I need trouble you further.'

In my heart I knew that nothing Heatherlegh could do would lighten the burden that had been laid upon me.

With that knowledge came also a sense of hopeless, impotent rebellion against the unreasonableness of it all. There were scores of men no better than I whose punishments had at least been reserved for another world; and I felt that it was bitterly, cruelly unfair that I alone should have been singled out for so hideous a fate. This mood would in time give place to another where it seemed that the 'rickshaw and I were the only realities in a world of shadows; that Kitty was a ghost; that Mannering, Heatherlegh and all the other men and women I knew were all ghosts and the great, grey hills themselves but vain shadows devised to torture me. From mood to mood I tossed backwards and forwards for seven weary days, my body growing daily stronger and stronger, until the bedroom looking glass told me that I had returned to everyday life, and was as other men once more. Curiously enough, my face showed no signs of the struggle I had gone through. It was pale indeed, but as expressionless and commonplace as ever. I had expected some permanent alteration – visible evidence of the disease that was eating me away. I found nothing.

On 15 May I left Heatherlegh's house at eleven o'clock in the morning; and the instinct of the bachelor drove me to the club. There I found that every man knew my story as told by Heatherlegh, and was, in clumsy fashion, abnormally kind and attentive. Nevertheless I recognised that for the rest of my natural life I should be among, but not of, my fellows; and I envied very bitterly indeed the laughing coolies on the Mall below. I lunched at the club, and at four o'clock wandered aimlessly down the Mall in the vague hope of meeting Kitty. Close to the bandstand the black and white liveries joined me; and I heard Mrs Wessington's old appeal at my side. I had been expecting this ever since I came out and was only surprised at her delay. The phantom 'rickshaw and I went side by side along the Chota Simla road in silence. Close to the bazaar, Kitty and a man on horseback overtook and passed us. For any sign she gave I might have been a dog in the road. She did not even pay me the compliment of quickening her pace; though the rainy afternoon had served for an excuse.

So Kitty and her companion, and I and my ghostly Light-o'-Love, crept round Jakko in couples. The road was streaming with water; the pines dripped like roof pipes on the rocks below, and the air was full of fine, driving rain. Two or three times I found myself saying to myself almost aloud, 'I'm Jack Pansay on leave at Simla – *at Simla*! Everyday, ordinary Simla. I mustn't forget that – I mustn't forget that.' Then I would try to recollect some of the gossip I had heard at the club: the prices of so-and-so's horses – anything, in fact, that related to the workaday Anglo-Indian world I knew so well. I even repeated the multiplication table rapidly to myself, to make quite sure that I was not taking leave of my senses. It gave me much comfort, and must have prevented my hearing Mrs Wessington for a time.

Once more I wearily climbed the convent slope and entered the level road. Here Kitty and the man started off at a canter, and I was left alone with Mrs Wessington. 'Agnes,' said I, 'will you put back your hood and tell me what it all means?' The hood dropped noiselessly and I was face to face with my dead and buried mistress. She was wearing the dress in which I had last seen her alive; carried the same tiny handkerchief in her right hand; and the same card case in her left. (A woman eight months dead with a card case!) I had to pin myself down to the multiplication table and to set both hands on the stone parapet of the road to assure myself that that at least was real.

'Agnes,' I repeated, 'for pity's sake tell me what it all means.' Mrs Wessington leaned forward, with that odd, quick turn of the head I used to know so well, and spoke.

If my story had not already so madly overleaped the bounds of all human belief I should apologise to you now. As I know that no one – no, not even Kitty, for whom it is written as some sort of justification of my conduct – will believe me, I will go on. Mrs Wessington spoke and I walked with her from the Sanjowlie road to the turning below the commander-in-chief's house as I might walk by the side of any living woman's 'rickshaw, deep in conversation. The second and most tormenting of my moods of sickness had suddenly laid hold upon me, and like the Prince in Tennyson's poem, 'I seemed to move amid a world of ghosts.' There had been a garden party at the commander-in-chief's, and we two joined the crowd of homeward-bound folk. As I saw them then it seemed that *they* were the shadows – impalpable, fantastic shadows – that divided for Mrs Wessington's 'rickshaw to pass through. What we said during the course of that weird interview I cannot – indeed, I dare not – tell. Heatherlegh's comment would have been a short laugh and a remark that I had been 'mashing a brain-eye-and-stomach chimera'. It was a ghastly and yet in some indefinable way a marvellously dear experience. Could it be possible, I wondered, that I was in this life to woo a second time the woman I had killed by my own neglect and cruelty?

I met Kitty on the homeward road – a shadow among shadows.

If I were to describe all the incidents of the next fortnight in their order, my story would never come to an end; and your patience would be exhausted. Morning after morning and evening after evening the ghostly 'rickshaw and I used to wander through Simla together. Wherever I went, there the four black and white liveries followed me and bore me company to and from my hotel. At the theatre I found them amid the crowd of yelling *jhampanies*; outside the club veranda, after a long evening of whist; at the birthday ball, waiting patiently for my reappearance; and in broad daylight when I went calling. Save that it cast no shadow, the 'rickshaw was in every respect as real to look upon as one of wood and iron. More than once, indeed, I have had to check myself from warning some hard-riding friend against cantering over it. More than once I have walked down the Mall deep in conversation with Mrs Wessington to the unspeakable amazement of the passers-by.

Before I had been out and about a week I learned that the 'fit' theory had been discarded in favour of insanity. However, I made no change in my mode of life. I called, rode and dined out as freely as ever. I had a passion for the society of my kind which I had never felt before; I hungered to be among the realities of life; and at the same time I felt vaguely unhappy when I had been separated too long from my ghostly companion. It would be almost impossible to describe my varying moods from 15 May up to today.

The presence of the 'rickshaw filled me by turns with

horror, blind fear, a dim sort of pleasure and utter despair. I dared not leave Simla; and I knew that my stay there was killing me. I knew, moreover, that it was my destiny to die slowly and a little every day. My only anxiety was to get the penance over as quietly as might be. Alternately I hungered for a sight of Kitty and watched her outrageous flirtations with my successor – to speak more accurately, my successors – with amused interest. She was as much out of my life as I was out of hers. By day I wandered with Mrs Wessington almost content. By night I implored heaven to let me return to the world as I used to know it. Above all these varying moods lay the sensation of dull, numbing wonder that the seen and the unseen should mingle so strangely on this earth to hound one poor soul to its grave.

27 August – Heatherlegh has been indefatigable in his attendance on me; and only yesterday told me that I ought to send in an application for sick leave. An applica-tion to escape the company of a phantom! A request that the government would graciously permit me to get rid of five ghosts and an airy 'rickshaw by going to England. Heatherlegh's proposition moved me to almost hysterical laughter. I told him that I should await the end quietly at Simla; and I am sure that the end is not far off. Believe me that I dread its advent more than any word can say; and I torture myself nightly with a thousand speculations as to the manner of my death.

Shall I die in my bed decently and as an English gentleman should die; or, in one last walk on the Mall, will my soul be wrenched from me to take its place for ever and ever by the side of that ghastly phantasm? Shall I return to my old lost allegiance in the next world, or shall I meet Agnes loathing her and bound to her side through all eternity? Shall we two hover over the scene of our lives till the end of time? As the day of my death draws nearer, the intense horror that all living flesh feels towards escaped spirits from beyond the grave grows more and more powerful. It is an awful thing to go down quick among the dead with scarcely one half of your life completed. It is a thousand times more awful to wait as I do in your midst, for I know not what unimaginable terror. Pity me, at least on the score of my 'delusion', for I know you will never believe what I have written here. Yet as surely as ever a man was done to death by the Powers of Darkness I am that man.

In justice, too, pity her. For as surely as ever woman was killed by man, I killed Mrs Wessington. And the last portion of my punishment is ever now upon me.

W. W. JACOBS
(1863–1943)

Raised in Wapping, east London, William Wymark Jacobs joined the civil service as a second-class clerk while still a teenager. He found it a job of mind-numbing tedium: 'I cannot flatter myself I was a very good clerk,' he remarked disconsolately, 'nor has anyone else attempted to do so.' While there he began to submit short stories to magazines. In 1896 his first collection, *Many Cargoes*, was published to great acclaim and his fame reached a feverish peak with the publication of what is still his best-known story, 'The Monkey's Paw', in 1902. In person, he was shy and subdued: Evelyn Waugh described his habit of 'speaking through the side of his lips in furtive, almost criminal tones, disconcerting in a man of transcendental respectability'. His wife, Nell, however, was a militant suffragette who was arrested and sentenced to two months' hard labour for carrying a hammer concealed in her muff.

THE TOLL-HOUSE

I T'S ALL NONSENSE,' said Jack Barnes. 'Of course people have died in the house; people die in every house. As for the noises – wind in the chimney and rats in the wainscot are very convincing to a nervous man. Give me another cup of tea, Meagle.'

'Lester and White are first,' said Meagle, who was presiding at the tea table of the Three Feathers Inn. 'You've had two.'

Lester and White finished their cups with irritating slowness, pausing between sips to sniff the aroma, and to discover the sex and dates of arrival of the 'strangers' which floated in some numbers in the beverage. Mr Meagle served them to the brim, and then, turning to the grimly expectant Mr Barnes, blandly requested him to ring for hot water.

'We'll try and keep your nerves in their present healthy condition,' he remarked. 'For my part I have a sort of half-and-half belief in the supernatural.'

'All sensible people have,' said Lester. 'An aunt of mine saw a ghost once.'

White nodded.

'I had an uncle that saw one,' he said.

'It always is somebody else that sees them,' said Barnes.

'Well, there is the house,' said Meagle, 'a large house at an absurdly low rent, and nobody will take it. It has taken toll of at least one life of every family that has lived there – however short the time – and since it has stood empty caretaker after caretaker has died there. The last caretaker died fifteen years ago.'

'Exactly,' said Barnes. 'Long enough ago for legends to accumulate.'

'I'll bet you a sovereign you won't spend the night there alone, for all your talk,' said White suddenly.

'And I,' said Lester.

'No,' said Barnes slowly. 'I don't believe in ghosts nor in any supernatural things whatever; all the same, I admit that I should not care to pass a night there alone.'

'But why not?' enquired White.

'Wind in the chimney,' said Meagle, with a grin.

'Rats in the wainscot,' chimed in Lester.

'As you like,' said Barnes, colouring.

'Suppose we all go?' said Meagle. 'Start after supper and get there about eleven? We have been walking for ten days now without an adventure – except Barnes's discovery that ditch water smells longest. It will be a novelty, at any rate, and, if we break the spell by all surviving, the grateful owner ought to come down handsome.'

'Let's see what the landlord has to say about it first,' said Lester. 'There is no fun in passing a night in an ordinary empty house. Let us make sure that it is haunted.'

He rang the bell and, sending for the landlord, appealed to him in the name of our common humanity not to let them waste a night watching in a house in which spectres and hobgoblins had no part. The reply was more than reassuring, and the landlord, after describing with considerable art the exact appearance of a head which had been seen hanging out of a window in the moonlight, wound up with a polite but urgent request that they would settle his bill before they went.

'It's all very well for you young gentlemen to have your fun,' he said indulgently; 'but, supposing as how you are all found dead in the morning, what about me? It ain't called the Toll-House for nothing, you know.'

'Who died there last?' enquired Barnes, with an air of polite derision.

'A tramp,' was the reply. 'He went there for the sake of half a crown, and they found him next morning hanging from the balusters, dead.'

'Suicide,' said Barnes. 'Unsound mind.'

The landlord nodded. 'That's what the jury brought it in,' he said slowly; 'but his mind was sound enough when he went in there. I'd known him, off and on, for years. I'm a poor man, but I wouldn't spend the night in that house for a hundred pounds.'

He repeated this remark as they started on their expedition a few hours later. They left as the inn was closing for the night; bolts shot noisily behind them, and, as the regular customers trudged slowly homewards, they set off at a brisk pace in the direction of the house. Most of the cottages were already in darkness and lights in others went out as they passed.

'It seems rather hard that we have got to lose a night's rest in order to convince Barnes of the existence of ghosts,' said White.

'It's in a good cause,' said Meagle. 'A most worthy object; and something seems to tell me that we shall succeed. You didn't forget the candles, Lester?'

'I have brought two,' was the reply; 'all the old man could spare.'

There was but little moon and the night was cloudy. The road between high hedges was dark and in one place, where it ran through a wood, so black that they twice stumbled in the uneven ground at the side of it.

'Fancy leaving our comfortable beds for this!' said White again. 'Let me see, this desirable residential sepulchre lies to the right, doesn't it?'

'Further on,' said Meagle.

They walked on for some time in silence, broken only by White's tribute to the softness, the cleanliness and the comfort of the bed which was receding further and further into the distance. Under Meagle's guidance they turned off at last to the right and, after a walk of a quarter of a mile, saw the gates of the house before them.

The lodge was almost hidden by overgrown shrubs and the drive was choked with rank growths. Meagle leading, they pushed through it until the dark pile of the house loomed above them.

'There is a window at the back where we can get in, so the landlord says,' said Lester, as they stood before the hall door.

'Window?' said Meagle. 'Nonsense. Let's do the thing properly. Where's the knocker?'

He felt for it in the darkness and gave a thundering rat-tat-tat at the door.

'Don't play the fool,' said Barnes crossly.

'Ghostly servants are all asleep,' said Meagle gravely, 'but *I'll* wake them up before I've done with them. It's scandalous keeping us out here in the dark.'

He plied the knocker again and the noise volleyed in the emptiness beyond. Then with a sudden exclamation he put out his hands and stumbled forward.

'Why, it was open all the time,' he said, with an odd catch in his voice. 'Come on.'

'I don't believe it was open,' said Lester, hanging back. 'Somebody is playing us a trick.'

'Nonsense,' said Meagle sharply. 'Give me a candle. Thanks. Who's got a match?'

Barnes produced a box and struck one, and Meagle, shielding the candle with his hand, led the way forward to the foot of the stairs. 'Shut the door, somebody,' he said; 'there's too much draught.'

'It is shut,' said White, glancing behind him.

Meagle fingered his chin. 'Who shut it?' he enquired, looking from one to the other. 'Who came in last?'

'I did,' said Lester, 'but I don't remember shutting it – perhaps I did, though.'

Meagle, about to speak, thought better of it and, still carefully guarding the flame, began to explore the house, with the others close behind. Shadows danced on the walls and lurked in the corners as they proceeded. At the end of the passage they found a second staircase and, ascending it, slowly gained the first floor.

'Careful!' said Meagle, as they gained the landing.

He held the candle forward and showed where the

balusters had broken away. Then he peered curiously into the void beneath.

'This is where the tramp hanged himself, I suppose,' he said thoughtfully.

'You've got an unwholesome mind,' said White, as they walked on. 'This place is quite creepy enough without you remembering that. Now let's find a comfortable room and have a little nip of whisky apiece and a pipe. How will this do?'

He opened a door at the end of the passage and revealed a small square room. Meagle led the way with the candle, and, first melting a drop or two of tallow, stuck it on the mantelpiece. The others seated themselves on the floor and watched pleasantly as White drew from his pocket a small bottle of whisky and a tin cup.

'H'm! I've forgotten the water,' he exclaimed.

'I'll soon get some,' said Meagle.

He tugged violently at the bell handle and the rusty jangling of a bell sounded from a distant kitchen. He rang again.

'Don't play the fool,' said Barnes roughly.

Meagle laughed. 'I only wanted to convince you,' he said kindly. 'There ought to be, at any rate, one ghost in the servants' hall.'

Barnes held up his hand for silence.

'Yes?' said Meagle, with a grin at the other two. 'Is anybody coming?'

'Suppose we drop this game and go back,' said Barnes suddenly. 'I don't believe in spirits, but nerves are outside anybody's command. You may laugh as you like, but it really seemed to me that I heard a door open below and steps on the stairs.'

His voice was drowned in a roar of laughter.

'He is coming round,' said Meagle, with a smirk. 'By the time I have done with him he will be a confirmed believer. Well, who will go and get some water? Will you, Barnes?'

'No,' was the reply.

'If there is any it might not be safe to drink after all these years,' said Lester. 'We must do without it.'

Meagle nodded and, taking a seat on the floor, held out his hand for the cup. Pipes were lit and the clean, wholesome smell of tobacco filled the room. White produced a pack of cards; talk and laughter rang through the room and died away reluctantly in distant corridors.

'Empty rooms always delude me into the belief that I possess a deep voice,' said Meagle. 'Tomorrow I –'

He started up with a smothered exclamation as the light went out suddenly and something struck him on the head. The others sprang to their feet. Then Meagle laughed.

'It's the candle,' he exclaimed. 'I didn't stick it enough.'

Barnes struck a match and, relighting the candle, stuck it on the mantelpiece and, sitting down, took up his cards again.

'What was I going to say?' said Meagle. 'Oh, I know; tomorrow I –'

'Listen!' said White, laying his hand on the other's sleeve. 'Upon my word I really thought I heard a laugh.'

'Look here!' said Barnes. 'What do you say to going back? I've had enough of this. I keep fancying that I hear things too; sounds of something moving about in the passage outside. I know it's only fancy, but it's uncomfortable.'

'You go if you want to,' said Meagle, 'and we will play

dummy. Or you might ask the tramp to take your hand for you, as you go downstairs.'

Barnes shivered and exclaimed angrily. He got up and, walking to the half-closed door, listened.

'Go outside,' said Meagle, winking at the other two. 'I'll dare you to go down to the hall door and back by yourself.'

Barnes came back and, bending forward, lit his pipe at the candle.

'I am nervous, but rational,' he said, blowing out a thin cloud of smoke. 'My nerves tell me that there is something prowling up and down the long passage outside; my reason tells me that that is all nonsense. Where are my cards?'

He sat down again and, taking up his hand, looked through it carefully and led.

'Your play, White,' he said, after a pause.

White made no sign.

'Why, he is asleep,' said Meagle. 'Wake up, old man. Wake up and play.'

Lester, who was sitting next to him, took the sleeping man by the arm and shook him, gently at first and then with some roughness, but White, with his back against the wall and his head bowed, made no sign. Meagle bawled in his ear and then turned a puzzled face to the others.

'He sleeps like the dead,' he said, grimacing. 'Well, there are still three of us to keep each other company.'

'Yes,' said Lester, nodding. 'Unless – Good Lord! Suppose –'

He broke off and eyed them, trembling.

'Suppose what?' enquired Meagle.

'Nothing,' stammered Lester. 'Let's wake him. Try him again. *White!* WHITE!'

'It's no good,' said Meagle seriously; 'there's something wrong about that sleep.'

'That's what I meant,' said Lester; 'and if *he* goes to sleep like that, why shouldn't –'

Meagle sprang to his feet. 'Nonsense,' he said roughly. 'He's tired out; that's all. Still, let's take him up and clear out. You take his legs and Barnes will lead the way with the candle. *Yes? Who's that?*'

He looked up quickly towards the door. 'Thought I heard somebody tap,' he said, with a shamefaced laugh. 'Now, Lester, up with him. One, two – *Lester! Lester!*'

He sprang forward too late; Lester, with his face buried in his arms, had rolled over on the floor, fast asleep, and his utmost efforts failed to awake him.

'He – is – asleep,' he stammered. 'Asleep!'

Barnes, who had taken the candle from the mantel-piece, stood peering at the sleepers in silence and dropping tallow over the floor.

'We must get out of this,' said Meagle. 'Quick!'

Barnes hesitated. 'We can't leave them here –' he began.

'We must,' said Meagle, in strident tones. 'If you go to sleep I shall go – Quick! Come!'

He seized the other by the arm and strove to drag him to the door. Barnes shook him off and, putting the candle back on the mantelpiece, tried again to arouse the sleepers.

'It's no good,' he said at last, and, turning from them, watched Meagle. 'Don't you go to sleep,' he said anxiously.

Meagle shook his head and they stood for some time in uneasy silence. 'May as well shut the door,' said Barnes at last.

He crossed over and closed it gently. Then, at a scuffling

noise behind him, he turned and saw Meagle in a heap on the hearthstone.

With a sharp catch in his breath he stood motionless. Inside the room the candle, fluttering in the draught, showed dimly the grotesque attitudes of the sleepers. Beyond the door there seemed to his overwrought imagination a strange and stealthy unrest. He tried to whistle, but his lips were parched, and in a mechanical fashion he stooped and began to pick up the cards which littered the floor.

He stopped once or twice and stood with bent head listening. The unrest outside seemed to increase; a loud creaking sounded from the stairs.

'Who is there?' he cried loudly.

The creaking ceased. He crossed to the door and, flinging it open, strode out into the corridor. As he walked his fears left him suddenly.

'Come on!' he cried, with a low laugh. 'All of you! All of you! Show your faces – your infernal ugly faces! Don't skulk!'

He laughed again and walked on; and the heap in the fireplace put out its head tortoise fashion and listened in horror to the retreating footsteps. Not until they had become inaudible in the distance did the listener's features relax.

'Good Lord, Lester, we've driven him mad,' he said, in a frightened whisper. 'We must go after him.'

There was no reply. Meagle sprang to his feet.

'Do you hear?' he cried. 'Stop your fooling now; this is serious. *White! Lester!* Do you hear?'

He bent and surveyed them in angry bewilderment. 'All right,' he said, in a trembling voice. 'You won't frighten me, you know.'

He turned away and walked with exaggerated careless-
ness in the direction of the door. He even went outside and
peeped through the crack, but the sleepers did not stir. He
glanced into the blackness behind and then came hastily
into the room again.

He stood for a few seconds regarding them. The
stillness in the house was horrible; he could not even hear
them breathe. With a sudden resolution he snatched the
candle from the mantelpiece and held the flame to White's
finger. Then, as he reeled back stupefied, the footsteps
again became audible.

He stood with the candle in his shaking hand, listening.
He heard them ascending the further staircase, but they
stopped suddenly as he went to the door. He walked a little
way along the passage, and they went scurrying down the
stairs and then at a jog-trot along the corridor below. He
went back to the main staircase and they ceased again.

For a time he hung over the balusters, listening and
trying to pierce the blackness below; then slowly, step by
step, he made his way downstairs and, holding the candle
above his head, peered about him.

'Barnes!' he called. 'Where are you?'

Shaking with fright, he made his way along the passage
and, summoning up all his courage, pushed open doors and
gazed fearfully into empty rooms. Then, quite suddenly,
he heard the footsteps in front of him.

He followed slowly for fear of extinguishing the candle,
until they led him at last into a vast bare kitchen, with damp
walls and a broken floor. In front of him a door leading into
an inside room had just closed. He ran towards it and flung

it open, and a cold air blew out the candle. He stood aghast.

'Barnes!' he cried again. 'Don't be afraid! It is I – Meagle!'

There was no answer. He stood gazing into the darkness, and all the time the idea of something close at hand watching was upon him. Then suddenly the steps broke out overhead again.

He drew back hastily and, passing through the kitchen, groped his way along the narrow passages. He could now see better in the darkness and, finding himself at last at the foot of the staircase, began to ascend it noiselessly. He reached the landing just in time to see a figure disappear round the angle of a wall. Still careful to make no noise, he followed the sound of the steps until they led him to the top floor, and he cornered the chase at the end of a short passage.

'Barnes!' he whispered. 'Barnes!'

Something stirred in the darkness. A small circular window at the end of the passage just softened the blackness and revealed the dim outlines of a motionless figure. Meagle, in place of advancing, stood almost as still as a sudden horrible doubt took possession of him. With his eyes fixed on the shape in front, he fell back slowly and, as it advanced upon him, burst into a terrible cry.

'Barnes! For God's sake! Is it *you?*'

The echoes of his voice left the air quivering, but the figure before him paid no heed. For a moment he tried to brace his courage up to endure its approach, then with a smothered cry he turned and fled.

The passages wound like a maze and he threaded them blindly in a vain search for the stairs. If he could get down and open the hall door –

He caught his breath in a sob; the steps had begun

again. At a lumbering trot they clattered up and down the
bare passages, in and out, up and down, as though in search
of him. He stood appalled, and then, as they drew near,
entered a small room and stood behind the door as they
rushed by. He came out and ran swiftly and noiselessly in
the other direction, and in a moment the steps were after
him. He found the long corridor and raced along it at top
speed. The stairs he knew were at the end, and with the
steps close behind he descended them in blind haste. The
steps gained on him and he shrank to the side to let them
pass, still continuing his headlong flight. Then suddenly he
seemed to slip off the earth into space.

Lester awoke in the morning to find the sunshine streaming
into the room, and White sitting up and regarding with
some perplexity a badly blistered finger.

'Where are the others?' enquired Lester.

'Gone, I suppose,' said White. 'We must have been asleep.'

Lester arose and, stretching his stiffened limbs, dusted
his clothes with his hands and went out into the corridor.
White followed. At the noise of their approach a figure which
had been lying asleep at the other end sat up and revealed the
face of Barnes. 'Why, I've been asleep,' he said, in surprise. 'I
don't remember coming here. How did I get here?'

'Nice place to come for a nap,' said Lester severely, as he
pointed to the gap in the balusters. 'Look there! Another
yard and where would you have been?'

He walked carelessly to the edge and looked over. In
response to his startled cry the others drew near, and all
three stood staring at the dead man below.

A. F. KIDD

(1953–)

Born in Nottingham and now living in West London, Chico (A. F.) Kidd is an award-winning writer and illustrator who has taken up the story of Thomas Carnacki, a supernatural detective created by the writer, photographer, poet and strongman William Hope Hodgson in 1910. Kidd's work reveals the events behind a series of unexplained episodes in Hodgson's original tales. Rivalling Sherlock Holmes's reference to the 'giant rat of Sumatra … a story for which the world is not yet prepared' in its tantalising potential, the events of 'The Black Veil' are hinted at uneasily in Hodgson's 'The Gateway of the Monster' story as 'that horrible Black Veil business. You know how *that* turned out.'

The Black Veil

I asked him whether he would object to my drawing
a pentacle round him for the night and got him to
agree, but I saw that he did not know whether to be
superstitious about it or to regard it more as a piece
of foolish mumming; but he took it seriously enough
when I gave him some particulars about the Black Veil
case, when young Aster died. You remember, he said
it was a piece of silly superstition and stayed outside.
Poor devil!

William Hope Hodgson, 'The Horse of the Invisible'

W E HAD ALL SEEN the newspapers, although
each of us knew that what we read there could
only be a part, at best, of the full story. So none of us
was surprised to receive a card in the usual vein from
Carnacki, and none of us would willingly have refused
the invitation.

No sooner had the four of us – Jessop, Arkwright,
Taylor and myself – all presented ourselves at No. 472
than we were ushered in to dinner, during which our host

was even more taciturn than was his wont. Afterwards, however, he settled himself comfortably in his great chair much as usual and waited for us to take our accustomed places.

'I dare say you fellows have seen the newspapers,' he remarked, puffing at his pipe. 'Though you won't have got much sense out of them. But you know that, of course. It's entirely due to that sort of materialistic scepticism that Aster died. An altogether curious and unpleasant affair and I can't say I am entirely blameless.

'Charles Aster was a newspaper reporter. Now as you know I won't, as a rule, have any truck with them, but there was something about his persistence which was rather – endearing, for want of a better word. The man was more like an importunate puppy than anything else, and he pestered me until I began to think I'd have to take him along on a "safe" case – as much as anything in this line could be termed "safe". As you know, it's a rather relative description!

'However, before a suitable case presented itself, Aster himself sent me a rather intriguing letter. It appeared that an uncle of his, a Mr Jago, had recently purchased a property in the West Country and was experiencing what Aster described as "some odd trouble" and begged me to come and investigate. In view of what I had been thinking, I decided to agree to this request.

'It appeared that the house had a long-standing reputation for being "queer" but Jago, far from being discouraged by this, had apparently viewed it as a positive asset! This is just the sort of thing I meant about the newspapers.

However, one night spent in the house had been sufficient to disabuse him of these notions and convert him into a fervent believer in the power of the Ab-natural, with the result that Aster had suggested contacting me.

'"What exactly was it that happened?" I asked Aster when he met me on the train.

'"I can't tell you, exactly," he replied. "But there's something about the silence in that house that makes a chap beastly frightened."

'It was clear that Aster's uncle was in quite a funk. He was one of those big, fleshy men – you know the type – who bluster a lot, but when they snap, they've nothing to fall back upon. He was almost pathetically glad to see us when we arrived at the station, and prattled nervously all the way to the house.

'When we turned in at the gates – the house stands in its own grounds – Jago began to cast quick, tense little glances at it as if he were trying to catch it unawares – as if it were doing something furtive that he only suspected. Then suddenly he caught Aster's arm and whispered, "Look, look, the upper window!" His voice was that of a man who expected some horror, but who is still surprised by its appearance. Do you know what I mean?

'By that time, it was twilight, and logically it was quite absurd to suppose that either of us saw anything, for the windows were all in deep shadow. Still Aster and I were both convinced that we saw the figure of a woman silhouetted in the window Jago was indicating. Not only that, but I had the distinct impression that she was a young woman, although her features were obscured by a long, black veil. Now as neither Aster nor I had any indication of what form the "haunting" took, there was no suspicion of auto-suggestion – indeed, had it not been for the very odd fact that we could see her at all in that light, I for one would have taken her for the housekeeper.

'However, the effect which the sight of this woman had on Jago was extraordinary. With a cry of "The woman, the woman!" he shrank into the corner of the carriage, his face as white as cheese. But curiously enough, neither Aster nor I felt, at that stage, any sense of fear or even revulsion.

'As soon as we entered the house, though, the silence overwhelmed me. It was like an ocean swell – wave upon wave of it. I can't begin to describe the suddenness with which that sickening feeling overwhelmed me, and I recalled Aster's words. I knew there was something merciless in it – something brutal. My hands started to perspire, and glancing at Aster I could see that he, too, was sweating. He turned to Jago, who stood behind us outside the doorway, unable to cross the threshold.

'"What is it, uncle?" he asked, and his voice was not quite steady. "Is it that woman?"

'"Not just her," Jago whispered. "I thought it was just her at first, and she couldn't harm me. I thought I'd give her a bit of company. But it isn't just her." He had actually decided to sleep in the haunted room out of sheer perverseness!

'After a while we got him indoors and I managed to extract the story from him. Having seen, as we had, the figure of the woman from the outside, he had gone up the stairs and located the room whose window it was, with the intention, as I said, of spending a night there. I must say I marvelled at his nerve, because I had not been in the house an hour and the "creep" was crawling all over me. But according to Jago, it was not until he actually entered the room that anything happened to him.

"'As soon as I stepped inside the door of that room, I began to have my doubts," he said. "It was so beastly quiet in there that it made me think – though I'm not a fanciful sort of chap – that something was holding its breath, and waiting. And then, you know, everything went black. I don't mean I passed out – I don't think I was scared enough for that, then. No, it was as if I'd been struck blind, and if I hadn't had my hand on the doorknob, I think I wouldn't have got out. As it was, I gave a kind of backwards leap out into the corridor and slammed the door as I did it. And then I was outside and I could see again. I haven't been near the room since."

'You remember what I told you about "making a darkness"? At first I thought that was what Jago meant, but he was quite insistent. His candle had not gone out. He repeated the words, "struck blind".

'By then it was too dark to do anything about investigating the room, although it was not late by any standards. I have to admit I was grateful for this excuse. Now I've gone into too many cases connected with "ghostly" things to be accused of being a cowardly chap; but sometimes, you know, there are things you just can't face. That was one of those occasions. There was something pretty unholy in that house, and maybe I was being warned against tackling it without proper preparation. You never know, do you?

'So I didn't feel too bad about funking matters, but decided to go to bed and start fresh in the morning.

'I waited until full daylight before beginning my investigations – which at this early stage consisted simply of sealing up the room in such a way that I would be able to tell instantly if something material had entered it during the coming night. First I checked every inch of the walls, ceiling and floor, tapping then with a little hammer – the room was completely empty of furniture save for a wooden window seat.

'Aster was tremendously interested in all this and I told him I didn't mind him watching, as long as he kept out of the way. Even in daylight, the atmosphere in the room was pretty beastly, and I didn't want any distractions of any kind.

'The room was not too large – only about twelve feet by ten – but it still took me a long time to cover every surface with the colourless sticky wafers I use to detect any material activity. I find them pretty foolproof for this purpose; I used to use chalk, as you know, until that "Locked Room" case in which the hoaxer was using the ceiling rose for access to the sealed room. After that I stretched hairs across the window and the window seat, which had registered as hollow, of course, but resisted all my attempts to open it. The house was only about a hundred years old and therefore unlikely to contain such things as priest's holes, but the builder could well have put in secret passages for his own purposes. You can never take anything for granted in this sort of case.

'As I was in the process of sealing the door, Aster asked

me why I used hairs for this purpose, rather than, say, cotton thread. I explained briefly, but he seemed unconvinced, and I was too busy with my work to pursue the matter further – I wish I had realised what it would mean. After that there was nothing to be done until the following day, so I convinced Jago that he should put up at a hotel for at least the next couple of nights. It was not difficult to persuade him, and shortly I prevailed upon Aster to accompany his uncle into town.

'You can imagine that I felt pretty small and lonely after they had gone. The winter evening was already darkening the sky, and I sat downstairs in the library with my revolver to hand, although I was more than half convinced by this time that this was a genuine "haunting". I spent the time reviewing the notes I had recently made from the Sigsand MS. You know what I told you about the "Defences" he mentions? Naturally I had assumed them to be simply the superstitions of the time, which had been superseded by other methods of protection – the Circle of Solomon, for one. But it occurred to me subsequently to wonder whether these old, old formulae would still be valid today, in the twentieth century; and I have, as you know, tried some of his suggestions before, with modest success.

'Still it is one thing to seal a door or window with hair and certain signs – quite another to trust one's own self to a type of barrier unused since the fourteenth century. And that is what I was contemplating, if the seals were unbroken in the morning. I had provided myself with the requisites for constructing such a barrier – certain herbs, for instance, candles, water vessels, and some things which

I might call "creative interpretations" of Sigsand. But I am anticipating, here. There was nothing further that I could do that night and so I went to bed.

'About midnight I went up to the room and loitered in the corridor for a little while, but that malevolent silence got on my nerves. I had intended to open the door and have a quick look inside, and had popped a couple of cloves of garlic into my pockets for protection – but I tell you, it would have taken more pluck than I had that night to open that door, in the end. I had the feeling that something rotten and monstrous was waiting on the other side, and that it was *smiling* at me – smiling with a kind of mean, gloating anticipation. What an odd thought – eh?

'Of course, there was no sign of any disturbance the following morning. I had hardly expected it, but I went over the room very carefully, nonetheless, as I cleared away my paraphernalia.

'I had just unsealed the window when a cab drove round the corner of the drive and came to a halt in a flurry of gravel below me, to disgorge young Aster. He stood looking up at the window where I was, and suddenly I wondered what it was that he could see – me, or the woman? I thought I had better hail him, and knelt on the window seat to attempt to open the casement.

'The catch was infernally stiff, but at last I got it dislodged with a shriek of disused metal and leaned out to call to Aster. As I did so I heard a sharp "snick" – like the tumblers of a lock being turned – but ignored it for the moment.

'"Aster!" I called.

"'I say, Carnacki, is that you?" he cried. "I've found out something about the ghost. Any luck your end?" But he was gone out of sight into the house before I could reply. I stood up from the window seat to try and see what had made the noise; and, do you know, it was loose! The sound I had heard was the releasing of some internal catch, which had snapped open when I opened the window.

'Carefully, I eased open the lid. Remember, I had no idea of what, if anything, I should find in there; but I admit I was disappointed to see that it contained nothing but a mass of sooty cobwebs – or so I thought at first.

'By that time Aster had arrived. I heard his footsteps clattering down the corridor – at least, I hoped they were his! – and now he put his head round the door and asked if he could come in.

"'Come and tell me what you make of this," I said.

"'By Jove! You've got it open," he exclaimed, and before I could stop him he had reached into the window box and brought out a handful of the black stuff, revealing it to be not cobwebs at all, but a couple of yards of cloth so fine or so old that his fingers tore through it as he lifted it.

"'The black veil!" he cried excitedly. I begged him to calm down and tell me what he was talking about, and at length he explained, and explained, too, why he had returned so soon. He had got the story of the ghost from some folk in the town, where apparently it was common knowledge.

'It was a nasty little story of the sort that one hears all too often as being behind "hauntings". The original inhabitant of the house, one Arthur Green, had been the worst sort of brute, given to beating not only his servants and animals but his unfortunate wife as well. She, poor woman, had appealed for help to some young man, and Green, assuming that she had taken a lover, had thrashed her so savagely that he blinded her. Green then imprisoned her in her room, where she remained until her death, but was often seen standing at her window clad in a long black veil; and after she died, she was to be seen still.

'"This must be her veil, Carnacki! What will you do with it? Bury it? Will that stop the haunting? Or does it have to be exorcised, or blessed, or something?"

'I told him rather shortly that I knew my business better than he did, and that I intended to burn the thing, but that it was by no means certain that this would put an end to the manifestations in the house.

'"There may be other circumstances we are not aware of," I told him. "We shan't know one way or another until tonight."

'"Do we spend the night in here?"

'"I can't tell you at this stage. First of all this veil must be burned."

'I had, as I have told you, equipped myself with a number of items out of which to construct a "Defence", and I employed some of these to construct a pentacle around the veil before burning it. Aster watched these proceedings with a very queer look on his face, but said nothing.

'When we went back into the house, I could tell at once that *something* had changed, but it seemed like a change without direction – I could not tell whether it was for the better, or not. It was just, somehow, different. I wonder if you know what I mean?

'I spent some time checking the room once more, and by about midday had more or less decided to chance it and spend a night in there. I was fairly sure that I had achieved at least a partial advance against the haunting, and it seemed like an ideal opportunity to test the Sigsand barriers. I told Aster what I intended and invited him to observe the preparations which I should be making. He nodded thoughtfully and after a scratch luncheon I set to work.

'Now as you know the powers and properties of herbs are well documented, and so I felt quite justified in using certain of them specified by Sigsand – hyssop, vervain, St John's wort and so on. To this I added garlic, which I have found to be most efficacious, in a limited but most specific sort of way, and ended up with a form of protection which I thought – I hoped! – would be peculiarly powerful.

'First I inscribed a circle, the outline of which I rubbed with garlic and swept with a spray of hyssop, the holy herb. Inside this I made a "Ringe of water and fyre", joining lighted candles with crescents of water using the Second Sign of the Saamaa Ritual; and then drew a pentacle, making sure that each of its points touched the circle. In each of its five points I placed a wafer of certain bread and in the "vales" a small dish of holy water.

'All this took rather longer than I had anticipated, and by the time I had completed these precautions the sky outside the window was growing dark and I was glad of the light cast by the candles in my defence. Then Aster, who had grown bored with watching, put his head round the door and remarked, in a conversational sort of way, "Are you going to let me into the joke, old man?"

"'I assure you this is quite serious," I replied curtly.

"'Well, it ain't science," Aster retorted. "I thought you were a scientist, Carnacki."

"'I don't discount things simply because modern opinion laughs at them," I told him. "Nor should you, Aster; an open mind is the best asset a journalist can possess."

"'The best thing this journalist possesses is a flashlight," he replied, drawing one from his pocket and switching it on, "not a piece of silly superstition."

'The bright light dazzled me momentarily and I screwed up my eyes against it, but before I could admonish Aster, an awful chill swept over me. I knew what it was at once.

"'Get inside the barrier – or get out!" I shouted at him. *"Hurry,* Aster!" He turned a puzzled face to me, and I actually reached over the defence to try and seize his arm, fearful of breaking the barrier but somehow more fearful for Aster himself.

'Then, just as Jago had described, everything went dark – a stifling blackness that you *knew* would not admit any light, ever. And in that Stygian darkness I heard Aster scream, followed by a thud and soft rumble as his flashlight hit the floor and rolled away somewhere.

"'I've gone blind – blind!" he cried. I tried to call to him, but my throat had closed up and I could not make a sound, although I was in mortal dread that he would blunder into my defence and make a path for whatever was in that room. Then he screamed again, and the sound was one I hope I never hear a man make again. All semblance of humanity had gone from his voice – I can't begin to describe the sick feeling of horror I felt at it. It was the negation of all that is clean and sane and wholesome to us, as is the touch of the outer monstrosities. No, it's no good – I am quite unable to convey to you the sheer *depth* of vileness in it.

'I crouched in the centre of the pentacle, all sense of direction lost. I had no idea where the door was, or the window, or even Aster – the thing which had been Aster – although I could hear him crawling round, making a sick, inhuman moaning noise which was somehow worse than the scream. In the utter silence it sounded like a voice from the pit.

'Even now I do not know how I got through that night. I felt physically and spiritually ill, and almost paralysed with fear – although if I had been able to see the door, I think I might have made a run for it. Thank goodness I didn't.

'At some stage the noises coming from Aster ceased, and at long last light began to grow outside the window – the cold and wholesome light of a winter morning. I found I could see again, and sure enough, my candles were still alight. Aster's body was huddled in a corner, and his flashlight glowed where it had rolled, just outside my outer circle. I made a move to pick it up, and then, you know, the most horrible thing of all happened.

'What made me look in Aster's direction then I don't know, for I was sure he was dead. But as I moved, his eyes snapped open and met mine. Their very *lack* of expression was so monstrous that I was paralysed, not with physical fear, but with the hideous conviction that I was actually on the brink of being dragged down into some foul depths beyond anything we humans are ever meant to know. And all that stood between me and the instrument of that descent which stared at me with its dead and gleaming eyes was a pentacle and a ring of garlic!

'Aster began to shuffle towards me, with an odd, broken-limbed crawl. I fumbled for my revolver and then paused. Aster's progress had halted. As I watched, he snuffled at the outer circle of my defence and drew back; crept around a little way and sniffed again – I felt a thrill of hope. The barriers were holding him back! The pathological, spiritual change which he had suffered – put simply, soul destruction – had transformed Aster into something so totally unhuman that he was as unable to cross as any purely aetheric manifestation.

'Then, as suddenly as it had become animated, Aster's body went limp and collapsed in front of me. It took me an instant to realise that it lay in a beam of weak sunlight which had just that moment struck through the window. Nevertheless I waited until full daylight before venturing out of the defence, and even then I had to "take my courage in both hands" before I could bring myself to touch Aster's body. He was quite dead.

'The house was demolished last week. There was absolutely nothing in the way of physical remains to suggest how the haunting had reached such a tremendous pitch.'

'No pathetic little skeleton buried in the cellars, then?' queried Arkwright.

Carnacki shook his head. 'Possibly the simple fact of the woman's dying a lonely, painful death in that room was sufficient to imbue its fabric with the feelings of her last months.'

'And Aster?' I asked. 'Do you think the defence would have protected him, since he didn't believe in it in the first place?'

'That particular brand of metaphysics is not my field,' replied Carnacki sternly. 'Out you go! I want a sleep.' And he ushered us all out on to the quiet Embankment, as always.

SAKI

(1870–1916)

Hector Hugh Munro, who wrote as 'Saki', had a short life marked by the sort of black comedy which is the distinguishing mark of his fiction. His father was a senior officer in the Burmese police force, while his mother died of shock after being chased by a cow in a Wessex lane; as a result, Munro's childhood, with his sister Ethel, was effectively an orphaned one, ruled with a rod of iron by two maiden aunts, Ethel and Augusta. After an abortive start in the Burmese police force (cut short by malaria), he embarked on a literary career with a series of vignettes in the *Westminster Gazette*. He later became the *Morning Post*'s foreign correspondent in the Balkans, Russia and Paris and an acclaimed writer of coruscating and acidic satires on Edwardian society. When war came he immediately joined up, refusing a commission, and was killed by a sniper at Beaumont-Hamel in 1916. His last words were said to be: 'Put that bloody cigarette out.'

THE HEDGEHOG

A 'MIXED DOUBLE' of young people were contesting a game of lawn tennis at the rectory garden party; for the past five-and-twenty years at least mixed doubles of young people had done exactly the same thing on exactly the same spot at about the same time of year. The young people changed and made way for others in the course of time, but very little else seemed to alter.

The present players were sufficiently conscious of the social nature of the occasion to be concerned about their clothes and appearance, and sufficiently sport-loving to be keen on the game. Both their efforts and their appearance came under the four-fold scrutiny of a quartet of ladies sitting as official spectators on a bench immediately commanding the court. It was one of the accepted conditions of the rectory garden party that four ladies, who usually knew very little about tennis and a great deal about the players, should sit at that particular spot and watch the game. It had also come to be almost a tradition that two ladies should be amiable and that the other two should be Mrs Dole and Mrs Hatch-Mallard.

'What a singularly unbecoming way Eva Jonelet has taken to doing her hair in,' said Mrs Hatch-Mallard; 'it's ugly hair at the best of times, but she needn't make it look ridiculous as well. Someone ought to tell her.'

Eva Jonelet's hair might have escaped Mrs Hatch-Mallard's condemnation if she could have forgotten the more glaring fact that Eva was Mrs Dole's favourite niece. It would, perhaps, have been a more comfortable arrangement if Mrs Hatch-Mallard and Mrs Dole could have been asked to the rectory on separate occasions, but there was only one garden party in the course of the year, and neither lady could have been omitted from the list of invitations without hopelessly wrecking the social peace of the parish.

'How pretty the yew trees look at this time of year,' interposed a lady with a soft, silvery voice that suggested a chinchilla muff painted by Whistler.

'What do you mean by this time of year?' demanded Mrs Hatch-Mallard. 'Yew trees look beautiful at all times of the year. That is their great charm.'

'Yew trees never look anything but hideous under any circumstances or at any time of year,' said Mrs Dole, with the slow, emphatic relish of one who contradicts for the pleasure of the thing. 'They are only fit for graveyards and cemeteries.'

Mrs Hatch-Mallard gave a sardonic snort, which, being translated, meant that there were some people who were better fitted for cemeteries than for garden parties.

'What is the score, please?' asked the lady with the chinchilla voice.

The desired information was given her by a young

gentleman in spotless white flannels, whose general toilet effect suggested solicitude rather than anxiety.

'What an odious young cub Bertie Dykson has become!' pronounced Mrs Dole, remembering suddenly that Bertie was rather a favourite with Mrs Hatch-Mallard. 'The young men of today are not what they used to be twenty years ago.'

'Of course not,' said Mrs Hatch-Mallard; 'twenty years ago Bertie Dykson was just two years old, and you must expect some difference in appearance and manner and conversation between those two periods.'

'Do you know,' said Mrs Dole confidentially, 'I shouldn't be surprised if that was intended to be clever.'

'Have you anyone interesting coming to stay with you, Mrs Norbury?' asked the chinchilla voice hastily; 'you generally have a house party at this time of year.'

'I've got a most interesting woman coming,' said Mrs Norbury, who had been mutely struggling for some chance to turn the conversation into a safe channel; 'an old acquaintance of mine, Ada Bleek –'

'What an ugly name,' said Mrs Hatch-Mallard.

'She's descended from the de la Bliques, an old Huguenot family of Touraine, you know.'

'There weren't any Huguenots in Touraine,' said Mrs Hatch-Mallard, who thought she might safely dispute any fact that was three hundred years old.

'Well, anyhow, she's coming to stay with me,' continued Mrs Norbury, bringing her story quickly down to the present day; 'she arrives this evening and she's highly clairvoyant, a seventh daughter of a seventh daughter, you know, and all that sort of thing.'

'How very interesting,' said the chinchilla voice; 'Exwood is just the right place for her to come to, isn't it? There are supposed to be several ghosts there.'

'That is why she was so anxious to come,' said Mrs Norbury; 'she put off another engagement in order to accept my invitation. She's had visions and dreams, and all those sorts of things, that have come true in a most marvellous manner, but she's never actually seen a ghost, and she's longing to have that experience. She belongs to that Research Society, you know.'

'I expect she'll see the unhappy Lady Cullumpton, the most famous of all the Exwood ghosts,' said Mrs Dole; 'my ancestor, you know, Sir Gervase Cullumpton, murdered his young bride in a fit of jealousy while they were on a visit to Exwood. He strangled her in the stables with a stirrup leather, just after they had come in from riding, and she is seen sometimes at dusk going about the lawns and the stable yard, in a long green habit, moaning and trying to get the thong from round her throat. I shall be most interested to hear if your friend sees –'

'I don't know why she should be expected to see a trashy, traditional apparition like the so-called Cullumpton ghost, that is only vouched for by housemaids and tipsy stable boys, when my uncle, who was the owner of Exwood, committed suicide there under the most tragical circumstances and most certainly haunts the place.'

'Mrs Hatch-Mallard has evidently never read *Popple's County History*,' said Mrs Dole icily, 'or she would know that the Cullumpton ghost has a wealth of evidence behind it –'

'Oh, Popple!' exclaimed Mrs Hatch-Mallard scornfully; 'any rubbishy old story is good enough for him. Popple, indeed! Now my uncle's ghost was seen by a rural dean, who was also a Justice of the Peace. I should think that would be good enough testimony for anyone. Mrs Norbury, I shall take it as a deliberate personal affront if your clairvoyant friend sees any other ghost except that of my uncle.'

'I dare say she won't see anything at all; she never has yet, you know,' said Mrs Norbury hopefully.

'It was a most unfortunate topic for me to have broached,' she lamented afterwards to the owner of the chinchilla voice. 'Exwood belongs to Mrs Hatch-Mallard and we've only got it on a short lease. A nephew of hers has been wanting to live there for some time and if we offend her in any way she'll refuse to renew the lease. I sometimes think these garden parties are a mistake.'

The Norburys played bridge for the next three nights till nearly one o'clock; they did not care for the game, but it reduced the time at their guest's disposal for undesirable ghostly visitations.

'Miss Bleek is not likely to be in a frame of mind to see ghosts,' said Hugo Norbury, 'if she goes to bed with her brain awhirl with royal spades and no trumps and grand slams.'

'I've talked to her for hours about Mrs Hatch-Mallard's uncle,' said his wife, 'and pointed out the exact spot where he killed himself, and invented all sorts of impressive details, and I've found an old portrait of Lord John Russell and put it in her room, and told her that it's supposed to be a picture of the uncle in middle age. If Ada does see a ghost at all it certainly ought to be old Hatch-Mallard's. At any rate, we've done our best.'

The precautions were in vain. On the third morning of her stay Ada Bleek came down late to breakfast, her eyes looking very tired, but ablaze with excitement, her hair done anyhow, and a large brown volume hugged under her arm.

'At last I've seen something supernatural!' she exclaimed, and gave Mrs Norbury a fervent kiss, as though in gratitude for the opportunity afforded her.

'A ghost!' cried Mrs Norbury, 'not really!'

'Really and unmistakably!'

'Was it an oldish man in the dress of about fifty years ago?' asked Mrs Norbury hopefully.

'Nothing of the sort,' said Ada; 'it was a white hedgehog.'

'A white hedgehog!' exclaimed both the Norburys, in tones of disconcerted astonishment.

'A huge white hedgehog with baleful yellow eyes,' said Ada. 'I was lying half asleep in bed when suddenly I felt a sensation as of something sinister and unaccountable passing through the room. I sat up and looked round, and there, under the window, I saw an evil, creeping thing, a sort of monstrous hedgehog, of a dirty white colour, with black, loathsome claws that clicked and scraped along the floor, and narrow, yellow eyes of indescribable evil. It slithered along for a yard or two, always looking at me with its cruel, hideous eyes, then, when it reached the second window, which was open, it clambered up the sill and vanished. I got up at once and went to the window; there wasn't a sign of it anywhere. Of course, I knew it must be something from another world, but it was not till I turned up Popple's chapter on local traditions that I realised what I had seen.'

She turned eagerly to the large brown volume and read: 'Nicholas Herison, an old miser, was hung at Batchford in 1763 for the murder of a farm lad who had accidentally discovered his secret hoard. His ghost is supposed to traverse the countryside, appearing sometimes as a white owl, sometimes as a huge white hedgehog.'

'I expect you read the Popple story overnight, and that made you *think* you saw a hedgehog when you were only half awake,' said Mrs Norbury, hazarding a conjecture that probably came very near the truth.

Ada scouted the possibility of such a solution of her apparition.

'This must be hushed up,' said Mrs Norbury quickly; 'the servants –'

'Hushed up!' exclaimed Ada, indignantly; 'I'm writing a long report on it for the Research Society.'

It was then that Hugo Norbury, who is not naturally a man of brilliant resource, had one of the really useful inspirations of his life.

'It was very wicked of us, Miss Bleek,' he said, 'but it would be a shame to let it go further. That white hedgehog is an old joke of ours; stuffed albino hedgehog, you know, that my father brought home from Jamaica, where they grow to enormous size. We hide it in the room with a string on it, run one end of the string through the window; then we pull it from below and it comes scraping along the floor, just as you've described, and finally jerks out of the window. Taken in heaps of people; they all read up Popple and think it's old Harry Nicholson's ghost; we always stop them from writing to the papers about it, though. That would be carrying matters too far.'

Mrs Hatch-Mallard renewed the lease in due course, but Ada Bleek has never renewed her friendship.